Blood Wings is the latest exciting … Series which will keep you immersed in following the action. A great read from author Phil Ward, a decorated Vietnam combat veteran and former Ranger School Instructor. An exciting book written by a knowledgeable special operations veteran who I had the honor of serving with in the Mekong Delta of 1968 and 1969.

— WAYNE BLESSING,
A/2-39/9 ID REPUBLIC OF VIETNAM 1968-69

During my tour in Vietnam, I had the pleasure of serving with some of the greatest soldiers I've known in my 20 years of military service. LT Ward was one of those soldiers. In wartime, you learn about brotherhood and trust. To this day we are still united in brotherhood... as well as in remembering our brothers who did not return. No matter how much training a soldier receives, Airborne, Air Assault, Ranger school etc., nothing prepares you for taking a life or the loss of a comrade. If called to war by our country again, I would be proud to serve with Phil Ward.

— LARRY TROXEL,
A/2-39/9 ID REPUBLIC OF VIETNAM 1968-69
B/2/502/101 ABN REPUBLIC OF VIETNAM 1970-71
B 2ND RANGER BN GRENADA 1983

Visit www.raidingforces.com and www.facebook.com/raidingforces to read more about the Raiding Forces Series.

BOOK THREE IN THE RAIDING FORCES SERIES

BLOOD WINGS

PHIL WARD

This book is a work of fiction. Names, characters, businesses, organizations, places, events, and incidents are either a product of the author's imagination or are used fictitiously. Any resemblance to actual persons, living or dead, events, or locales is entirely coincidental.

Published by Military Publishers LLC
Austin, Texas
www.raidingforces.com

Distributed by Military Publishers LLC

For ordering information or special discounts for bulk purchases, please contact Military Publishers LLC at 8871 Tallwood, Austin, TX 78759, 512.346.2132.

DEDICATION

THIS BOOK IS DEDICATED TO MIKE R. LARY, COUSIN, LIFELONG FRIEND, football star, attorney, entrepreneur, and gentleman rancher, RIP.

Randal's Rules for Raiding

RULE 1: The first rule is there ain't no rules.

RULE 2: Keep it short and simple.

RULE 3: It never hurts to cheat.

RULE 4: Right man, right job.

RULE 5: Plan missions backward (know how to get home).

RULE 6: It's good to have a Plan B.

RULE 7: Expect the unexpected.

SITUATION

PROLOGUE

THERE IS NO OFFICIAL RECORD THAT A FORCE N EVER OPERATED in the central part of Abyssinia in 1940 and 1941. A request for information on the subject provoked this response: "Special Operations Executive's records were destroyed in a fire at the end of World War II."

1
WIRE NOOSE

MAJ. JOHN RANDAL, DSO, MC, STARED THROUGH THE DARK GLOOMY night as the inkblot coastline of enemy-occupied France swam into focus after a high-speed run from his headquarters located at Seaborn House in the southern portion of England. Anticipation spiked among the small group of Raiding Forces officers on the bridge of Motor Gunboat 345 as they inched their way in toward a purple-shaded signal lamp beckoning from the rocky shore. Tonight they were working for the fledgling Escape and Evasion organization, MI-9, making the first-ever attempt to bring out an evading British officer on the run from the Nazis.

The powerful engines of MGB 345 warbled as the heavily-armed craft stealthily worked in toward the faded violet light. Six pairs of night glasses strained to pierce the night fog. This was a hasty operation, launched in response to an urgent request from MI-9 to evacuate a high-value escaper about whom little was known. The only information Raiding Forces' mission planners had to go on was the coordinates of the pickup point, the type of signal to be expected upon arrival and the fact that they were bringing out a senior British officer tonight.

Purple meant the landing point was clear. Any other color was a wave-off, indicating the mission was compromised. At this point, the pick-up was a go.

"Stand-by, landing party," Major Randal ordered, never lowering the powerful Zeiss field glasses he had captured from a German Panzer leader at Calais, what now seemed like a lifetime ago but in reality was less than a year.

There was a rattle of equipment as six Commandos made last-minute checks and prepared to go ashore in the MGB's Goatly dory. Two Lifeboat Servicemen were primed to launch the dinghy upon command. Members of the famous Royal National Lifeboat Institute, they were a couple of the top rough-water small-boat handlers in the world. The Raiding Forces troops in the landing party were the most experienced small-scale amphibious operators in the British Armed Forces. Tonight may have been MI-9's maiden mission as an Escape & Evasion organization, but the personnel carrying it out for them were the best in the business, led by the most capable small-unit special operations officer that Combined Operations possessed.

Nevertheless, they were winging it. No one really knew what to expect. You never do on first operations.

Major Randal looked at the luminous green Coke bottle-shaped hands on his Rolex and noted that it was 2330 hours. The watch was a gift from his fiancée, Capt. the Lady Jane Seaborn, OBE, Royal Marines; a fabulously wealthy widow of a Royal Navy officer killed early in the war when the destroyer he commanded was sunk by Stuka dive bombers off Norway. Captain Lady Jane was generally described by any man who ever laid eyes on her – and by most women – as "drop-dead gorgeous."

The watch was an exact copy of the official hardhat diver's model the Royal Navy had specially purchased from the Rolex Company. Originally it had been intended as a surprise birthday present for Captain Lady Jane's husband, but he had sailed on his last voyage before she had been able to present it. Major Randal thought about her every time he glanced at the watch, which, in his line of work was often. A reliable source had privately confided that this was the very reason Lady Jane had given it to him.

"Bring her around, Randy, and be ready for us to get the hell out of Dodge the minute we come back on board," Major Randal ordered MGB 345's young commander, Lt. Randy "Hornblower" Seaborn, DSC, RN, as he made a last-minute check of his equipment.

Tonight Major Randal was going ashore armed to the teeth with his Browning A-5 auto-loading 12-gauge shotgun with the short barrel and extension magazine holding eight rounds; a Colt .38 Super at his waist; a High Standard Military Model D .22 with the silencer mounted in a chest holster; a Fairbairn fighting knife laced to that; and four Mills No. 36 grenades tucked into the bellows pockets of his sand-green Denison parachute smock. What the Commandos called "dressed for success." The mission was not intended to be a fighting patrol but he planned to be prepared for any contingency.

"Expect the unexpected" had been one of Raiding Forces' "Rules for Raiding" before they had learned from hard experience the rule was worthless since the unexpected was always the worst-case scenario and never anything anyone had ever even remotely anticipated.

The new rule to replace it was: "When the unexpected happens, press on."

The rest of the men in the landing party were all armed with Thompson .45-caliber submachine guns as well as the personal sidearm of their choice, Fairbairn daggers, and an assortment of hand grenades. Lt. "Pyro" Percy Stirling, MC, 17/21 Lancers, the "Death or Glory Boys," was equipped with a small amount of explosives.

The young cavalry officer had recently been undergoing an intensive course of demolitions training provided by the Territorial Regiment stationed near Seaborn House, the Kent Fortress Royal Engineers. Lieutenant Stirling had achieved "living legend" status in Raiding Forces, having blown up a lighthouse on OPERATION TOMCAT by ordering one hundred pounds of guncotton explosives to be placed under the two-story storage tank of acetylene fuel that powered the light. The resulting explosion had struck terror into the hearts of a lot of brave men (most of them his own) and earned him the lasting nickname "Pyro."

Sgt. Mike "March or Die" Mikkalis, a baby-blue-eyed professional who looked exactly like the dreamy soldier of fortune in a white kepi staring off into space on French Foreign Legion recruiting posters, had been tapped to be the interpreter tonight. He actually had completed a tour in the legendary 13th Demi-Brigade of the Legion. Tough as nails, he spoke French like a native.

The remaining four men of the landing party consisted of two cavalrymen from the swanky Blues Regiment of the Household Guards, one rifleman from the Kings Royal Rifle Corps and one rifleman from the Rifle Brigade. RM Butch Hoolihan rounded out the team. All personnel were graduates of the British Parachute School and the Commando School at Achnacarry, Scotland and were veterans of a number of small-scale Commando raids, including the first-ever British parachute raid on a German installation on the continent and the cutting-out of three enemy ships from the Port of San Pedro – OPERATION LOUNGE LIZARD.

Major Randal was an American volunteer serving in the British Forces. Originally he had been commissioned into The Rangers, a Territorial Regiment recently activated as the 9th Battalion "The Rangers", King's Royal Rifle Corps. He had served four years previously as a junior officer in the 26th United States Cavalry Regiment (Philippine Scouts). Two years of that tour of duty were spent on intensive operations against the elusive and deadly Huk guerrillas.

Tonight was his first back-on-duty after recovering from a serious wound he had received on an off-the-books pin-prick raid unofficially known in Combined Operations circles as the "Gunfight at the Blue Duck."

"You men all know your jobs," Major Randal said as he prepared to lead the way down into the gently-rocking dinghy being held against the side of the MGB 345 by Lifeboat Servicemen Tom Tyler and Jimmie Dodd. "Let's go do it."

The purple lantern was their objective. The mission was a quick in and out. The idea was for them to slip ashore, retrieve the high-value evader waiting at the water's edge, return to the MGB and be away and gone before anyone was the wiser. All good plans are simple. And this one was as simple as it gets.

Maj. Norman Crockatt, the officer commanding MI-9, was onboard tonight as an observer for this very first evader retrieval operation. He was along to evaluate Raiding Forces' performance with an eye to entering into a long-term commitment with them for joint operations in the future. Thus far he had been keenly impressed with the high degree of professionalism and teamwork exhibited by Major Randal's men.

Everything had gone like clockwork.

The Lifeboat Servicemen rowed the dinghy with powerful strokes. As the small cockleshell of a craft approached land it became clear that they were coming in to a rugged rocky shore. White foam lapped around a large stone that appeared right in front of them as they made landfall. These were the kind of landing conditions that would defeat most small-boat handlers but in which the Lifeboat Servicemen excelled.

Lieutenant Stirling leapt from the bow of the dinghy carrying the landing line and landed silently on the big rock. The rubber soles of his canvas-topped raiding boots gave him a secure grip on the slippery surface and were completely silent. He helped hold the boat in place as the Lifeboat Servicemen paddled furiously to bring the stern of the dinghy against the rock and tossed the young officer another line to secure the fragile craft from the pounding of the tide.

Sergeant Mikkalis followed him on to the rock. Next out was Major Randal, Royal Marine Hoolihan and the four remaining Commandos. The Raiders fanned out and immediately set up a ragged security perimeter. Terrain dictated that they position themselves halfway up a rocky cliff in a ragged, diamond-shaped formation.

A tiny cadaverous Frenchman clad in a thread-worn black suit topped by a nasty-looking beret was holding the purple-shaded lamp. The man was excitedly gesturing to Sergeant Mikkalis and speaking in a high-pitched rapid-fire voice.

When Major Randal came up, Sergeant Mikkalis announced, "Sir, we have a situation," sounding like he enjoyed delivering bad news, as usual.

"Let's hear it."

"Fritz says the police nabbed our man on the way to the rendezvous tonight. The bloody idiot was apparently in the village up the road having dinner with a woman in a public eatery and got caught during a routine inspection. Fritz arrived in time to see the policemen leading our evader and his dinner companion away in handcuffs."

Major Randal knew from his map reconnaissance prior to the mission that there was a tiny village two miles west of the rendezvous point called Le Muy. The place consisted of no more than a dozen buildings, making it not much more than a wide spot in the road. No German forces were permanently stationed there, according to the intelligence provided by Major Crockatt, MI-9.

"Military?"

"Metropolitan Police – they patrol the rural areas. Vichy, which means they cooperate with the Gestapo. Mean bastards, every bit as bad as the SS, sir."

"How many?"

After a lengthy back-and-forth with the shabby little man in the worn black suit, Sergeant Mikkalis translated, "A mobile squad, Fritz is not sure exactly how many there were. He thinks he saw approximately half a dozen but did not hang around long enough to get an exact head-count, sir."

"How many police cars did Fritz say were in the village?"

"Three, sir."

"What do you think, Sergeant Mikkalis?"

"We ought to go home and let the Germans keep the bloody fool, Major," the ex-Legionnaire said in a flat tone. "The man failed to follow instructions to lay low. He deserves what he gets. Whoever the evader is, he's a dangerous fool."

"I meant how many policemen do you estimate are in Le Muy?"

"That is what I was afraid you meant, sir," the tough sergeant grinned, which came across more like a homicidal snarl. "Probably no more than six or eight. Metropolitan Police seldom expect to find much in remote areas like this."

"Where's the evader now?"

"Locked up in the local post office, sir," Sergeant Mikkalis said, "in the only public building in town, dead center in the middle of the village according to Fritz." He had not needed to go through the Frenchman for the answer, having already asked the question – anticipating Major Randal the way really good sergeants do.

"Will he take us there?"

"Not a chance, sir."

"Have Lieutenant Stirling report to me."

"Yes, sir," the NCO responded in a resigned tone. Sergeant Mikkalis knew his commanding officer and he knew what was coming next.

Major Randal turned to the Lifeboat Serviceman standing alongside, "Tom, you hear everything we just said?"

"Yes, sir."

"All right, report back on board the 345 and brief Lieutenant Seaborn and Major Crockatt on the situation. Tell them we'll be going into Le Muy to retrieve our evader," Major Randal ordered. "Inform the Lieutenant he is to wait until 0300 and if we are not back by then, head home immediately. Is that clear?"

"Wait 'till 0300 hours, sir," the Lifeboat Serviceman repeated, clearly not liking the sound of the message he was to deliver, "then shove off."

"Roger that, move out."

"Godspeed, Major."

Lieutenant Stirling walked up with Sergeant Mikkalis as Lifeboat Serviceman Tyler headed back to the dinghy.

"You understand what's happening here, Percy?"

"Sergeant Mikkalis filled me in, sir."

"Good. Have your garrote with you?"

"Always, sir."

Major Randal took the weapon, fashioned a wire loop, then whipped it over Fritz's head and pulled the noose tight before the startled Frenchman knew what was happening, causing him to emit a noise that sounded like something you might expect to hear from a startled duck. Then he took the ends of the garrote and wrapped them around the barrel of Lieutenant Stirling's Thompson submachine gun behind the Cutts compensator, twisted them down tight and tied them off so the muzzle was wired in place about three inches from the back of Fritz's neck.

"If the man so much as wiggles," Major Randal ordered through clenched teeth, "blow his head clean off."

"Yeeeeehaaaaa!" Lieutenant Stirling responded in a stage whisper. "Death or Glory, Fritzie!"

"Sergeant Mikkalis, tell him what I just said," Major Randal instructed. "Make sure you include Lieutenant Stirling's comment."

"With pleasure, sir!"

After listening to a short, unhappy exchange in French, Major Randal commanded, "OK Fritz, lead the way."

2
BAD DOG

WITH LT. "PYRO" PERCY STIRLING ON POINT HOLDING HIS THOMPSON submachine gun with the muzzle wired to the neck of reluctant guide Fritz, the team of Raiding Forces Commandos climbed up the steep steps that had been roughly hacked out of the side of the cliff. Off shore, MGB 345 was a dark shadow in the gloomy night. A light fog swirled.

Fritz was not happy but he was not stupid. He led the way as ordered and moved out smartly. At the top of the steps, the Commandos came to the coast road, a narrow, single-lane hard ball typical of rural country lanes everywhere.

The party did not have time to waste. MGB 345 was going to sail for home in a little over three hours with or without them onboard. When the team reached the road, Lieutenant Stirling shepherded his guide left face, nudging him forward with the big .45-caliber muzzle of the Thompson, and the team broke into a trot headed in the direction of Le Muy.

Most infantry tactical manuals discourage the practice of jogging down the center of a high-speed avenue of approach behind enemy lines in the dark of night. It is an invitation for trouble. However, tonight time was more of a real threat than the possibility of a chance encounter with Germans or a blue-on-blue clash with the French underground.

No resistance forces were believed to be operating in the area for the simple reason that, thus far, Special Operations Executive, the organization charged with arming and equipping the French resistance movement in order to "set Europe ablaze," had not been able to complete a single mission to France to organize and equip resisters. There were no friendly forces.

To date, the only British officer to actually carry out SOE's instructions was Lieutenant Stirling, when he blew the lighthouse sky high. All hands present at the time it exploded were in complete agreement – "Pyro" Percy had "really set Europe ablaze."

Moving at double-time, the patrol took a little over twenty minutes to cover the distance to Le Muy. Raiding Forces was trained to move faster than that, but Fritz was not in the best physical condition. The diminutive Frenchman was almost in cardiac arrest by the time the village swam into sight.

Lieutenant Stirling held up one hand, signaling the formation to slow to quick-time and deploy into a tactical column formation traveling with one file on each side of the road. Fritz suddenly developed the dry heaves and fell heavily into the ditch retching, dragging the muzzle of the Thompson submachine gun down with him like the tip of a fly rod with a hooked trout on the line.

Maj. John Randal moved up to the head of the column to talk to his Lieutenant. "Set up an Objective Rally Point in that clump of trees over there. Sergeant Mikkalis and I are going in to Le Muy to do a quick leader's reconnaissance. If we're not back in one hour, return to the boat and go home."

"Yes, sir," Lieutenant Stirling responded, clearly not happy to be left behind, or with the orders to return to the MGB in the event the recon team did not return in the allotted time.

"We'll be back in less than thirty minutes, Percy."

"Roger, sir."

Sgt. Mike "March or Die" Mikkalis led the way in the event they were challenged, since Major Randal did not speak a word of French. The two strode rapidly down the lane in the direction of Le Muy. The night was spooky with evil-looking fog swirling. Anything seemed possible.

There was no snow, but the weather was uncommonly cold. Like every other city or town on the continent of Europe in 1940, the village was completely blacked out.

Le Muy was typical of farming communities everywhere – residents went to bed early. The village was woefully short of nightlife. In fact, there was no entertainment to be found in the entire place, not even a pub. Only one small eatery was in business, but it had long ago closed for the night.

Major Randal and Sergeant Mikkalis slipped into the village without any trouble. Sticking to the shadows, they located the post office and the small inn where the Metropolitan Police were thought to be spending the night. The inn was easy to identify in the dark and fog by the three black Citroëns parked out in front. The Commandos took the precaution of letting the air out of the tires on two of them.

The post office was a small, single-room affair, notable for the heavy iron bars on the windows. The bars presumably protected the mail, though it wasn't clear what the mail needed to be protected from in Le Muy. The French postal system mandated post offices be constructed so that they could be secured.

Heavy blackout curtains made it difficult to see inside, but after carefully working their way around the building, the Raiders were able to locate one window where they could peek through a crack left in the drapes. In this way, they determined there was only a single policeman in the room, sitting in a chair with his feet propped up on a desk, listening to a radio. The French police officer was a heavyset, rumpled individual with his shirt collar undone and his tie loosened. He was smoking and occasionally drinking from a tall green bottle. A manacled prisoner was lying on the floor in the back of the room.

No weapons were in sight.

For a moment Major Randal considered breaking in and effecting the rescue right then and there. He knew it was a bad idea for a number of reasons, not the least of which was that the manacled man might be seriously injured, making it difficult to move him without additional help. Even so, the thought was tempting.

He made eye contact with Sergeant Mikkalis, and they slid around the side of the building in search of a rear door. They found one, but when they carefully tested the knob, it was firmly locked. That was all they needed to know.

Silently, the two made their way back to the ORP. Major Randal conducted a short briefing on what they had found in the village, then assigned individual tasks for the rescue attempt.

"Sergeant Mikkalis, Marine Hoolihan and I will compose the snatch team that enters the post office to bring out the evader. Lieutenant Stirling, you and the remainder of the team will set up a perimeter around the inn where the policemen are staying, securing the building a full 360 degrees. We've let the air out of the tires on two of the police cars. There's no sense walking all the way back to the boat, so when we pull out of Le Muy we'll be traveling in a police car.

"Have it ready to go, Percy," Major Randal ordered, making eye contact with his young Lieutenant. "Make sure you take the one with the air in the tires."

"Wilco."

"You'll have to hotwire it."

"Not a problem, sir."

Hotwiring was a well-honed skill in Raiding Forces. All the Commandos had practice with "borrowing" unauthorized vehicles to drive back to Seaborn House at the end of their passes. Stealing cars was a unit tradition.

"When we come out of the post office I'll clap my hands three times. That's the signal to rally on the police car. Have it running when we get there. Three men in the back, two in front with the evader and two on the running boards. I'll drive. What are your questions?"

"What should I do with Fritz, sir?"

"Cut him loose when we move out."

The Raiders took a minute to check their equipment. The drill was an automatic, very reassuring act to men who had done this sort of thing before. The time also allowed each of the men to gather his individual thoughts and rehearse in his mind what actions he would perform from the moment they moved out until they withdrew from their objective. Every man present was a seasoned professional. They knew the drill.

"Let's do it."

The small force patrolled quietly to Le Muy. The order of march was Sergeant Mikkalis, Major Randal, RM Butch Hoolihan, and Lieutenant Stirling, followed by the four Raiding Forces Commandos.

Major Randal was clicked on. He was super aware. His decision-making process was effortless. Every thought was crystal clear. This transformation was something that had been happening to him as far back as tactical training exercises as a student in ROTC at UCLA. He could not explain how he did it – the clicking-on was not a conscious effort. The sensation, one he had come to take for granted, was not something he ever discussed with anyone, and he had never heard anyone else describe it.

But Major Randal never felt as alive as he did when he was in command of troops making a tactical movement to contact.

The Commandos crept through the town like phantoms. Nothing stirred. Le Muy was all quiet, at peace with the world. When the patrol came to the small inn, Lieutenant Stirling peeled off, followed by the four men who would secure the building. Moving silently, they took up their positions.

Sergeant Mikkalis continued on to the post office. His rubber-soled canvas-topped raiding boots were completely silent on the concrete. The Raiders padded along, stalking through the swirling fog.

Suddenly, a large black dog with his fangs bared leapt out of the dark and buried his foaming teeth in the former Legionnaire's calf. The ferocious canine clamped down with his huge slobbering jaws, growling furiously and whipping his head back and forth as fast as he could. The enraged animal was doing his dead-level best to chew Sergeant Mikkalis' leg off.

The Sergeant swung the steel-capped butt of his Thompson submachine gun at the dog's soccer ball-sized head but missed, lost his balance and went down. Lights began to show in windows up and down the street as people pulled back their blackout curtains to peer outside and see what was causing the disturbance.

To his credit, Sergeant Mikkalis did not make a sound though he had to be in tremendous pain.

Major Randal quickly drew his High Standard Military Model D automatic with the silencer mounted and shot the animal three times – to no effect. The monster seemed as undaunted by the .22-caliber rounds as a werewolf that could be killed only when shot with a silver bullet – or maybe a bullet with a virgin's blood rubbed on the tip.

It was that kind of night.

The door to the post office cracked open, and the big, disheveled policeman carrying his green bottle by the long neck made eye contact with Major Randal, standing in the street with a pistol in his hand. Without hesitation, the Raiding Forces' Commander jumped over the fighting slobbering dog and his struggling Sergeant the instant he saw the policeman attempt to close the door.

Major Randal hit the heavy oaken door full-speed with his shoulder as it was slamming shut. He crashed into the room, quickly shooting the policeman four times as he stumbled past and fell to the ground. Then he shot twice more from where he ended up on the floor before the heavyset man crumpled.

Outside, the dog let out a high-pitched scream probably heard all the way back on MGB 345. Royal Marine Hoolihan had rammed his stiletto-sharp Fairbairn knife into its heart, killing the vicious animal – but not instantly. So much for stealth. *When the unexpected happens*, Major Randal thought, *press on*. This rule was not working out so great either. What choice did they have?

A policeman ran out of the inn with his revolver in hand to investigate. He was immediately shot dead by a hail of Thompson submachine gun fire. This was followed immediately by a fusillade that erupted from what seemed like every window in the front of the two-story inn. Police pistols were popping like flash bulbs on the red carpet at a Hollywood movie premiere.

Lieutenant Stirling's team engaged, and a general firefight ensued. That put the final nail in the plan of slipping in, freeing their man and stealthily withdrawing safely home to England with no one the wiser.

Militarily, the situation was not good.

Sergeant Mikkalis limped into the post office cursing in three languages. He searched the dead policeman for keys and unlocked the manacles on the man lying in the back of the room.

Seeing that his Sergeant had the evader well in hand, Major Randal went back out into the street to evaluate the situation. He found Royal Marine Hoolihan crouched down firing bursts up the block into the second story of the inn. Before he could determine a course of action, he heard a burst of loud, angry shouting coming from inside the post office behind him suddenly cut short, then silence.

Sergeant Mikkalis came to the door, "We have another situation, sir."

Major Randal dashed back inside to see the evader lying on the floor unconscious, with the manacles back in place. He noted that whoever the officer was, he was a big handsome devil. "What happened?"

"The bloody fool has a woman over at the inn being held by the police. He tried to break away from me to rush over to rescue her. Major, I warned you this man was going to be trouble."

"Who's the woman?"

"Hard to say. He was shouting about not leaving without her – pulling rank, claiming to be a commander in the Royal Navy. Says he is going to have us all keelhauled if we don't go retrieve her. I had to knock the fool out to prevent him running out in the street and getting shot."

"Keep him under tight control while I try to sort this out," Major Randal ordered. "Be ready to move to the police car as soon as I give you the word."

"Sir!"

Outside, the firefight had not slackened. Fortunately, the policemen were armed only with their service revolvers. Unfortunately, they had an impressive supply of ammunition, and they did not seem to be the least bit bashful about shooting it up.

"Come on, Butch," Major Randal called, bounding past the Royal Marine as he headed up the street to check on Lieutenant Stirling. The Raiding Forces troopers were continuing to blaze away at the front of the inn.

"How many do you estimate, Percy?"

"Hard to say, sir. Sounds like more than we initially thought."

"The bad guys have a woman in there with some connection to our evader. I need to get her out. Any ideas?"

"We have a Raider stationed at back," Lieutenant Stirling replied. "So far, there has not been any firing from his position, sir."

"OK, Percy, I'll see if we can effect entry from there. Butch, you're on me," Major Randal ordered, already moving.

When he and Royal Marine Hoolihan arrived behind the inn, they found the rear security man crouched down with his Thompson submachine gun aimed at the back door.

"We're going in," Major Randal informed him. "When we come out, I'll shout "*Remember Calais*" three times. Shoot anyone coming out that door who doesn't remember Calais."

"Bloody unlikely I shall ever forget it, Major."

Major Randal and Royal Marine Hoolihan made a dash to the door. When they made it, Major Randal reached out to test the door. To his surprise the knob turned and the door swung open without anyone shooting at them.

Making eye contact with the Royal Marine, Major Randal nodded, then slipped through the door, staying low. Firing was continuous from the second floor, and there was the loud sound of pistol shots coming from the front room of the building. The gunshots were greatly amplified inside the inn. The kitchen was in the back. They crept in carefully and found it empty.

Moving warily down a narrow hall beside the stairway, Major Randal inched his way slowly and carefully to a spot where he could see into the front room. Tied to a wooden chair in the center of the room was a naked woman with a huge mop of pale blond hair partially covering her face. Her arms, feet and neck were lashed to the chair. A gag was tied in her mouth. With no nightlife in Le Muy, the Vichy policemen had managed to organize their own entertainment.

Even with the firefight raging, Major Randal could not help but notice that the blond was a stunner. The woman saw him. Right behind her were two policemen with their backs turned, intent on firing their pistols out the front windows at Lieutenant Stirling's men in the street.

When Royal Marine Hoolihan slid forward on his signal to take up a position to cover the stairs, Major Randal swung his Browning A-5 around on his back by its sling and drew his holstered Colt .38 Super pistol. As the blond's eyes grew large, he brought the Colt up in both hands and shot the two men behind her, fast. *Bang! Bang!*

He had elected to use the Colt in hopes the shooters upstairs would not realize the ground-floor men had been killed. Had the big 12-gauge Browning been touched off inside the room, it would have sounded like a cannon and all the policemen would have known instantly that the inn had been breached. The silenced .22 High Standard might have been best for stealth, but it did not pack the punch to put the men down quick, as evidenced by the dog he had shot to little or no effect.

While Royal Marine Hoolihan kept the stairs covered, Major Randal advanced to the woman in the chair. Drawing his Fairbairn knife, he quickly cut the bindings strapping down her neck, arms and legs. He pulled her up by one hand and led her to the back door while the tattoo of firing continued unabated above.

Royal Marine Hoolihan pulled in behind them, providing rear security. He managed to roll two Mills bombs back into the room as he withdrew.

"*REMEMBER CALAIS, REMEMBER CALAIS, REMEMBER CALAIS.*"

"Pull out!" Major Randal ordered as the trio came running past the rear-security man, and the grenades inside the inn cooked off. The party sprinted around to the front of the building.

"Do it now, Sergeant Mikkalis!" he shouted down the block.

"Prepare to break contact, Percy!"

Major Randal shoved the naked woman in the front seat of the Citroën then piled in behind the wheel. The motor was ticking over. Lieutenant Stirling was an officer you could depend on, he noted – not for the first time. Cramming the gearshift into reverse, he backed down to the post office, tires smoking the whole way.

Sergeant Mikkalis dragged the semi-conscious evader out the front door, shoved him into the car's trunk, slammed it shut and then jumped into the passenger's seat in front, next to the blond. Events were moving too fast for anyone to have had the time to offer a jacket or even take the gag out of her mouth.

"No wonder our man wanted to rush that building," Sergeant Mikkalis said. "Where do you reckon he latched on to her?"

On signal, the Raiders started throwing Mills bombs at the windows of the inn as fast as they could to cover their withdrawal. The Commandos jumped on the front fenders and running boards of the car when it pulled back up to the inn, all the while maintaining a steady rate of fire. From the backseat, someone tossed a coat left by one of the Vichy cops over the woman's shoulders.

Major Randal put the pedal to the metal. The overloaded Citroën fishtailed out of town with its passengers hanging on, blazing lead. Behind them the grenades were thundering like the grand finale of a New Year's Eve fireworks show.

Two miles later, they screeched up to the edge of the cliff. The Commandos jumped out, abandoning the car and sprinting down the stairs, dragging the groggy evader and his consort, who was clutching her policeman's coat. They quickly piled into the waiting Goatly dinghy for the short row out to the 345.

Once on board, the blond and the evader were hustled below while Lt. Randy "Hornblower" Seaborn cranked up the Motor Gun Boat and made his best effort to set the all-time surface-speed record for home. With shaky hands, Major Randal lit cigarettes all around with his old battered Zippo – the one with the gold, crossed sabers of the U.S. 26th Cavalry Regiment embossed on the front.

Maj. Norman Crockatt remarked, "Nicely done, old man."

To be perfectly honest, this first hasty mission for MI-9 had turned out to be a little more than bargained for.

Later, when MGB 345 began its run up the small river to its dock at Seaborn House, the tall evader joined them on the bridge. He had on a borrowed sailor's pea jacket and was no longer wearing manacles. Lieutenant Seaborn recoiled like he had seen a ghost.

The evacuee laughed and called out, "Randy, is that you, lad?"

Through the smoke of his cigarette, Major Randal watched the exchange.

"Sir," Lieutenant Seaborn announced in a quaking voice, "let me introduce you to my uncle – Commander Mallory Seaborn. Welcome home, Uncle Mallory. The family is certainly going to be in for a big surprise. We thought you were dead."

Major Randal flicked his cigarette overboard, unlatched the Rolex on his wrist and handed it over to Commander Seaborn – his fiancée's formerly dead husband.

"I believe this belongs to you."

3
CHEESE

MAJ. LAWRENCE GRAND, THE IMPECCABLY-DRESSED SPECIAL operations Executive Chief of Section D (Destruction), was wearing his trademark red carnation pinned in the lapel of his grey, pinstripe, Savile Row suit two days after the raid when he found Maj. John Randal in the Morning Room of the swanky Bradford Hotel, nursing a world-class hangover. Normally, the hotel employees buzzed around the young Raiding Forces officer but this morning none of them would so much as even glance in his direction, much less come near his table. Word must have reached the Bradford that Cdr. Mallory Seaborn had miraculously reappeared from the dead.

Never a heavy drinker, Major Randal's normally lightning-quick decision-making process had been hampered by the hangover. It dawned on him as he sat sipping a tall glass of tomato juice heavily spiked with lime and a dose of salt – hoping against hope to offset the effect of the sledge hammer banging away in his brain – that this might be his last stay at the exclusive Bradford. His suite of rooms was provided by his ex-fiancée, drop-dead gorgeous Capt. the Lady Jane Seaborn, wife of the previously-thought-deceased evader he had rescued for MI-9.

As Capt. "Geronimo" Joe McKoy was known to say, "Life'll twist off on you." Major Randal had never actually understood what that meant. Now he did.

"By Jove, the only bloke I ever saw who looked as bad as you was in Shanghai," Major Grand called cheerfully, "laying dead in a gutter."

"I feel worse than I look."

"Suspected that. No good deed goes unpunished, what?"

"Do you want something?"

"Not I," Major Grand replied, nonplussed. "You have been requested by name for a Most Secret covert operation somewhere a long way from merry old England. I dare say it could not have come at a more opportune time, what?"

"Operation?"

"All in good time, John, you will be going out to the Middle East straight away. Today, in fact, by way of Turkey.... Istanbul to be exact. And there is this small favor you could do for us while you are laid over in the wicked city before traveling on to Cairo."

"Anything else you care to tell me, Larry?"

"Simply that while you are in Egypt it would be time well-spent for you to be keeping an eye open for a good location to establish a forward-operating base out there where an element of Raiding Forces can set up permanent shop. How have you been progressing with your recruiting?"

"Not so good," Major Randal admitted. "Regimental commanders are increasingly resentful about us poaching their best men."

"Nevertheless, be thinking about how quickly you can double the size of your unit. Your Raiders are wanted out in Africa, and we have an operational requirement to keep a detachment of them here as well."

"When do I leave?"

"Within the hour, John. I am going to drive you to the BOAC terminal. You will be traveling incognito as a civilian. Your kit, to include personal weapons, will be flown out to Cairo on a military aircraft and waiting there when you arrive."

"In that case, arrange for a confidential stenographer to ride to the terminal with us unless you can take dictation. I'll need to issue marching orders for Raiding Forces while I'm gone."

"Captain Pelham-Davies will assume command in your absence, I take it?"

"With Terry banished to Egypt, he's next in the chain of command. Pelham-Davies is a brilliant tactical commander but he's going to need help liaising with the intelligence agencies now that Lady Jane is out of the picture."

"On my word he shall have it," Major Grand promised. "We have no desire to let Raiding Forces' efficiency diminish one iota while you are away. Finish your snakebite medicine, John. We leave as soon as you change into the mufti my men have delivered to your suite."

The British Overseas Airline Company's flying boat took off with Maj. John Randal aboard wearing a superbly cut navy blue suit, courtesy of Pembrooks Military Tailors. His cover story was that he had been discharged from the Army because of the wound he had suffered at the Blue Duck. As the story ran, he was making his way home to Los Angeles.

Why he needed a cover story was not explained.

All Major Randal knew was that he was ordered to fly to Istanbul and check into the five-star Palace Hotel & Casino where he would be met by an "agent or agents known to you." The last time he had been given similar instructions was during OPERATION LOUNGE LIZARD. On that trip, Raiding Forces had invaded the neutral island protectorate of Rio Bonita.

That gave him something to think about.

The flight to Istanbul took three days. While the BOAC plane was a nice aircraft, it was a far cry from the plush Flying Clipper he and Capt. Sir Terry "Zorro" Stone, KBE, MC, had flown aboard to Africa when they traveled to the Gold Coast to set up the raid on Rio Bonita. Although the stewardesses on the BOAC flight were attractive, they were not in the same league as "Red," the spectacular Clipper Girl they had met on that trip.

Red was responsible for Captain Stone being exiled to Egypt by no less a personage than His Majesty the King because of what he described as a "salacious incident" in the Life Guards' mess. The couple had been drinking Black Jacks, the regimental drink of the 2nd Life Guards. Ancient tradition demands the secret concoction be imbibed standing on your head (at least that is what Red had been led to believe).

The 2nd Life Guards are such a high-tone regiment that the troops do not call themselves soldiers, preferring to refer to themselves as "The gentlemen of the Life Guards." So when Captain Stone's incident became known to the King, it was *adios* Sir Terry for conduct unbecoming... banished to the desert.

The quality of stewardesses on the flight to Istanbul was not a problem. Major Randal was not much in the mood for female companionship. A professional soldier (some might call him a mercenary since he was an American serving in the British Army), he was about as mentally hard as a man could possibly be. The disintegration of his engagement did not make him feel sad or depressed in any conventional way. It felt no different to him than losing one of his men in battle, which meant he felt nothing at all except an ice-cold absence of happiness.

The lack of emotion was not something he was proud of.

To say Major Randal felt nothing was a stretch. Actually, ever since the hard-fought action at Calais quite awhile ago, his emotions were cut against the grain. He no longer experienced highs and lows.

Major Randal thought of the way he felt as "*the edge*" – it kept him dialed in, focused on the moment. *The edge* kept him alive. Privately, he had come to like the sensation which could best be described as always feeling "ready."

Like all combat commanders who specialize in high-risk independent operations, Major Randal was always alone – even when he was with his men, his friends or a woman. He was comfortable with that.

Lady Jane had been the exception.

She was special.

When Maj. John Randal walked into the exotic Istanbul Palace Hotel and Casino, the mystery identity of the "agent or agents known to you" was cleared up instantly. A life-sized cardboard cutout of Capt. "Geronimo" Joe McKoy was standing in the lobby, propped up on a big wooden easel advertising his show. The silver-haired ex-Arizona Ranger was in full cowboy regalia. He was crouched down, raring for action with a highly-engraved, ivory-stocked .45 Colt Single Action revolver in each hand.

The handsome cardboard cowboy had a great big grin on his face.

Upon checking in, Major Randal arranged to have his bags sent to his room, then made his way to the area behind the stage where he had been advised by the hotel's concierge he would find Captain McKoy's dressing room. The time was approximately 2000 hours, though he had no way of knowing precisely since he no longer owned a watch, a personal equipment deficiency he would to need to address.

"Come on in," Captain McKoy barked when he knocked on the door with the oversized silver star painted on it. "It ain't locked."

The look of surprise on the San Juan Hill veteran's face could not have been described as *happy* when Major Randal walked into the dressing room. "Whatever you're 'a fix'n to do, John, my advice to you is don't do it."

"I'm to meet an 'agent or agents' known to me."

"Listen, John, espionage ain't your line of work ol' son. You're a combat commander, not a clandestine operative," Geronimo Joe warned. "Istanbul is the crossroads of every kind of bad actor on Planet Earth. What we have going here is double agents, triple agents, political assassins… all kinds of intrigue. We got German Nazis, Italian Fascists, Vichy French, the Muslim Brotherhood, Greek Cypriots and a whole bunch of other freelance bad-guy operators I ain't never even heard of before.

"On top o' all that you got your Turkish, British, Free French, Russian and U.S. intelligence spooks a-hidin' behind every potted plant, ready to do an evil deed. You're not a cloak-and-dagger man, and Istanbul ain't the place for on-the-job training. This is the big show."

"Are you my contact?" Major Randal cut him off.

"I'm your man," Captain McKoy conceded with a shake of his thick, silver mane. "Heard about you rescuing Lady Jane's husband and all. Made you a mite testy, did it? They are a-talkin' about giving you another decoration, said it was a right neat piece of work. You're running up quite a score, medal-wise."

"Finding you there ahead of me everywhere I go is the only thing making me edgy," Major Randal said. "I think it's about time to declare your credentials, Captain."

"All I'm doing is a favor for a mutual friend," Captain McKoy responded in a semi-innocent, semi-hurt tone that came across gunfighter cool. "Be at the roulette wheel at 2200 hours where you'll be met by an agent or agents known to you. Wear your tux. It'll be in your room.

"Have a nice night."

The former Rough Rider reached into a much-traveled, hand-tooled leather tote bag sitting on the floor and produced the Browning 9mm pistol Sgt. Mike "March or Die" Mikkalis had given then-Lieutenant Randal the first day at Calais when Swamp Fox Force was formed. The pale blue-eyed Sergeant claimed he had taken it off of a Belgian Admiral… and maybe he had.

"Touched up the trigger like you asked me to and put the same gold bead sights on it you got on your Colts. Took a little longer than I thought, P-35's trigger's a might pesky to smooth up. Better give it to you now. I may not get the chance later."

Major Randal racked back the slide and chambered a round. The weapon's action ran like it was on ball bearings. The tune-up had obviously consisted of more than changing the sights and smoothing out the rough trigger for which Browning P-35s are infamous. He carefully lowered the hammer on the loaded chamber (which is not the recommended method of carry), then tucked the Browning in the back of his pants under the suit jacket.

Noting Major Randal had put the hammer down on a loaded chamber, Captain McKoy inquired mildly, "Ain't that pistol dangerous?"

"I wouldn't carry it if it wasn't."

"Watch yourself, John," the ex-Arizona Ranger grinned. "This place is like Abilene, Kansas on a Saturday night when the drovers hit town with a pocket full of money. Everybody's packing."

Major Randal said, "Nice job on the Browning."

In his hotel room, Major Randal took a shower and indulged in a short nap before putting on the evening clothes, which had been thoughtfully provided by Maj. Lawrence Grand of Special Operations Executive,

Section D with a little help from Mr. Chatterley of Pembrooks Military Tailors. Major Randal wondered idly how much the exquisite, shawl-collared tuxedo had cost.

It fit like a glove.

Arriving early at the roulette table, Major Randal immediately spotted a platinum-blond bombshell in a silver cocktail dress looking like she stepped right out of a Vargas Girl drawing. She was surrounded by a cadre of cosmopolitan male admirers in immaculate dinner jackets. He recognized her as RM Pamala Plum-Martin, OBE, Capt. the Lady Jane Seaborn's personal assistant. Royal Marine Plum-Martin was also a member of MI-6, the Secret Intelligence Service. She was easily the best-looking woman in the room, if not all of Istanbul.

Uncertain what to do next, Major Randal stood awkwardly and observed his former fiancée's aide at play, fairly sure she was his contact. At this point he was beginning to have second thoughts about so readily agreeing to perform whatever favor Major Grand had requested.

He clicked on. After a time, Royal Marine Plum-Martin wandered his direction while her entourage of admirers looked on, despairing to see her leave. Brushing past Major Randal, she snapped, "Room 914 right now!"

Then, without breaking stride, she continued past him to the long bar while the tuxedoed gentlemen began to break away from the roulette table and drift in that direction.

Across the casino, Major Randal caught a brief glimpse of Lt. Cdr. Ian Fleming, RN, the originator of the idea for OPERATION RUTHLESS, standing at the baccarat table.

The door to Room 914 opened to the first light tap. Maj. John Randal and RM Pamala Plum-Martin stood staring at each other. They had a lot of history. Not only was she Capt. the Lady Jane Seaborn's personal assistant, there had been the little matter of OPERATION LOUNGE LIZARD where she and her boss, working in conjunction with Capt. "Geronimo" Joe McKoy, had performed the forward reconnaissance for the raid on Rio Bonita.

And later, during the "Gunfight at the Blue Duck," where she and the ubiquitous Lady Jane had each shot up a car full of German Stuka pilots with .45-caliber Thompson submachine guns.

"What are you doing here?" Royal Marine Plum-Martin demanded angrily as she quickly pulled him into the room.

"A favor for a mutual friend," Major Randal replied, thinking it had sounded better when Captain McKoy said it.

"Tonight's assignment requires an experienced operative. Besides, you have barely recovered from your wound." The glamorous blond was clearly upset. She felt partially responsible for him being shot in the "Gunfight at the Blue Duck," and as a matter of fact, she was.

"I can go back to my room," Major Randal said helpfully, "and fly on to Cairo first thing in the morning."

"Too late, the game is in play." Royal Marine Plum-Martin was so unhappy she actually stamped her silver, 6-inch stiletto pump. "I only have time to provide my contact, meaning you, a quick briefing and then we shall have to blunder on and hope for the best."

Major Randal liked the Royal Marine. There would have to be something wrong with any man who was not attracted to her, but he had always suspected her heart had been chopped out of a solid block of ice. Now he thought he might have been a little harsh.

"We are attempting to mouse trap the Abwehr Station Chief in Istanbul tonight. The idea is to lure him out by offering up someone that German intelligence would dearly love to have fall into their hands. The plan is for a team of SIS agents to move in and ambush the Nazi when he comes out in the open to take our bait."

"I'm good at setting up ambushes."

"You idiot – *you're* the cheese in the mousetrap!"

"Oh!"

"Tonight you will be picked up in the casino by a female Abwehr operative; wined, dined, drugged, interrogated, tortured and then murdered. John, I never suspected we were planning to use you for this, but from the Nazi's perspective you are irresistible. The Germans are especially interested in British Special Operations capabilities and no one knows that subject any better than you do. I am so terribly sorry to get you involved."

"What's the drill, Pam?"

She handed him a red folder. Inside was a single 8x10 glossy photo of a striking brunette in a SS uniform sporting the three-diamond insignia indicating she held the equivalent rank of captain. "SS-Hauptsturmführer Gretchen von Coffenhauser; the photo does not do her justice.

"Currently she is detached from SS intelligence on temporary duty to the Abwehr as an interrogator. The Hauptsturmführer speaks five languages, is a gymnast, a fencer and a member of the SS equestrian team. She is a bi-sexual nymphomaniac known to frequent the local sadomasochist scene... a giver not a taker."

"Could be a long night," Major Randal said.

"John, be serious! This is a dangerous woman, completely amoral, totally dedicated to National Socialism. She thinks Hitler is God. Men find her irresistible, as do women. Few survive her interrogations, which have been described as "imaginative."

"The German plan for tonight is for von Coffenhauser to pick you up here at the hotel, take you night clubbing until at some point you eventually end up at the same location as the Abwehr Chief of Station. Our plan is for a team of agents to shadow the two of you, then swoop in as soon as it is established the German spy chief is actually on the premises.

"You have nothing to worry about until she takes you to a private residence or manages to get you alone somewhere. Never forget for one moment you are dealing with a highly trained, totally depraved, Nazi killer."

"I see," said Major Randal.

"No, John, you do not. Whoever selected you for tonight is a complete fool."

On the way down to the lobby in the elevator Royal Marine Plum-Martin said, "I am terribly sorry about how things have worked out for you and Jane. I know she is madly in love with you, John. Life can be so dreadfully complicated."

Then, just as the elevator doors were opening, she suddenly kissed him passionately, full on the lips. Shaken by the violence of the kiss, Major Randal dumbly followed the glittering blond into the bar area of the hotel where they ran straight into Hauptsturmführer Gretchen von Coffenhauser.

In fact, they practically collided.

After that, things happened quickly. Royal Marine Plum-Martin spat something in French that sounded angry. She swept a champagne glass off the tray of a passing waiter, then splashed it full in Major Randal's face before storming off.

Major Randal found himself standing there with champagne dripping down on his Pembrooks tuxedo, looking directly at the woman who had come to kill him. When they made eye contact, something happened that no one in the British Secret Service had anticipated. The two connected.

In an instant, Major Randal forgot he was the victim of a broken engagement. He forgot he was on a mission for the Secret Intelligence Service. He did not forget that the hypnotically beautiful SS woman staring him full in the eyes enjoyed all the forbidden vices. The black-and-white photo had most definitely not done her justice.

SS-Hauptsturmführer von Coffenhauser sported wild, jet-black hair, faded turquoise eyes, razor-sharp cheekbones and glossy scarlet lips that were all curves – making her seem, to someone briefed on her background, spectacularly decadent.

Without comment, the SS woman offered him a napkin, studying him like a hungry panther. The SS must really train their women hard. Her ab muscles rippled through the thin silk of her simple sheath when she moved. It's difficult to think clearly, Major Randal noted, when a woman's ab muscles ripple like that.

Royal Marine Plum-Martin, watching covertly from across the room, realized instantly that the best laid plans of MI-6 had been blown sky high. No one ever counted on the two of them actually being physically attracted to each other. Frantically she flashed the abort signal to the members of her team.

Without a word he could recall being exchanged or any recollection of how he was transported there, Major Randal found himself in the empty stairwell of the hotel with SS-Hauptsturmführer von Coffenhauser ripping his tuxedo shirt so violently that the mother-of-pearl studs went flying and bounced down the concrete steps. Flashes were going off in his head like a battery of artillery field pieces rapid-firing at night.

Then the two were upstairs, having been levitated somehow to her suite, and Major Randal distinctly heard her tell him to make himself "very, very comfortable" while she disappeared to run a shower. He followed her suggestion and made himself very, very comfortable indeed.

Shortly, the door to the bath opened, allowing a cloud of steam to billow into the room. The giant, bald head of six-foot, six-inch Feldwebel Karl Swatcharzwolfen of the Special Purpose Company, Brandenburg Battalion – the in-house Commando unit of the Abwehr – emerged from the towel closet just inside the door of the bathroom. He was holding a truncheon in one hand and a syringe in the other. The Nazi storm trooper weighed in at 260 pounds, all of it muscle.

There was an evil grin on his ugly face.

Major Randal was lying on the bed with his hands clasped behind his neck, or so it appeared. Actually, one of them was tucked under the pillow, fondling the checkered walnut grip of his finely tuned 9mm Browning P-35 automatic. He brought it out and shot the Brandenburg Feldwebel in the third wrinkle of his giant shaved head, the exact spot you are supposed to shoot charging elephants.

The trigger, he noted, broke crisp like the proverbial glass rod.

SS-Hauptsturmführer von Coffenhauser ran out of the shower, dripping wet, clasping a profusely engraved, pearl-handled Walther PPK .32-caliber pocket pistol. Major Randal observed Gretchen's ab muscles were rippling again, which was a distraction.

He shot her through the heart, twice.

When the MI-6 team, trailed by Royal Marine Plum-Martin and Lieutenant Commander Fleming burst into the room, weapons drawn, Major Randal was surveying the remains of his shredded tuxedo shirt in the full-length mirror. He tossed the Walther PPK to the platinum-blond secret agent.

"Reckon room service could send me up a replacement?"

4
PORT OF SUDAN

THE BOAC FLIGHT FROM ISTANBUL ARRIVED AT THE CAIRO AIRPORT on time. Maj. John Randal took his carry-on bag from the overhead luggage bin and made his way down the steps to the tarmac. As he exited the aircraft, the dry Egyptian desert heat nearly suffocated him; then it felt good. The sky was china blue. Having grown up in Southern California, he suddenly realized how much he missed sunshine. Most of the last year had been spent in rain and fog.

Before that had been the jungle.

Standing at the foot of the unloading ladder was a tan and fit Capt. Sir Terry "Zorro" Stone. He was wearing a faded khaki shirt with the sleeves rolled up, khaki shorts, desert boots and a white cloth kaffiyeh headpiece like the ones worn by sheiks of the golden sands in the movies. In fact, he looked exactly like Errol Flynn… only tougher. Pinned to the headdress was a circle of silver with a scorpion in the center, the insignia of the Long Range Desert Group.

Captain Stone was grinning from ear to ear.

Major Randal felt better immediately. Better than he had in a long time. The dashing cavalry officer was his best friend as well as the former deputy commander of Raiding Forces.

"Welcome to Cairo, John. I hope you are well rested because we have another plane to catch, and time is short. How was Istanbul, land of mystery, eroticism and romance?"

"Had its moments."

"Certainly did when I passed through, old stick."

"I'm supposed to meet an 'agent or agents known to me.' That you, Terry?"

"That would be me. I shall explain later. Right now we have a tight schedule to maintain."

Captain Stone dispatched his driver to collect the luggage. Then he led the way into the airport terminal to the latrine where another one of his men was waiting with Major Randal's gear that had arrived in the bay of a Lancaster bomber. Two complete sets of khaki battle dress uniforms on hangers had been added to the gear.

"That will be all, Trevor," Captain Stone said, dismissing his trooper. "Wait outside. You are free to begin your debauchery after you take the Major's bags to my room at Shepard's Hotel. I should be back here in three or four days. Until then, you lads are on your own. Do try not to get into too much trouble."

"See you later, Zorro," the big, bearded New Zealand private responded cheerfully. "Try to stay out of trouble yourself, mate."

Noting Major Randal's surprise at the familiarity, Captain Stone was quick to explain. "The LRDG is a very democratic outfit. Everyone, including the officers, is called either by their first name or their nickname."

Major Randal took off his civilian suit. Then both he and Captain Stone changed into battle dress. The BDUs were sporting a large flash on the left sleeve that proclaimed in bold, scarlet stitching "1st SPECIAL AIR SERVICES" with British parachutist wings stitched underneath. If that were not advertisement enough, there was also another pair of parachutist wings pinned above the left shirt pocket. Sand-colored berets with "1st SPECIAL AIR SERVICES" stitched on the front over still another pair of parachutist wings completed the ensemble.

"The 1st Special Air Services sure do like to advertise, whoever they are," Major Randal observed, as he buckled on one of his Colt .38 Supers and the Fairbairn knife. He put the other Colt .38 Super and the Browning P-35 into his canvas carrying case with his silenced High Standard Military Model D .22.

"Yes we do. That's our job, advertising. As for who they are, well, it's you and me, old stick," Captain Stone explained with a laugh as he adjusted his beret in the mirror. "1st SAS only exists on paper... what Colonel Clarke calls a *notional unit.* You and I constitute the entire regiment.

"Notionally, you are the battalion commander of the 10th Abyssinian Parachute Battalion, 1st Special Air Services and I am your No. 2. We are a little vague whether 1st SAS is a regiment or a brigade, but it's the only parachute unit in the whole of Africa and we want everyone to know it's here – even if it's not. For some nefarious reason, Colonel Clarke is particularly interested in the enemy believing we have a parachute battalion of Abyssinians in theatre. Do not ask me why."

"I see."

"No, probably not. Frankly, I am not absolutely sure I do myself. It is a bit complicated, John. Extraordinarily hush-hush. Better if we wait until we return from the little trip you and I are getting ready to take for me to explain more fully. "Need to Know" and all that rot. Suffice to say, we are back working for Lt. Col. Dudley Clarke again and life as you have known it is never going to be the same."

What Captain Stone did not tell him because he did not know himself was that they were actors in what was to be Lieutenant Colonel Clarke's first-ever deception scheme called OPERATION ABEAM. The purpose of the exercise was to convince the Italian High Command that the British were capable of landing a strong airborne force deep in their rear in Italian East Africa – any time they wanted to.

All things considered, that notion was ridiculous, there being almost no qualified parachutists, very few parachutes, no troop-transport aircraft and a complete absence of the support resources in the Middle East Command necessary to carry out so much as a squad-sized airborne operation.

From radio intercepts (British Signals Intelligence was reading 90 percent of Italian radio traffic in Italian East Africa) it was known that the Blackshirts were extremely paranoid about the threat parachutists posed to their lines of communication. Armed with that information, Lieutenant Colonel Clarke was doing everything in his power to keep them worried.

Captain Stone led Major Randal out to a pink and buff desert camouflage-painted Chevrolet truck with the cab removed. The vehicle was bristling with gun mounts, a Boys .55 Anti-Tank rifle and two .303 Lewis machine guns. "I would dearly love to have a few Bren guns, but there are simply none to be had. Can you believe there is not a single Bren gun in the entire Middle East Theatre of Operations?"

"Lovely."

After a short drive, they came to a remote airplane hangar. A Royal Navy Catalina amphibian was parked outside with the engine ticking over. Major Randal and Captain Stone hurried aboard, and after a short time the plane began to taxi.

Once they were airborne, Captain Stone broke out a map, laid it over a crate and showed it to Major Randal. "For tonight's entertainment, we are flying up to a secret air base south of the Port of Sudan. There we will load onto a Vickers Valentia from No. 216 Bomber Transport Squadron and be flown to the Dahlak Archipelago located in the Red Sea off the coast of enemy-occupied Eritrea, specifically the island of Bela.

"Bela is a tiny privately-owned paradise situated six nautical miles off the coast of the port town of Massawa, where the Command Headquarters of the Italian East African Navy resides. The officer in command, Admiral Count Emmanuel Lombardi, commutes daily by floatplane or motor launch to and from his headquarters in Massawa to his island plantation estate.

"The only Italian troops on Bela are a handful of support personnel stationed there to service the floatplane and motor launch. This information is current and reliable. Colonel Clarke has an agent in residence on the island.

"Tonight, acting on a signal from that agent, you and I are going to parachute onto Bela and kidnap the Admiral. Waiting for us a quarter of a mile from the plantation house on a small, isolated beach will be a Royal Air Force Search and Rescue crash boat capable of speeds up to 40 knots per hour. After capturing the Admiral we will spirit him aboard the crash boat and return with all due speed to Sudanese territorial waters.

"What are your questions?"

"Is this a variation of LIMELIGHT?"

"Very perceptive, old stick. That is precisely what we will be doing.

"Tonight we are going to drop a dozen parachutes weighed down by blocks of ice on Bela to make the Italians think a raiding party from the 10th Abyssinian Parachute Battalion was used to snatch the Admiral. All the parachute gear and some other stuff we leave behind will be clearly marked 10th APB, 1st SAS."

"You dream this up?"

"No, it was all Dudley all the way – I merely suggested using the blocks of ice to weigh down the parachutes. Colonel Clarke thinks I am a military genius. Naturally, I never actually bothered to mention LIMELIGHT being the source of my inspiration.

"I did recommend sending for you."

"How do we get into the house?"

"The Admiral's mistress is going to leave the back door open for us."

"Now that's convenient. Anything else I need to know?"

"Not a thing… that is basically the plan."

"In that case, I've had a long day so I'm going to catch some zzz's before the fireworks begin."

"Good idea, we have awhile before we change planes in Port Sudan. By the way, there is this one little thing I am dying to know," Captain Stone inquired dryly. "Tell me, John, exactly how did it feel to rescue your betrothed's husband?"

"I could but then I'd have to…"

"Rotten luck, or maybe not," Captain Stone laughed. "Now we can get back to the serious business of chasing women again. Wait till I introduce you to the fleshpots of Cairo."

"Can't wait," Major Randal said. "You always did have good taste in bad women."

"Too true, but there is this one little distracter," Captain Stone said. Reaching into the pocket of his khaki battle dress uniform, he produced a heavy, black Rolex watch and handed it to Major Randal.

"Lady Jane wants you to have your trinket back. She shipped it out with the rest of your equipment.

"Orders are for you to wear it."

"You're kidding."

"My guess is your personal life is about to become enormously complex, old stick."

When the Catalina landed at the airbase outside of Port Sudan the two officers quickly off-loaded and went into a hanger where they linked up with the pilot who was to fly the night's mission. Capt. Sir Terry "Zorro" Stone gave a short pre-mission briefing.

"Situation: The Italians occupy Eritrea, British and French Somaliland and Abyssinia – called Italian East Africa.

"Enemy Forces: Conservative estimates show the Italians now have in excess of three hundred fifty thousand men under arms in IEA with a healthy mixture of regular stiffeners to native troops. The Italian troops consist of some of the finest regiments in the Italian Armed Forces. The Wops have approximately two hundred armored fighting vehicles, sixty of them tanks and four hundred fifty pieces of artillery.

"The IEA Air Force consists of approximately three hundred twenty-five warplanes.

"Italian Forces in IEA are expected to invade the Sudan at any moment in a coordinated pincer attack with the approximately two hundred fifty thousand Blackshirt Army striking out of Libya. The giant pincer movement will crack the Middle East Command like a walnut. If the Wops launch their assault, the result will be a walkover. The two armies will link up in Cairo.

"Friendly Forces: We have fewer than nine thousand troops in the Sudan consisting of three British line battalions, the four thousand five hundred-man Sudan Defense Force and a few small border outposts that are manned by Sudan Defense Force personnel and commanded by British reserve officers called up for emergency hostilities service. We have no tanks. However, there are a number of locally made armored cars created by welding turrets onto truck frames and mounting .55-caliber

Boys Anti-Tank rifles and Vickers .303-caliber machine guns. Aside from two ceremonial saluting guns at Government House, there is no artillery in the whole of the Sudan.

"Mission: Tonight, elements of the *notional* 10th Abyssinian Parachute Battalion, 1st Special Air Services, accompanied by two *actual* Raiding Forces officers will parachute onto the island of Bela in the Dahlak Archipelago located six nautical miles off the Coast of Massawa, a deep-water port inside Eritrean waters. Immediately upon landing, a two-man team consisting of Major Randal and myself will enter the plantation house, effect the capture of Admiral Count Emmanuel Lombardi and move him by the most direct route to the small beach located below the estate. There we will rendezvous with a RAF Search and Rescue boat that will be waiting in concealment there to transport us back to the Sudan.

"Execution: The concept of the operation is to depart this airfield aboard a Vickers Valentia provided by No. 216 Bomber Transport Squadron. Flying Officer Shawn Flannigan, the pilot for tonight's adventure, will brief the route immediately following this portion of the operations order. Our scheme of maneuver is to be as follows: the snatch party will drop by parachute, proceed to the rear door of the estate, which will be left unlocked by a confederate residing in the house, move to the bedroom located at the top of the stairs and take Admiral Lombardi prisoner. The snatch party – to include the inside operative – will then move to the extraction site by the most direct route, as briefed.

"Command and Signal: Our agent on the island has confirmed the Admiral is in residence on Bela tonight. En route to the drop zone, the jump aircraft will maintain radio silence. Upon arriving at the extraction point on the beach, the "challenge" is "*Remember*" and the "reply" is "*Calais.*" Anyone failing to "*Remember Calais*" when challenged is subject to being shot, which means they will be.

"Administration and Logistics: We are here, the jump aircraft is on station, parachutes are onboard the jump aircraft, the mission is a green light… we are going.

"Questions?"

When Major Randal responded with a thin smile, Flying Officer Flannigan stepped up to the map. "As briefed, we will be flying a Vickers

Valentia rigged for dropping parachutists. The Valentia is an open cockpit-type aircraft with two open cupolas in the back. Tonight you will exit from the rear cupola. The Valentia was never intended to drop people, only bombs. So as far as I am able to discern, this will be the first ever parachute jump from one. I can state unequivocally that it will be the maiden drop for the crew and pilot, meaning myself.

"The jump should be interesting. On the signal of my bombardier, who is acting in the capacity of dispatcher for the night's mission, you will have to simultaneously climb out and exit the aircraft from both sides of the fuselage. Unfortunately, our bombardier has never dispatched anything before except a bomb and rarely ever hits what he aims at.

"The flight time to the drop zone is thirty minutes. Tonight we will be dropping from an altitude of 400 feet. The drop zone is the front lawn of the estate. We will make a second pass over the island to drop the other parachutes and the ice blocks which will be carried in external bundles under the wings.

"Tally-ho and good hunting, gentlemen. I wish you all the luck. You are bloody well going to need it, what!"

As they double-timed out to the Vickers with their gear slung over their shoulders, Major Randal summarized to Captain Stone, "We're flying a World War I-era, open cockpit, bi-plane bomber never designed to drop paratroopers, piloted by a man who has never dropped a parachutist, with a dispatcher/bombardier who has a spotty record. We're making a low-level jump onto a tiny island behind enemy lines of a country I have barely ever heard of, in an archipelago for sure I never heard of. We have no way to confirm the wind conditions on the ground beforehand, which if they are excessive we crash and burn in our chutes or miss the drop zone all together and land in the sea.

"I leave anything out?"

"You managed to capture the essence of the exercise marvelously, old stick."

"Why does this not sound like a good idea?"

5
NIGHT DROP

THE ANCIENT VICKERS VALENTIA BI-WINGED BOMBER CLAWED ITS way out to sea. The African night was beautiful – clear and salted with neon-silver stars. They sparkled like diamonds lying on dark blue velvet, millions of stars – so many that they seemed to be stacked in layers on top of layers, glittering way up high. The night sky in Africa has a 3-D effect, making it seem much bigger than in England where the fog always seems to shut everything in.

The African sky looked even larger than Maj. John Randal was used to seeing in California. Tonight the panorama seemed especially majestic since he was sitting in the rear, open-topped cupola of a RAF bomber, winging his way toward enemy territory under the gleaming Southern Cross on what could only be described as a high-risk mission. Wearing aviator goggles but with his face in the slipstream, he was exposed to all the elements. This was what old-school flying was all about. If it rained, you got rained on; if it snowed, you got snowed on. Iron men crewed these open-cockpit canvas aircraft.

The adrenalin rush kicked in early.

Major Randal could see the back of Capt. Sir Terry "Zorro" Stone's head up front in the midsection cupola. The dashing Life Guards officer turned and gave him a grin and a thumbs-up signal. There was no one he would rather be joining on a dangerous enterprise. The wind screamed through Major Randal's hair, and he had the feeling he was rushing toward something... but what?

It felt as if Major Randal somehow had crossed through a time warp to find himself transported back to an old-fashioned 19th-century war. In fact, that was almost exactly what had occurred. The remote war in East Africa was like turning back a page in history, improvised day to day, complete with spear-carrying warriors, feudal chieftains, slaves, mule cavalry, homemade cannons, camel caravans, communication carried by messenger in the forked cleft of sticks and a passive-aggressive Abyssinian Emperor-in-exile who had a Royal Umbrella.

And Major Randal was flying straight into it as fast as the old airplane could sputter. The Vickers Valentia seemed to be streaking through the diamond-studded sky, but in fact it was crawling along since top speed was only 120 mph. Captain Stone turned in the cupola again and held up both hands with his fingers splayed wide, the international jumpmaster signal indicating "10 minutes." Normally, that meant they had ten minutes flight time until the green light came on, only there was no green light on this airplane. Suddenly, Captain Stone ducked down, completely disappearing from the cupola.

Major Randal did the same and waited for him to come crawling back through the communications tunnel that ran the length of the aircraft's fuselage. They would both be jumping from the rear cupola, which was going to be a bit of a challenge. No one had ever done it before. In a few seconds, Captain Stone came worming along followed by the goggle-faced bombardier who would be acting as the dispatcher.

Since the RAF man had never ever dispatched a parachutist before, this mission was on-the-job training all the way. The two officers had taken the precaution of wearing their parachutes onboard so they would not have to perform in-flight rigging – a feat that is tricky under the best of circumstances. The Vickers Valentia was not fitted with a static line.

Two cheap-looking metal handles that looked suspiciously as if they had been unscrewed from the drawers of one of the squadron desks (which is exactly what had happened) had been bolted to each side of the airframe to provide a place to hook their static lines.

Each of the two jumpers took the snap hook on his static line and snapped it to the handle on the side of the aircraft from which he would exit – Major Randal from the left and Captain Stone from the right. The improvised desk handles/static line devices raised the meaning of the term "field expedient" to a new level.

"Check equipment," Captain Stone commanded, acting in the role of jumpmaster because the rookie dispatcher did not know the sequence of the jump commands. Both officers ran their hands over their pistols, knives, and the buckles of their parachute harnesses and patted their pockets. At this point, the two Commandos were merely going through the motions. The drill was a wasted exercise.

The two were going to jump no matter what they discovered.

"Check static line!" On this command, both officers jerked on their static lines, hoping against hope the handles would not come free from the airframe. The kitchen furniture hardware looked decidedly unprofessional.

Major Randal felt reasonably confident the drawer handles had not undergone any preflight testing to establish tensile strength. They would probably work fine. Probably, however, is not reassuring when you are getting ready to exit an aircraft at an altitude of 400 feet with no reserve parachute. A paratrooper has to depend on a lot of things when jumping from an aircraft in flight. Hope should not be one of them.

The bombardier/dispatcher relayed into the headset of the radio he was wearing, "One minute to target."

Now came the tricky part. Both jumpers had to climb out of the cupola and take up a position outside the fuselage of the aircraft directly across from each other while holding onto their static line like it was a rope, and making sure not to accidently activate their parachutes. Once in place, they assumed the mountaineering "on rappel" position with their knees bent and the rubber soles of their canvas-topped raiding boots flat against the skin of the plane.

The idea was this: when the signal was given to "Go," the jumpers would each thrust out vigorously like they were raapelling off the side of the Vickers Valentia. And it was critical to ensure that at any point in the process they did not kick a hole in the side of the fabric covering the airframe, thus finding themselves trapped and being towed upside-down by the leg, or manage to get the static line wrapped around their neck.

Little details like that are important when jumping from an aircraft while in flight.

In theory, parachuting from a Vickers Valentia sounded possible, only no one had ever actually jumped from one. When Major Randal climbed over the side of the cupola, the slipstream started to whip and crackle, but he was pleasantly surprised to find that he had no trouble maintaining his balance. The lightweight, rubber-soled boots Capt. the Lady Jane Seaborn had custom-made for Raiding Forces based on a pattern used by water fowlers stuck to the side of the airplane like glue. He made sure each boot was firmly planted on a support strut under the fabric covering the fuselage.

Across the top of the cupola he could barely make out Captain Stone's padded jump helmet. Stitched boldly on the front in big, bold, scarlet letters was "1st SPECIAL AIR SERVICES." The bombardier/dispatcher was standing up, leaning back against the front of the cupola with his back to the direction of flight, concentrating on the radio strapped to his chest.

Up ahead, looking down the side of the bi-winged Vickers Valentia, Major Randal could see a white line of breakers coming up fast. This was the best view he had ever had of a jump in progress. The mission was unfolding right before his eyes, sending a fresh dose of adrenalin surging through his system.

His brain was screaming *Go, Go, Go...*

The breakers and the beach flashed below. Major Randal could see the RAF crash boat as they sailed over and actually saw what appeared to be two white faces turned skyward, then the plantation house was in sight. He turned his head back to watch the bombardier, but kept the drop zone in the edge of his peripheral vision.

Major Randal was ready.

Savagely, the bombardier/dispatcher chopped his hand: "Go!"

Major Randal kicked out vigorously with his legs and let go of the yellow static line. He was away from the aircraft, falling backward, watching in semi-detachment as his canopy deployed over his shoulder. He actually saw the canopy being pulled out – and he thought – the retaining bands snapping off and the white thread tie pop from his body weight and snap free from the tie-off on the static line.

Up to that point, the jump was playing out in slow motion, but then things shifted into real time, real quick. He took one swing – *KERBLAAAAAM* – and slammed into the ground, barely having taken up the "prepare-to-land" position with his fists clenched together in front of his helmet, forearms and elbows touching, head bent, feet, ankles, knees touching, knees bent and relaxed – not locked.

Major Randal never saw the ground coming up. He was down, instinctively doing a rear parachute landing fall that must have been pretty close to textbook perfect, at least in part because he ended it standing on his head (which is not one of the five points of contact) before crashing back down. And he did not kill himself or break a single bone. Though that was not entirely clear at first.

The pilot must have been flying lower than 400 feet. This was one jump when he did not immediately bounce right back up, slap off the dust and shout AIRBORNE! In paratrooper speak, he had "crashed and burned."

Major Randal lay there checking himself for injuries and could not believe his luck when he did not find any major damage. My, did that hurt! Fortunately he had come down right in the middle of the manicured carpetgrass lawn.

Captain Stone limped up, "You OK?"

"I'm probably dying from internal injuries, but let's go."

The island was perfectly quiet. Suddenly there was a mighty thundering roar as the Vickers Valentia came around and made another low-level pass overhead to jettison the dozen parachutes weighted down by their ice blocks. The sky was dotted with chutes swinging their way silently to the ground. The men, both real and notional, of the 10th Abyssinian Parachute Battalion, 1st Special Air Services, were going into action.

While there were no serious jump casualties in the notional unit, the two actual paratroopers were dinged up a bit.

Major Randal slipped his silenced High Standard .22 automatic out of his chest holster. He and Captain Stone padded silently around to the back of the white house that appeared faintly blue in the mellow African moonlight. Everything seemed perfectly quiet – nothing was stirring on the island as far as they could tell. No lights were showing in the house.

As advertised, the back door was unlocked, but they were startled to find a woman waiting for them in the dark when they stepped inside. Major Randal came very close to shooting her. In the dim light they could see that she was dressed in riding habit, jodhpurs and boots, ready for a journey.

Was the woman their contact?

"The master bedroom is upstairs on the right," she whispered. "The Count is in bed, fast asleep. He woke up momentarily but thought your plane was merely one of his pilots buzzing the island. They do that occasionally to amuse themselves."

"Lead the way, lady," Major Randal ordered, "I'll be right behind you."

"You have no reason to be alarmed. We are quite alone. The Admiral is a heavy sleeper. He will not awaken again."

"For his sake let's hope not."

They crept to the top of the long spiral stairway and peeked into the room on the right. The master bedroom was as big as most houses. One whole wall was glass, showcasing a fabulous view of the ocean. The sight was breathtaking, only they were not there for the scenery. The man they had come to collect lay snoozing contentedly in a mammoth four-poster, high-canopied bed. He was dressed in a long, white, silk nightshirt, and they could see from the round mound protruding from the center of it that he was a tubby little fellow.

The woman, who was not the least bit tubby in her skin-tight jodhpurs, moved to the side of the bed and shook the Admiral gently. "Wake up, darling. There are some gentlemen here to see you."

That had to be one of the major understatements in the history of armed warfare. The only response from the sleeping sailor was to roll over and clutch at the covers. Apparently, Admiral Count Lombardi did not care for visitors or the notion of having his beauty rest disturbed.

Captain Stone, being a man of action, reached over and slapped him on the derrière with the flat slide of his Colt .38 Super, commanding cheerfully, "Rise and shine, old stick."

The metal slap must have really stung because the drowsy Admiral yelped, rolled over and sat up, startled, shouting "abuse" in Italian.

"You think he is threatening to have us court-martialed?"

Major Randal ignored the question, screwed the silencer on the .22 High Standard into Admiral Count Lombardi's left ear and snarled, "Shut up and get out of bed before I blow your head clean off."

The Admiral spoke flawless English. He responded with alacrity. You do not reach his station in life in a fascist dictatorship without knowing when to give orders and when to obey them. He shot out of bed like the tail of his silk sleeping shirt had burst into flames.

The Admiral's mistress had his best uniform all laid out waiting for him. Major Randal noted there were enough ribbons, badges, cords and orders pinned to it to have decorated every man in Raiding Forces, twice over. Gold braid covered all the places the medals left bare. The comic opera military costume would have made Napoleon blush.

Only, why was it laid out like that in the middle of the night?

Admiral Lombardi was a pampered prima donna, but not a stupid one. He could add two plus two. The melodrama commenced. He burst into tears uttering loud effusive recriminations in flowery Italian. The mistress burst into tears responding in kind. This went on for some time until Major Randal snapped, "Will you people put a cork in it. Get your pants on, or we'll drag you out of here in your underwear."

The Admiral petulantly commenced the involved process of suiting up. Major Randal took the precaution of slipping the man's beautifully engraved Beretta Model 1935 .32-caliber pocket pistol out of its tiny holster and into his own pocket. No sense taking a chance.

Italian Admirals, especially Counts, have their needs – and Admiral Lombardi was no exception. Getting him dressed was an involved process. Normally, his two naval aides arrived early by floatplane or motor torpedo boat and served as valets to assist the mistress in the elaborate morning ritual.

But not too early... Admiral Count Lombardi was not a morning person.

Considering the exigency of the circumstances, the two pseudo-

1st Special Air Services officers were certainly indulgent. Patience with recalcitrant prisoners when behind enemy lines on a dangerous mission is not known as a common Commando trait. Particularly when it was time to execute that age-old military maneuver popularly known in Raiding Forces as "getting the hell out of Dodge."

"I demand to know who I am surrendering to. I would prefer it to be an officer of my own rank, but in this situation a mere introduction will undoubtedly have to suffice," the Admiral complained.

"This is Maj. John Randal, DSO, MC, and I am Capt. Terry Stone, KBE, MC. British Commandos currently assigned to the 1st Special Air Services," Captain Stone replied, unruffled. "We apologize for the inconsequentialness of our grade, your Excellence; however, there is no one in all Africa of appropriate flag rank who knows how to parachute."

Captain Stone had quite a bit of experience breaking news they did not want to hear to members of the exalted class, as might be expected of the fabled black sheep of an ancient noble family. His father was a duke.

"If it is any solace, old stick," he added modestly, "I am a Knight of the Realm."

Even in the dim light they could see Admiral Count Lombardi had turned a sickly shade of green. "The pirates who purloined the *Giove* and the *Egadi* from San Pedro?"

"That would be us," Major Randal said. "Get a move on."

"My dear, you have placed me in the hands of ruthless brigands!" the Count wailed. "To criminals like these the Geneva Convention is a fool's scrap. What villainy, I am betrayed to cold-blooded murderers."

"Time to go, your lordship," Captain Stone ordered, losing patience. "Be nice or we shall be forced to turn you over to the platoon of Abyssinian paratroops that dropped in with us. I doubt they have ever heard of the Geneva Accords, much less read them."

The threat worked like magic. The rotund little sea warrior began trembling in terror and suddenly became passive and cooperative. Major Randal had never seen a bluff deliver a better result.

The Admiral's mistress had bags packed and waiting by the back door. The four moved out of the house and proceeded single file down the trail to the beach where the RAF crash boat was standing by with its powerful engines warbling. As they approached, a challenge rang out from a concealed position, "*REMEMBER*!"

"Don't shoot, Butch."

"Anyone following your party, sir?" RM Butch Hoolihan queried, aiming his Thompson submachine gun back up the trail.

"If anyone is, they aren't going to remember Calais," Major Randal said. "What are you doing here?"

"Lady Seaborn sent me out to deliver your gear. Did you get your watch, sir?"

"Yeah," Major Randal snapped, "I got it."

"I am under strict orders to make sure, sir," Royal Marine Hoolihan said sheepishly.

"Let's get the hell out of Dodge, sailor," Major Randal ordered, ignoring the young Royal Marine as he started to climb aboard to take the seat next to the boat captain, a slim sailor wearing a black baseball cap with the bill pulled down low.

"Hang on, John!" Mrs. Brandy Seaborn whooped, ramming the throttle forward. She was a competition-class, open-sea speedboat driver. A surprised Major Randal barely managed to pile in before the whiplash of the powerful engines nearly broke his neck.

"Brandy...?"

"I came out to work for Dudley," Brandy shouted over the roar of the powerful RAF boat, anticipating his question. "It was A-Force or be drafted."

The trip back to the Sudan was like riding on the tip of a speeding bullet. Nothing the Italian Navy had in their inventory could have caught them, although Brandy did not intend to give them the chance to find out. The daughter of a legendary Royal Navy fighting admiral, she loved to go fast in speed boats.

No one on the RAF Search and Rescue boat complained about the quality of the pounding ride. No one, that is, except the Admiral, who became nauseous from seasickness... or maybe he was simply taken ill when it became apparent there was no platoon of Abyssinian parachutists along on the raid.

As they pounded along, Admiral Count Lombardi began to grow concerned about appearances. It was not going to sit well with his superiors in Rome for a man of his stature to be kidnapped by a raiding party that consisted of a mere four people – one of which was a woman. The fortunes of war are capricious. An officer has to be prepared to accept the possibility of becoming a POW. Only he was, after all, an admiral and a count.

Any unit sent to capture such a man should consist of a battalion, at least, if not a full regiment.

Royal Marine Hoolihan leaned over the front seat as the boat shot across the Red Sea, pounding hard for the Sudan. "You and Captain Stone looked fantastic hanging out of that Vickers on rappel, sir. The plane was so low I was afraid your parachutes might not deploy at that altitude. We lost sight of you right after you flew over the tree line."

"Parachutes?" Brandy asked with a glittering smile. "I thought you and Terry slid down ropes."

Even Admiral Count Lombardi was forced to do a double-take. Mrs. Brandy Seaborn was a one-of-a-kind original. She also happened to be married to the first cousin of Captain the Lady Jane Seaborn's recently-returned-from-the-dead husband.

As the crash boat pulled into safety inside Sudanese waters, Brandy turned to Major Randal and said, "We need to talk."

6
PARTY IN CAIRO

THE CAPTURE AND ABDUCTION OF ADMIRAL COUNT EMMANUEL Lombardi was front-page news worldwide. Newspaper reporters, magazine feature writers and radio "press wallahs" were literally crawling all over Shepard's Hotel competing for a chance at an "exclusive" interview with Maj. John Randal and Capt. Sir Terry "Zorro" Stone. The press drank copious amounts of alcohol in the Long Bar while tantalizing each other with totally fictitious "inside" accounts from bogus participants in the operation, who quite naturally wished to remain anonymous.

The hotel was a zoo.

Lt. Col. Dudley Clarke was out of the city but he dispatched one of his officers – a rumpled author, Capt. Dennis Wheatly, who in civilian life had made a spectacular fortune writing bodice-ripping thrillers. Captain Wheatly was scheduled to spend a day interviewing the two heroes with an eye to producing a pamphlet for public distribution entitled *Jump on Bela*. The interview had not required anything like a full day. In fact, it had lasted less than an hour. After listening to a brief recital of events, the author began packing up.

"No need to waste your time with the minor details, chaps. The crux of the story, as I understand it, is the 10th Abyssinian Parachute Battalion, 1st Special Air Services, launched its maiden operation in Italian East Africa by dropping a platoon of crack Abyssinian Paratroops from a fleet of sleek modern RAF long-range troop transports onto the island of Bela, which was guarded by a force of suicidal Muslim fanatics all armed to the teeth with automatic weapons and curved swords sworn to fight to the death in the defense of their beloved commander, Admiral the Count Lombardi.

"You parachuted in, fought a pitched battle on the drop zone, wiped out the entire bodyguard in bloody hand-to-hand combat, then captured and spirited away the Count by submarine in a hail of gunfire. How am I doing so far?"

"Absolutely spot-on, Dennis," Captain Stone drawled. "You make it sound almost as if you were right there peeking over our shoulders taking notes during all the action, old stick."

"Those bad guys were tough sword fighters," Major Randal said.

"Excellent! I shall fill in the rest," Captain Wheatly said. "No need for you two to bother yourself unnecessarily supplying the background, it's all color anyway. I shall be off, then."

Three days later while they were sitting at the Gezira Club pool admiring the scenery, Captain Stone observed, "Methinks upon reflection, there is more to all this publicity than meets the eye, old stick."

"Like what?" Major Randal asked, ogling one of the long-legged secretaries who worked at the Free French Legation. She had a golden milk-chocolate tan and was wearing the tiniest bikini legal in public.

"Not quite sure. Normally our missions are classified 'Most Secret,' unless of course there is something to be gained by publicizing the operation. We might want to do it again someday, so why tell the opposition how we went about it. There are things it does not pay to advertise."

"Well, let me know when you figure it out, Zorro."

An armed messenger arrived poolside bearing a briefcase for them to sign for. Captain Stone initialed the chit and snapped open the case. Inside were two copies of a paperback book with an artist's drawing of a heroic figure firing a Thompson submachine gun from the hip with one hand while his parachute billowed out behind him. Prominent on his padded jump helmet was a "1st SPECIAL AIR SERVICES" flash. A big tear-shaped flame was coming out the barrel of the Thompson, and in the foreground an evil-looking, sword-swinging Muslim fanatic was biting the dust.

The title screamed, *JUMP ON BELA. The 10th Abyssinian Parachute Battalion, 1st Special Air Service gets their Man.*

"That was quick," Major Randal said.

"I told you something was afoot," Captain Stone muttered with a tinge of concern in his voice. *Jump on Bela* has to be the all-time world record for publishing a book."

"I bet it's good writing, too."

The two young officers took turns reading parts out loud to each other. "You are simply going to love this, John. *'Sir,' the leather-faced Abyssinian sergeant inquired of his commander, Maj. John Randal, the legendary pin-prick raider, 'what are your orders for dealing with the platoon of fanatical Muslim Commandos on Bela when we land?'*

" *'Kill 'em all,' Major Randal growled, 'and let Allah sort 'em out!'* " Captain Stone recited, barely able to contain himself.

"You're kidding me…"

"Pulitzer Prize-winning material!"

The two gave it up as a lost cause when they came to the part where *"Capt. Sir Terry 'Zorro' Stone climbed up the vines growing up the wall of the estate with a razor-sharp Fairbairn Commando dagger clenched in his teeth in high hopes of slipping inside and cutting a "Z" into the belly of the Admiral's faithful bodyguard, a giant known to guard the door to the bedroom suite while his master slept."*

"I remember I thought at the time," Major Randal said, "you looked really cool scaling that grapevine."

"As I recall, we simply walked up the staircase. I find it hard to believe Captain Wheatly actually put his name on this piece of trash. After all, the man does have a certain reputation to maintain."

When they both turned back to the cover of their books, they noticed Captain Wheatly's name was conspicuously absent. But in the lower right-hand corner, under the billowing parachute, was printed, *"as related by Maj. John Randal, DSO, MC, and Capt. Sir Terry 'Zorro' Stone, KBE, MC."*

"Oh, no..."

"We shall never live this one down. Dudley has ruined us."

"I should've let him bleed to death the night the Germans nearly shot his ear off."

"Rather wish you had, old stick. The Regiment will take a dim view of *Jump on Bela*. Exaggerating one's actions is something simply not done in the Life Guards. We are the acknowledged masters of the art of studied understatement."

"Can we put a stop to this?"

"Not a chance, Colonel Clarke is a law unto himself," Captain Stone said regretfully. "Some people say he reports to Wavell, some claim he reports directly to Churchill, while others believe he does not bother to report to anyone."

"Brandy said she was in A-Force. What's the 'A' stand for?"

"The A is a clever cover designed to mislead the Italians into thinking it means 'Airborne Force.' Rather odd, considering not one single member except Hoolihan and the two of us is parachute-qualified. Colonel Clarke is obsessed with the idea of parachutists."

"How and when did we get assigned, exactly?"

"Hard to say. The whole of Raiding Forces will be A-Force when it arrives out here. How it is going to work out in practice is anyone's guess. Most likely we shall be under its umbrella, like we are Combined Operations back home."

"Do you have any idea what A-Force does?"

"Actually, no. It is a Most Secret combination of intelligence, operations, escape and evasion, propaganda and deception functions. I doubt there has ever been a military unit like it. All hush-hush, completely compartmentalized, nobody knows everything A-Force is involved in, even those people working for it."

"I didn't even know I was working for it," Major Randal said. "Could be the kind of outfit that might have possibilities."

"When I came out, Dudley shipped me off to the Long Range Desert Group straight away to 'get desertized.' When we bring the first detachment of Raiding Forces out here, I recommend we do the same with them. Desert operations up to two thousand miles behind the Italian lines at a clip are a very specialized business. And they are very interesting."

"Can you set that up?"

"The Long Range Desert Group is a snooty bunch, particular about who they let in. It's made up mostly of officers who were pre-war cerebral desert rats, explorers, scientists, archeologists and the like. The LRDG is the brainiest bunch of cutthroats in Africa. Their primary mission is to perform strategic long-range reconnaissance for General Headquarters Middle East Command."

"Interesting...."

"Right now all the field troops assigned are New Zealanders. But that is getting ready to change soon. The LRDG plan to have patrols from a cross-section of the British regiments assigned out here. Most likely, Dudley can arrange for a Raiding Forces patrol to be attached for training purposes.

"Good idea, let's do it."

"The Colonel is set on having his own parachute-amphibious-desert-capable unit he can call on at a moment's notice to go anywhere, anytime, to carry out his special pet projects. That's why he sent for you. This definitely could work out to be a plum assignment, John."

"Raiding Forces can fit that bill," Major Randal said. "Not that it sounds like we have much choice."

"The Middle East Command is where all the action is," Captain Stone explained. "It covers the entire continent of Africa plus the Mediterranean and every country that borders it. The possibilities for raiding are unlimited.

"What have you done to increase the troop strength of Raiding Forces?"

"I gave instructions to Pelham-Davies to stand down, send the men on a ten-day recruiting leave with orders for each man to come back with his counterpart, or at least his name," Major Randal said. "Larry Grand is arranging the transfers. In about another six weeks or so we ought to have all our new recruits passing out of Parachute School and Achnacarry."

"Outstanding," Captain Stone produced his sterling silver cigarette case and held it out.

"My idea was our boys would pick only the best if they were recruiting their own wingmen."

"No doubt, neatly done, old stick."

"I couldn't think of anything else."

What Capt. Sir Terry "Zorro" Stone did not mention to Maj. John Randal because he did not have a "Need to Know" was before departing England for Egypt he had been summoned to White's for a discreet meeting with "C" – Col. Steward Menzies, DSO – the head of MI-6, the British Secret Intelligence Service. Captain Stone and "C" were officers of the 2nd Life Guards, graduates of Eton, members of the prestigious boy's club Pop, White's and the politically influential Beaufort Hunt.

In a brief meeting in the billiard room where "C" unofficially conducted much of MI-6's official business, Colonel Menzies explained to the young playboy that it was time for him to do his duty for King and Country.

"Sir Terry, from this moment forward you are my man. When you go to Africa I have need of trustworthy eyes and ears on the ground out there. One must never let the side down, and I am quite confident you shall not."

And that, as they say, was that. Welcome to the SIS. Once in, never out.

While Major Randal and Captain Stone were spending their days waiting for Lt. Col. Dudley Clarke to return to Cairo, they were having the officially sanctioned party of their lives. They were not on leave, and there were certain military obligations the two were required to perform, but the work was not onerous.

Basically, the Raiding Forces officers were under orders to be seen in 1st SAS regalia in as many places as possible by as many people as possible in as short a period as possible. The two intrepid Commandos interpreted that to mean at the race track, polo club, every bar at which officers were authorized admittance, some they were not, and every social function – belly-dancing emporium, cabaret, house party, or any event where people gathered to entertain themselves.

The assignment was taking a toll.

Mornings they were met at their hotel by RM Butch Hoolihan, accompanied by two natives in starched khaki 1st Special Air Services uniforms. They were masquerading as parachutists from the 10th Abyssinian Parachute Battalion. In fact, the pseudo-1st SAS troopers were Kenyan houseboys borrowed from the fashionable bordello located at No.6 Sharia Qasr El-Nil that occupied the upper floor in the building Lieutenant Colonel Clarke had chosen for his A-Force Headquarters.

It was typical that the A-Force Commander would choose to set up offices on the ground floor of a house of ill repute and allow the ladies to continue operating their business as usual on the second floor. Also, good cover. No suspicions were aroused by a wide variety of officers coming and going at all hours.

The five SAS men would proceed to a nearby airfield where the jump-qualified members of the group – meaning Major Randal, Captain Stone and Royal Marine Hoolihan – donned parachutes and boarded one of a number of different obsolete RAF transport airplanes. They would then fly to a nearby drop zone that had been carefully selected so that it could be seen by thousands of people in Cairo from a distance – but by no one up close. Then they would parachute out at three times the normal combat jump altitude so that the maximum number of people on the ground would have ample time to observe their descent.

On each jump, Major Randal, Captain Stone and Royal Marine Hoolihan were accompanied out the door by a stick of dummy paratroopers improvised out of sand-filled duffel bags. It was hoped they looked like genuine parachutists from a distance. A crew from A-Force on the Drop Zone (DZ) collected the duffel bags the moment they hit the ground. The DZ personnel discreetly poured out their sand, rolled up the parachutes, and loaded everything into a tarp-covered truck that drove them back to the airfield to make ready for the next day's jump.

The two houseboys – being deathly afraid of heights – did not go anywhere near an airplane. They simply removed their starched khaki uniforms in the hangar, put work clothes back on and were returned by truck to resume their domestic duties with no one the wiser.

There were soon so many sightings of the 10th Abyssinian Parachute

Battalion that speculation began circulating around the bars of Cairo that the unit must actually be the advance party of the 1st Airborne Division known to be forming in England.

Additional misinformation exercises were conducted during the hours of darkness by the two intrepid 1st Special Air Services officers, which consisted mainly of chasing women. Major Randal and Captain Stone felt it was important to personally brief as many of the local lovelies as they possibly could on the highly-classified organizational details and future plans of the nonexistent Most Secret 10th APB in the time allocated.

In the interest of military deception, naturally.

As women were such well-documented gossips and most likely not signatories of the Official Secrets Act, the two reasoned they were getting the maximum bang for their buck by focusing on them almost exclusively – especially the good-looking ones. The women would immediately go and tell their girlfriends all the juicy details. At least, that was the plan.

All in all, it was probably a good thing they did not have to clear that part of the deception campaign with any senior grade officer. Not even with Lieutenant Colonel Clarke, who never showed up.

A photo of the two 10th APB officers soon appeared in the local newspapers. The two Commandos were seated, hunched over a table in a smoke-filled room in intense conversation. The cutline on the photo read, *"Raiding aces Major John Randal, DSO, MC, and Captain Sir Terry Stone, KBE, MC, who recently returned from their daring capture of the Italian commander of the Port of Massawa, plot the next mission to be carried out by the famed 1st Special Air Services. No high-ranking enemy officer anywhere in Africa should sleep soundly knowing these two gentlemen might drop in unannounced to pay them a visit."*

In fact, when the photo was taken the duo was watching a floorshow at the Kit Kat Club and were debating the merits of who would get the bleached blond and who would get the redhead. On the seventh day, Captain Stone had to return to the field with the Long Range Desert Group. Major Randal bravely soldiered on alone.

He and Royal Marine Hoolihan made a jump every morning, then drove around town in full 10th APB dress. Cairo smelled of dung, kerosene, jasmine and Jackalberry trees. The green, palm tree-lined boulevards by the Nile, with the desert sun glittering off the river, was a stark contrast to the fog, rain and gloom they had left behind in England.

The city was magical, especially as the sun sank into the desert blazing gold, scarlet and silvery turquoise. Horns honked, military trucks and staff cars weaved in and out of traffic, and the shrill cries of vendors pierced the air. A throng of Arabs, Englishmen, French, Greek, Egyptians, Maltese, Cypriots, Turks, Muslims, Jews, Coptic Christians and Syrian Christians milled in the bazaars or sipped from tiny cups in the cafés. The city pulsated with music and exotic prospects. Anything was possible in Cairo. And anything might just happen… for a price.

After a drink at the bar in the Continental, where it was said that sooner or later you would run into every officer serving in the Middle East Command, Major Randal would head over to the terrace at Shepard's, which was always packed. The crowd consisted of a variety of uniformed officers and their ladies. Later he would pay a visit to the Turf Club, or he might decide to drop in on a cricket match at the Sporting Club.

Afternoons were always spent poolside at the Gezira Club. Except for Brandy Seaborn, Major Randal did not know a single woman in Cairo, but he was never alone. Evenings after a drink at the Long Bar at Shepard's it was dinner at Groppi's or the posh Mohammad Ali Club.

Women simply threw themselves at him. The females in Cairo were insatiable. Major Randal could not understand what caused the girls to act the way they did. He had always been lucky with women, though never anything like this. Without overthinking things, he did his duty. His was not to reason why.

Major Randal mostly gravitated toward Egyptian hostesses, French secretaries, Hungarian actresses and Greek refugees. He stayed away from the British expatriates. Some were married or recently widowed by the war. He made a point of avoiding anyone who might possibly know Capt. the Lady Jane Seaborn or know someone who knew her.

He tried not to spend one minute of time thinking about or being reminded of his ex-fiancée, which was not all that easy since he was wearing the Rolex she had given him. All he was looking for was the anonymity to have a good time, though that too was proving difficult with his picture in the papers and strangers coming up asking him to sign their copy of *Jump on Bela.*

1940 Cairo was the kind of place where you did not have to explain your actions to anyone. Anything short of outright homicide was legal, and even murder was permissible under certain circumstances. It was the perfect place for a fighting soldier to blow off steam with no regrets.

Major Randal took full advantage of the opportunity.

Lt. Gen. Sir Archibald Percival Wavell looked across his desk at the Royal Navy officer tasked with clearing the Red Sea of Italian submarines by unconventional means, Cdre. Richard "Dickey the Pirate" Seaborn, VC, OBE. In as few words as possible he outlined his immediate problem.

"Commodore, we need a man to command a guerrilla force deep behind the lines in Abyssinia and we need him right now. Do you know of any officer who might be a candidate for the assignment?"

Since clearing the Italian East African coastline of Italian Air and Navy military bases along the Red Sea was a precondition of qualifying for the soon-to-be-enacted United States Lend Lease Act, the ground conquest of IEA was of principal concern to the Royal Navy.

Commodore Seaborn had been charged with that assignment using irregular means. The upcoming East African Campaign in Abyssinia was in fact going to be an army land battle fought to accomplish an Air Force and Navy objective. It was arguably the most important military operation of the war.

He was well-briefed on the subject.

Coincidentally, in his pocket Commodore Seaborn had a cable which had arrived that morning from his cousin, the recently returned-from-the-dead Cdr. Mallory Seaborn which read:

> AM UNDER CLOUD WITH THE ADMIRALTY STOP JANE DIFFICULT STOP FALLEN FOR AMERICAN OFFICER KNOWN TO YOU WHO IS TEMPORARILY ON ASSIGNMENT MIDDLE EAST COMMAND STOP IMPERATIVE YOU

ARRANGE FOR SAID OFFICER TO REMAIN IN THEATRE UNTIL I PUT THINGS RIGHT WITH ADMIRALTY AND JANE STOP
SIGNED MALLORY STOP

His cousin created something of a dilemma for Commodore Seaborn. England is a seafaring nation and a country that expects her subjects to do their duty during times of national emergency. That goes double for members of the Six Hundred, the wealthy, titled families who control the Empire and whose men are expected to lead from the front during times of war.

While Royal Navy captains are not actually required to go down with their ship it is considered good form for the commander to be the last man to abandon ship in the event it should ever sink. What is not such a terrific idea is for the skipper of a warship lost in action to be the sole survivor, like Mallory.

Commodore Seaborn loved his cousin like a brother, yet he was torn in this situation. Until Maj. John Randal had requested him by name to participate in OPERATION LOUNGE LIZARD, the cutting-out operation at Rio Bonita, he had been an obscure convoy-router, slaving in the bowels of the Admiralty. Most likely it would have been his fate to be buried alive there for the duration of the war had the young American not intervened.

Now promoted with a Victoria Cross he was not sure he deserved *and* a prestigious new assignment, the request from his cousin put him between a rock and a hard spot. A man of honor, he would never intentionally do anything to harm the Raiding Forces officer or interfere with his career other than to further it. Clearly Commodore Seaborn owed Major Randal a debt of gratitude he could never repay.

On the other hand, he loved his cousin.

Commodore Seaborn understood as well as anyone that the narrow neck of water where the Red Sea emptied into the Gulf of Aden known as the Bab el-Mandeb passage was the most strategically important single piece of real estate in the entire world right at this precise moment in history. If the Italians choked it off, the Middle East Command would be left twisting in the wind. There would be no Lend Lease, and in all likelihood the war would be lost.

Maybe it was possible to kill two birds with one stone.

"Sir," he said, "I believe I know the man for the job."

Maj. John Randal was sitting alone at a table at the Kit Kat Club taking in the floorshow and killing time in high anticipation for closing time to roll around. The feature dancer had invited him to escort her to a private party on a Nile River houseboat after last call. A big man with a ginger toothbrush moustache, wearing an ill-fitting, off-white linen suit that had seen better days, strolled up and sat down at his table, uninvited.

The interloper gave him a yellow-toothed smile.

Major Randal did not know what to make of the situation but did not welcome the intrusion. He did not have any interest in making a new friend. The bulge under the left shoulder of the man's coat was a dead giveaway… the stranger was a member of the Field Security Branch of the Cairo Military Police. Now what could *he* want?

The man said, "*Frogspawn*!"

All things must come to an end.

Within the hour, Major Randal found himself (along with all his gear and RM Butch Hoolihan) in the back of a lumbering RAF transport airplane so old he had never seen one like it before, not even in a picture. He had no idea why they were on this aircraft or where it was going.

Oh well, Cairo had been good while it lasted.

MISSION

7
LONE RANGER

THE SUDAN'S SPECIAL OPERATIONS EXECUTIVE CHIEF OF STATION Jim "Baldie" Taylor was sitting in the sandwich shop of the Khartoum Airport talking quietly to one of his agents who had recently returned from Istanbul. He was waiting to meet a Royal Air Force transport plane scheduled to arrive shortly from Cairo with a very important person onboard.

"Let me get this straight," Baldie demanded incredulously. "They used Randal as bait in a mousetrap operation and were surprised when he shot all the opposition before the show even got started? What did they think was going to happen?"

"No one knew he was armed," the agent explained. "Plum-Martin tried to abort the operation in the casino when she realized things were spiraling out of control, but it went down so fast."

The agent laughed, "Randal and the SS woman were not supposed to make a beeline straight for her bedroom. The idea was to follow the two of them bar-hopping around town until the Abwehr Chief showed up, then nab him. No one was supposed to get killed, except maybe Randal later on."

"Those SOE Istanbul people are complete idiots."

"Chief, that's exactly what Plum-Martin put in her report."

"Do the Turks know?"

"The locals are not happy; one of their Security Service officers accompanied by two muscle thugs escorted Major Randal to the airport the next morning, but nothing came of it. They even gave him his Browning 9mm back. Everyone concerned is trying to act like they have no idea anything happened."

"How about the Germans?"

"What are they going to do, Chief? Besides, they were planning to kidnap and murder Randal."

"Go get the car; here comes Romeo now."

Maj. John Randal and RM Butch Hoolihan were walking across the blazing hot tarmac to the terminal with their weapons and equipment slung over their shoulders. They had no idea where to go or what to do until Baldie walked outside and pointed them toward the waiting transportation.

"Make somebody else mad?" Major Randal said by way of greeting.

"I got expelled from the Gold Coast, thanks to you. Remember?"

"Dodging my question, Jim?"

"This is a promotion, Major. The Sudan may not seem like much, but it's the center of the universe for guys like you and me… where all the action is," the SOE Chief of Station smiled broadly. "Welcome to the sharp end of the stick."

Major Randal looked at Royal Marine Hoolihan, "Looks like we've been met by an agent or agents known to us, huh, Butch?"

Royal Marine Hoolihan took their gear and stowed it in the trunk of the dilapidated black 1926 Ford automobile Jim was using for ground transportation. Then they all climbed aboard with the SOE Chief and Major Randal sitting in the back.

Baldie briefed them as they drove. "The only things that stand between us and 350,000 Italians right this minute are three British battalions – the 2nd West Yorkshires, the 1st Worcestershires and the 1st Essex – and they have to defend Khartoum, Port Sudan and the railhead of Atbara. On the frontier, the Sudan Defense Force has 4,500 men organized into six motor machine-gun companies to patrol 1,200 miles of border. We have no tanks, no mobile artillery and in fact, no guns at all except for four small obsolete howitzers at the Governor-General's house that have never been used except to fire blanks to salute the Muslim Feast of Ramadan.

"For air cover, we have a ragtag air force of six flying relics euphemistically called 'Gladiators' to cover an area the size of Germany. Our only reserve on call is a long way off, and it consists of the Camel Corps. The numbers against us are better than sixty to one. Worse odds than those facing "Chinese" Gordon when he was here back in 1885."

"That's reassuring, Jim," Major Randal said, "considering Gordon's command was slaughtered to the last man."

"Yeah, well, Mussolini has visions of becoming a modern-day Pharaoh. The easiest way to accomplish his dream is for the Duke of Aosta to go over to the attack and advance straight through the Sudan to Egypt. And he just might go for it. Mussolini has already shipped over a white stallion to ride into Cairo in the victory parade when he does."

"What's stopping him?"

"Well, *you* are," Baldie said. "He's worried about the 1st Special Air Services, most especially the 10th Abyssinian Parachute Battalion. As long as the Duke thinks you are anywhere in the area, he is not about to set foot outside of Abyssinia for fear he might wake up with you tickling his whiskers with a Fairbairn knife.

"Did you really say *'Kill 'em all and let Allah sort 'em out?'* " the SOE Chief laughed. "Made me want to strap on a parachute."

"Absolutely, I distinctly recall saying that to the men just before the platoon jumped on Bela," Major Randal said. "You remember, don't you, Butch?"

"How could I ever forget, sir?" Royal Marine Hoolihan responded with a grin.

"Here's the big picture, Major," Baldie cut to the chase. "Our troops have to clear Italian Forces out of Abyssinia to make the Red Sea safe for Allied shipping. A land attack called the East Africa Campaign designed to accomplish exactly that task is gearing up to kick off sometime in the next three to five months.

"In the next few days you and Hoolihan will parachute into the central highlands of enemy-occupied Abyssinia to execute OPERATION ROMAN CANDLE, a mission to ferment a rebellion by raising an irregular guerrilla army. You are going to become a bandit king – the next Lawrence of Arabia, only in Abyssinia."

The agent driving the car was watching Major Randal closely in the rearview mirror to gauge his reaction. Royal Marine Hoolihan turned in the front seat and looked back at his Commander in surprise.

Baldie kept his face perfectly neutral. He had found it was generally a good idea not to string out bad news. Best, he always thought, to get it out there in the open fast. That way he could observe the effect on the receiving party before he had a chance to think about it.

Major Randal did not say a word. His eyes narrowed slightly, and he seemed to drift off to a distant place. A small smile played with the corner of his mouth – or possibly it was merely ironic reflection. "Can we get some of my Raiding Forces people out here?"

"Major, I can send for anyone you request and promise to make every effort to get them out here, but I have to advise you, availability of transport is an 'iffy' proposition at best. The Sudan is the dead-end of the Empire's supply chain.

"I can give you all the silver Maria Theresa thalers you can spend, a thousand U.S. Model 1903 A-1 Springfield .30-caliber rifles for starters, with 4,000 more at a later date as you need them. But that's about it.

"No need to mislead you, Major. What we have to work with out here – as far as equipment and available personnel are concerned – is not good. One of the officers already gone in-country is a man over sixty years old and more than a few who are getting ready to go are over fifty. We are scraping the bottom of the barrel."

"What do you say, Butch?" Major Randal asked.

"You and me against half a million bloody Wops," Royal Marine Hoolihan said with a slight catch in his voice. "Sounds about right, sir."

"Three hundred and fifty thousand in Abyssinia," Jim Taylor corrected, "give or take a few."

"Odds are getting better all the time, sir," Royal Marine Hoolihan quipped, hoping he sounded braver than he felt.

Baldie made eye contact with his driver in the rearview mirror and gave a small imperceptible nod as if to say "I told you so." He had worked with these men before and had been confident they would accept the challenge.

Still, what the SOE Chief was proposing, and Jim knew it better than anyone, was a highly perilous mission, the most dangerous he had ever been involved in. Major Randal was a friend, and it did not feel so good being responsible for sending him out into the great unknown. When the two Raiding Forces Commandos deployed to Abyssinia, they truly would be jumping in on the far side of the rainbow.

The country was the kind of place where a team could be swallowed up without a trace.

When the car arrived at the safe house on the outskirts of the city, Baldie turned to Major Randal, "Let me have your pistols."

Major Randal looked at him levelly for a moment, then handed over the two Colt .38 Supers and the High Standard .22.

"Now the Browning 9mm," Jim demanded in a monotone voice.

Producing the P-35 from the back of his pants where it was tucked under his desert khaki BDU blouse in a Yaqui slide holster, Major Randal reluctantly handed over the handgun. Baldie passed the weapons to his driver. "Be extremely careful with these and have them back here by nightfall."

"What's this about?" Major Randal asked in a brittle tone – one which the SOE operator had learned to recognize from other days as being similar to a rattlesnake buzzing his tail.

"A little surprise," Jim explained vaguely. "Abyssinians love to follow what they call a '*tillik sau*' – a big shot. Our plan is to turn you into one."

"I see."

"You will."

Since time was short, the pre-mission country background briefing began at once with a series of lecturers rotating all day and into the evening. Maj. John Randal and RM Butch Hoolihan were immediately immersed in mission prep. There was a lot to cover. The idea was for them to drop into Abyssinia within the week.

First up was an expert from the Foreign Office who had worked in the British Legation in Addis Ababa Office on the Abyssinian Desk.

"Abyssinia is a landlocked country bordered by the Sudan, Eritrea, Djibouti, Somalia and Kenya. One of the oldest nations in the world, it has remained independent for 4,000 years and is one of – if not the only – country in all Africa never to be colonized by the European powers. Abyssinia is recognized as the second-oldest Christian nation, having converted in the 4th century A.D. Historically, it has been a crossroads of African and Middle Eastern civilizations with a rich, diverse culture.

"Abyssinia is considered to be the location of the land known to ancient Egyptians as *Punt* or 'The Land of the Gods.' The Greeks believed the Fountain of Youth is located up-country. There is evidence of a Semitic-speaking people in Abyssinia as early as 2000 B.C. The country was isolated until 1855 when there was a mad scramble by the 'Great Powers' to acquire African territory.

"In 1890, the Italian Eritrean colony was established on the Red Sea with the inevitable result of border conflicts with the bordering landlocked Abyssinia. The imperialistic Italians repeatedly encroached on the passive, peace-loving Abyssinian national territory. These skirmishes escalated into a major conflict that culminated in the great historic Battle of Adowa in 1896 where the underdog Abyssinian defenders stunned the world by magnificently defeating the belligerent Italian aggressors in open battle.

"The early twentieth century was marked by the benevolent reign of His Imperial Majesty Haile Selassie I, Conquering Lion of Judah, Elect of God and King of Kings. His Majesty laid down the principle of primogeniture and took it upon himself to institute a rapid modernization and re-education program until forced to flee in 1936 by the cruel, unprovoked aggression of the evil Fascist Italian Armed Forces when they illegally invaded the passive, peace-loving Abyssinian nation seeking to avenge their humiliation at Adowa.

"Any questions… No?"

Baldie escorted the man from the room. He returned alone and said, "You can take most everything in that briefing with a grain of salt. Abyssinia remained independent for over 4,000 years for the simple reason that there is nothing, not one thing, in the entire country worth having. The King of Kings etc., etc. had very little power outside of the capital of Addis Ababa before the Italians overthrew him, and by that, I mean outside the city limits.

"There was no central government, the most modern building in the country at that time was the prison and to this day no real road structure exists. There is only one rail line, but it is a real beauty, and I expect you two thrusters to become intimately familiar with blowing it up in the near future.

"Abyssinian culture is based on myth. Their entire history is a lie. The Emperor claims to be a direct descendent of a one-night stand between Solomon and Sheba. Abyssinians resolutely maintain Sheba was an Abyssinian despite the inconvenient truth that no factual basis for the real-life existence of Sheba has ever been established. The fairy tale is also hindered by the fact that there has never been a continual, uninterrupted bloodline because the title of Emperor is not passed down from father to son – oh well.

"The Abyssinians even claim to have stolen the Ark of the Covenant when Sheba's son went to visit his father to tell him he preferred to live in Abyssinia. Legend has it the Ark is hidden on a small island situated in a remote lake somewhere in-country.

"The only export Abyssinia has ever produced is nubile slave girls. His Imperial Majesty Emperor Haile Selassie, known as '*Highly Salacious*' among those of us who have the displeasure to work with him, is not all that enlightened. No matter what claims are made by those consular service apologists like the one who just left, he never stopped slavery or even tried all that hard. HIM has personal slaves as a part of his entourage right here in Khartoum."

Warming to the subject, the SOE Chief of Station continued, "The Abyssinians are a quarrelsome bunch. Nonstop blood feuds rage throughout the country. In some tribes, a man has to kill an enemy in order to be allowed by his chosen bride's family to marry. They do not specify the enemy; any live person – man or woman – will do in a pinch.

"In other tribes, a boy has to kill an enemy in order to become a warrior – also enemy and gender unspecified. Naturally, the idiots whack whoever is handy, usually some unsuspecting innocent from across the fence. This results in automatic retaliation by the victim's family, and that breeds a self-perpetuating state of intertribal warfare.

"Your mission is to raise a guerrilla army to act as a force multiplier to assist conventional forces who will be attacking overland to clear the Italians from the territory bordering the Red Sea.

"Let me be very clear. You are not going in-country to return the Emperor to his throne; you are not tasked with liberating the oppressed Abyssinian people from the clutches of the evil Blackshirt Fascist aggressors. Securing the shore of the Red Sea is the one and only purpose of the exercise."

"Sounds like you don't much like Abyssinians, Jim."

"I hate the entire bloody country," the SOE Chief growled. "You will too. Never trust an Abyssinian."

The next speaker was a rumpled professor in a bowtie who had lived in the country until expelled by the Italians. "Abyssinia boasts 84 indigenous languages…"

So much for learning to speak Abyssinian, Major Randal thought to himself. He immediately tuned out as the professor droned on.

"Amharic is the primary language taught in the schools. It is possible to find the odd English-speaker scattered about the country. Abyssinia has its own alphabet, which is a complication.

"Christians make up over 70 percent of the religious, with the remainder spread between Muslims and practitioners of the traditional faiths. A small ancient group of Jews, the Beta Israel, live in the Northwestern section of the country. Abyssinia is also the spiritual homeland of the Rastafari movement whose adherents believe Abyssinia is Zion. The Rastafari view Emperor Haile Selassie I as Jesus, a view apparently not shared by the Emperor himself since he is Orthodox Christian.

"Abyssinian cuisine consists of various vegetable and meat side-dishes and entrées, usually a wat or thick stew served atop injera, a large sourdough flatbread. One does not eat with utensils, the common procedure is to use the sourdough bread to dip from a common bowl in the center of the table. The food is quite spicy.

"The music of Abyssinia is extremely diverse with each of the country's

80-plus ethnic groups having their own unique sounds. Abyssinian music uses a unique modal system that is pentatonic….."

Major Randal rolled his eyes at Royal Marine Hoolihan. Baldie interrupted, "Thank you professor, I think we get the picture."

Next up was a military officer, an impressive suntanned intelligence captain from the Sudan Defense Force. "In 1936, Italian forces led by Marshal Rodolfo Graziani invaded and conducted a short, brutal, highly effective campaign against the Abyssinians. It was a walkover.

"Many people, including our Prime Minister I understand, believe that if the League of Nations had stood up to Mussolini in 1935 when he chose to invade Abyssinia, the current war would have been averted. Hitler saw that the League of Nations could be bullied and what he took away from the experience was that he could bully England too. Who is to say?

"The Italians attacked Abyssinia using modern armored forces and lorry-mounted infantry. The Italian Air Force strafed anything that moved and sprayed copious amounts of mustard gas on the towns and villages along the line of march. During the war, the Italian armed forces intentionally targeted hospitals and Red Cross operations.

"The Italians hate the Abyssinian people. These hard feelings date to 1896 when the Abyssinians defeated them at the Battle of Adowa; the first and only time a European Army has ever surrendered *en masse* to Africans.

"After the battle, the gallant Abyssinian victors castrated the Italian prisoners."

Ah, that explains why Admiral Lombardi snapped to so fast when Terry threatened to turn him over to our platoon of Abyssinian paratroopers, Major Randal thought.

"Naturally, the Italians were bitter about Adowa. They hold a grudge to this day. The Blackshirts seize on every opportunity to exact revenge.

"Following a bungled assassination attempt on Marshal Graziani two years ago, over 9,000 Abyssinians in the capital of Addis Ababa were murdered in cold blood. Any Abyssinian with a European education was liquidated and over 400 monks at Debra Marcos were killed.

"Resistance to the Italians has flared up. However, no organized resistance movement exists as such, though there have been accounts filtering out of Italian units of up to brigade strength being attacked and dispersed by large bands of shifta. Personally, I make these reports of large-scale bandit attacks out to be flights of fancy, but we do continue to hear them.

"The shifta are more interested in banditry, slaughtering the odd neighbor and what have you, than fighting any so-called national enemy. There is not any profit in it."

"Are the Italians afraid of the Abyssinians?" Major Randal asked.

"Petrified of being taken prisoner," the Captain responded without hesitation. "The treatment of the soldiers captured at Adowa definitely scarred the macho Italian military psyche."

The noted big game hunter and explorer Capt. Lionel Chatterhorn followed. Since the day was getting long, he had been requested to be brief.

"In Abyssinia proper you will find all of the 'Big Five,' though rhinoceroses are reasonably rare, having been shot out to sell their horn to the Chinese confectionaries to grind into an aphrodisiac. Supposed to do wonders for your sex life, what? Never tried it myself, you chaps may want to give it a go. If you do, please be so kind as to provide me a detailed report on your return. I should like to know, ha ha, probably tally-rot!

"Queer place, Abyssinia. The crocodiles are the largest and most aggressive I have personally encountered anywhere, particularly those crocs along the Blue Nile, and I have hunted them on three continents. The blighters will actually rush off the bank into the river to pursue and attack small canoes. I saw one monster upward of 23 – 24-odd feet myself. Bear in mind, anyone who ever tells you they have encountered a crocodile over 19 feet in length is a bloody liar.

"The lion are far more aggressive than their Simba brothers elsewhere in Africa. I cannot say why that is exactly. If you track them, when bayed, the instant they straighten out their tail they are coming for you, right now… and by then it is too late to send in your insurance premium. The Abyssinian lions, in general, are not the biggest I have hunted; but they are, without question, the most likely to charge without provocation, and you have to stop them or they will get you right enough.

"Abyssinian leopards are sometimes called panthers because they are frequently jet-black in color. The leopard is a nocturnal hunter. You probably will never ever see one but beware if you should shoot one and merely wound it. Following a wounded leopard is strictly for professionals.

"Elephants in Abyssinia carry heavy ivory. I have encountered quite a few 200-plus-pound side-by tuskers over there. The rule in the country used to be one tusk for you and one for the Emperor, only he has not been home for the last five years, what? I am sorely tempted to pop over myself for a peek at how the elephant herd is faring. Good money in ivory. Be careful with Jumbo. They are smart; they are big, and if you shoot and wound one he will come for you with a vengeance.

"Quite a few snakes abide in the country – some poisonous, some not... so my rule of thumb is shoot first and ask questions later, and whatever you do please do not pet them.

"To summarize, the Big Five flourish in Abyssinia. The crocs and lion are peculiarly aggressive. Now here is the part to remember – you may be tested on it later... man-eaters are rampant over there, particularly lion. Any animals that specialize in eating people are the most dangerous creatures you will ever encounter anytime, anywhere. Never forget that.

"Man-eaters are generally rare in nature. Usually the big cats turn to it only because of some injury. However, where there are dead people lying about for them to nibble on and develop a taste for man meat, like in Abyssinia, the percentage of man-eaters explodes.

"The Italians have bathed the countryside in mustard gas from the air. They routinely strafe any group of natives on the off-chance they might be shifta. And as their truck convoys roll merrily down the roads, Wop soldiers pop away randomly at any natives they pass for the sport of it. The point I am trying to make, gentlemen, is for the last five years there have been a lot of dead Abyssinians lying around over there in the bush – left where they fell. And that means there must be frightfully large numbers of big cats that have developed a fondness for human flesh.

"The jungle telegraph reports man-eating lion in epidemic proportions. The tales I am hearing are downright scary, so watch out. You do not want to end up being the 'Blue Plate Special.'"

"A final word of advice.... consider every native you encounter hostile until proven otherwise. The experienced Abyssinian traveler generally follows the same policy for the locals that I recommended to you for the snakes.

"Why take a chance? And if you make a mistake, well, on that side of the wire, murder is not considered much of a crime. It's more like the national pastime."

Last to speak but definitely not least informative was the medical doctor who inoculated Major Randal and Royal Marine Hoolihan for yellow fever before he began his lecture, which was succinct.

The doctor's bedside manner left a lot to be desired. The man was either a burn-out case from a lifetime in the tropics fighting a losing battle against exotic diseases or a dry drunk… or maybe both.

"Gentlemen, in Italian East Africa 80 percent of the native population are infected with either syphilis, gonorrhea or soft chancre, the first being the most common. Twenty percent of the population as a whole has tuberculosis, and dengue fever is endemic. Malaria, typhus, and enteric fever are widespread throughout the country and there is significant incidence of epidemic meningitis, relapsing fever, leichmaiasis, leprosy, brucellosis, myiasis, tropical ulcer, smallpox, trachoma, diphtheria, worm infections, rabies, typhoid, paratyphoid, and both bacillary and amoebic dysentery.

"There are no medical supplies to be found anywhere in the country proper. Not to worry, most of the diseases I listed are incurable anyway. My professional medical opinion is to stay as far away from Abyssinia as possible if you value your health."

As the doctor was walking out the door, Jim's man returned, bringing with him Major Randal's pistols. All four were sporting brand-new, hand-carved grips made of ancient elephant ivory the color of pale butter. Carved in relief on the rectangular grip panel on each pistol was the RAIDING FORCES flash.

"I ordered those grips the minute I learned you were available for the assignment. Today all that was needed was to have them hand-fitted to your pistols. Big shots in Abyssinia sport ivory. The plan is to set you up to be a real *tillik sau*."

"Captain McKoy should see these," Major Randal said. "I'm going to look like the Lone Ranger."

"That is the general idea."

"Hi-ho, Silver," Royal Marine Hoolihan added, "away."

8
THANKS BALDIE

BRIGHT AND EARLY THE NEXT MORNING, RM BUTCH HOOLIHAN WAS dispatched to receive an intensive but brief – by necessity – course of instruction on the communications equipment they would be taking with them. Radios were in desperately short supply in the Sudan, as was practically everything else in the way of military stores.

The good news was that both Maj. John Randal and Royal Marine Hoolihan were trained in the rudiments of signaling. After experience gained in the fighting at Calais it had been laid down that each member of Raiding Forces be able to operate every kind of signaling device – from hand-and-arm wigwag to a battleship's radio.

While Royal Marine Hoolihan was away, Chief of Station Jim "Baldie" Taylor and Major Randal met in private for a highly classified briefing.

"Last time we operated together, John," the Chief of Station Khartoum said, "I worked for you. This time you report to me. Do you have any problem with that?"

"Moved up in the cloak and dagger world, Jim?"

"Well, ah... I may or may not have misrepresented my exact status when we were in the Gold Coast, but we did not know each other at the time. Fair to say LOUNGE LIZARD turned out so spectacularly I was allowed to, ah... gravitate to where the real action is."

"I can't think of anyone I'd rather work for."

"Ditto," the Chief of Station said. "Now that we have that out of the way, what I am getting ready to tell you is never to leave this room."

"Roger."

"The Abyssinian Campaign is my show. The entire ball of wax is an SOE mission. We fund everything – which means we own it. General Wavell has authorized the operation, designated the ground forces for the conventional phase and named the commanders... and that is the beginning, middle and the end of his direct involvement except to resolve conflict between the commanders if and when any arise.

"Both ground commanders, as well as the RAF and Royal Navy, report to me. That is strictly off the record, and no mention of it will ever appear in any report, to include the official history of the operation when it is eventually written after the war."

"Jim, I was in Cairo waiting to have a meeting with Colonel Clarke while he was off on some mysterious mission. Apparently, Raiding Forces has been assigned to a unit he's putting together called A-Force," Major Randal said. "Can you clear my assignment with him?"

"Dudley's with us on this," Baldie informed him with a conspiratorial wink. "Colonel Clarke devised the raid on Bela as part of OPERATION CAMILLA which is the cover/misinformation plan for OPERATION CANVASS, the liberation of Abyssinia. He knows you are out here now to take command of OPERATION ROMAN CANDLE, the raising of a guerrilla army in support of CANVASS.

"The original idea was to have you set up a permanent element of Raiding Forces in the Middle East Command to carry out high-priority operations A-Force is anticipating in the future. We intend to continue moving forward to implement that plan while you are on the ground in Abyssinia."

"Sounds like you have a lot of irons in the fire."

"Yes, we do. You were under orders to increase the troop strength of Raiding Forces before you left Seaborn House," Baldie continued, demonstrating knowledge of the Raiding Forces unit only a handful of people were cleared to have. "Tell me, how is that working out?"

"Raiding Forces should have doubled by now," Major Randal said, "with the new men fairly far along through their training."

"How is that possible? By last report I understood you were experiencing heavy going with the regiments refusing to allow you access to their soldiers."

"Before I left, orders were cut standing down the entire unit and sending it on a recruiting leave," Major Randal explained. "Each officer and man was ordered to bring back either his number two or the name of his number two."

The Chief of Station shook his head in admiration. "Now that is what I call an elegant military solution – Randal's Rules for Raiding – 'Keep it short and simple.'"

"It was all I could think of."

"How are you going to arrange the transfers?"

"Larry Grand is taking care of that. If there's any problem, Raiding Forces turns the name of the man they want over to SOE, and he swings into action."

"By the way, Major, I owe you an apology," Baldie said, changing the subject. SOE Cairo was ordered to keep an eye on you while you were decoying the Italians with that Special Air Services act."

"Apology?"

"Our man in Cairo noticed you had never been given a SOE security clearance… you know how there is always that 10 percent who don't get the word. Well, he decided to have you vetted on his own hook without informing anyone, meaning me."

"How'd I do?"

"Major, that lunatic ran every woman we have on the payroll in Egypt at you and even brought in some outside talent. The girls did not learn a thing except the 10th Abyssinian Parachute Battalion is one tough bunch of throat-slitters."

"There is no 10th APB."

"Exactly, but all those women keeping you such good company sure believe there is, which means SIM – Italian intelligence – thinks so too."

"Really?"

"SOE Cairo knows some of their girls happen to be on the Italian payroll as well as ours. You never gave away a thing. Not much for pillow talk, are you, John."

"So that was you," Major Randal said. "I *thought* it was too easy."

"Not me, that imbecile in Cairo," Baldie explained sheepishly. "The Services do not call SOE the 'Ministry of Ungentlemanly Combat' without some justification. No hard feelings?"

"Give me about six months to recover," Major Randal said, "then feel free to update my security clearance any time you want to."

The next order of business, on a more serious note, was a brief overview of the planned Abyssinian campaign.

Baldie plunged straight in, "OPERATION CANVASS is a land invasion of Italian East Africa designed to accomplish Royal Navy and Royal Air Force objectives. The mission is to clear the Italian Forces from the Red Sea area so the Prime Minister can assure the President of the United States the sea lane passing through it is not a hot combat zone in order to qualify for Lend Lease.

"The sole reason for OPERATION CANVASS is to clear the Red Sea for Lend Lease, period.

"Now, having stipulated that, it never hurts to get a little good press. Liberating the first conquered country from the evil Fascist Blackshirts sounds like something that might give cheer to the hard-pressed English people. Not to mention looking good to the American public whose support Great Britain desperately needs to stay in the war.

"There is this one other detail. ROMAN CANDLE is a test tube operation. Special Operations Executive has never raised a guerrilla army from scratch where we start with individual guerrilla resisters and build it up to an army to support a full-scale invasion by conventional forces coming in from the outside. SOE needs to master the art of how to go about it. We have all of Europe to liberate someday."

"In that case, Jim," Major Randal said, "you'd best explain exactly how you see my part of this military science project unfolding."

"Count on it, only we shall have to wait until another time," Baldie looked at his watch. "Right now you have to get ready for your command performance with His Imperial Majesty Emperor Haile Selassie. You need his blessing in order to take on this mission."

"The man we're not restoring to his throne," Major Randal said, "has to sign off on me?"

"I warned you it was complicated," Baldie shook his head. "In the spirit of getting everything out on the table, you should know, Major, that you were not my first choice for this mission. And to be perfectly honest, not even on my long list of candidates for this assignment."

"Somehow I suspected that."

"You barely speak English let alone even one of the 84 languages the professor briefed you about. You have never been to Abyssinia, and I am not entirely convinced you ever fully recovered from the gunshot wound you received in your shootout in the Blue Duck."

"I'm OK."

"Except for the fact you fought Huk guerrillas in the Philippine jungle and waged a hit-and-run delaying operation that might be described as 'guerrilla-like' at Calais, you do not have one single qualification for this job."

"Why not use the man you want?"

"Highly Salacious blackballed him," Baldie explained. "Major Courtney Brocklehurst, former game warden in the Galla country, the exact area you are getting ready to parachute into, was our dream mission commander. We had Major Brocklehurst primed to command Mission 106, the original name of ROMAN CANDLE, and ready to go when the Emperor pulled the plug.

"The problem arose because the Galla hate the Emperor's tribe, the Amhara. And, HIM hates them back. They want their own country with their own ruler. There is no chance of Highly Salacious granting the Galla independence. He rightly suspected Brocklehurst was a Galla man and possibly might be planning to help them start a civil war."

"I can see why the man might object."

"A lot of people, of which I am one, believe the Emperor is overrated as a rallying point for the Abyssinian peoples. The country is in a state of chaos, and banditry is out of control. Not all the tribes, and probably none of the shifta – as the bandits are called – will unite under any central figure, much less rally to a runaway coward who sat out the last five years of Italian occupation safe and sound at Bath in England."

"Why use the man?"

"HIM is all we have," Baldie said in resignation. "A passive-aggressive little dodger with his own agenda, the Emperor distrusts everyone and is loyal to no one. He bitterly resents the British because, although we let him live at Bath, we did not accord him the status, rank and privileges of a deposed king living in exile. He even had a problem paying his bills at the local bookstore.

"When the Emperor found out about the composition of Mission 106, aware that Major Brocklehurst was a friend of the Galla, he cabled Prime Minister Churchill behind my back, claiming Brocklehurst was unacceptable because of being pro-Italian, which is a red-hot lie."

"How did I wind up here, Jim?"

"Commodore Seaborn recommended you to General Wavell," the SOE Chief grinned. "Wonder if old 'Dickie the Pirate' is playing a double game to keep you marooned while his cousin works on explaining away his naked Norwegian girlfriend to the ravishing Lady Jane?

"What's the story on that blonde, John?" Baldie pressed, unable to keep from laughing. "The report I saw claimed she was a real looker."

"That would be affirmative."

"Remember, I warned you back in the Gold Coast there were likely going to be problems falling for a woman like Lady Jane. But it's OK now, you are out here and we are working together again. Do you think Zorro might want in on this? Get the old San Pedro raiding firm back together."

"Definitely," Major Randal said. "Can you arrange that?"

"I will have the orders cut immediately."

"Terry's out in the desert," Major Randal said, "with the Long Range Desert Group."

"Not a problem."

"Maybe you can get SOE Cairo to upgrade his security clearance."

While they changed into fresh uniforms for the night ahead, Baldie's man brought the car around. Maj. John Randal was slated for a private audience with His Imperial Majesty Emperor Haile Selassie I, King of Kings, Lion of Judah, Elect of God at his Khartoum residence, a place called the *Pink Palace*. He was not particularly looking forward to the experience.

When Major Randal walked out of his room he found Baldie dressed in the uniform of a Major General!

"Just a local rank," the SOE Chief explained casually, "to impress the natives. I plan to use the name 'James' when I wear it. Sounds more military than 'Jim'... Major General James 'Baldie' Taylor... now how do you like the sound of that?"

"Nice, General."

Major Randal knew the British Army did bizarre things like that – gave officers temporary or sometimes even local rank to suit the exigency of the moment. Though he had known of the practice, this was the first time he had run across anyone promoted locally.

He could not vouch for the natives, but *he* was certainly impressed.

Major General Taylor continued to brief Major Randal nonstop on the ride over to the *Pink Palace*. "When Maj. Orde Wingate – we like to call him 'Wingnut' because he is as mad as a hatter – the senior staff officer assigned to Mission 101 – which I will brief you on in detail later – went in for his audience with the Emperor he researched the protocol beforehand. 'Wingnut' knew the exact number of bows required – three or maybe it was five, he told me. The fool bowed his way in and walked out backwards afterward, bowing his way out.

"I'm reliably informed that during the audience he pledged fealty to the Emperor, promised to die in the cause of liberating Abyssinia and generally made an unmitigated ass out of himself."

"You want me to bow three to five times, sir?"

"That is precisely what I do not want you to do. Play it strictly military all the way. March in, salute, report, get the Emperor's endorsement, do an about-face and march the hell out. I find out you kowtowed to that little tin pot, I promise I will have you on the next plane out of Khartoum."

"Roger that, sir."

"You might want to give him one of your old U.S. Army Cavalry salutes with the palm down. Make it sharp. Play up the fact that you're a

U.S. citizen serving in the British Army to sanitize you politically. America has never had any designs on Abyssinia, which has to be good for us."

"Yes, sir."

"Never call me 'sir' again," Major General Taylor ordered. "Unless we are in public and need to keep up appearances. You and I are going to play this the same way we did on OPERATION LOUNGE LIZARD.

"I act as the chief of intelligence and you are going to be the ground commander. Major, you could have lorded it over me back in the Gold Coast but that's not your style, and I want you to know I noticed."

"OK, General, but for the record I won't be calling you 'Baldie' anymore."

"Fair enough."

Maj. John Randal's private audience with the Emperor was a weird, mellow anti-climactic affair at the *Pink Palace*, which was located two miles outside of Khartoum on the Blue Nile River below its confluence with the White Nile. Major Randal was ushered into a large room after being formally announced by Maj. Edwin Chapman-Andrews, the Emperor's British Political Liaison Officer.

The Emperor turned out to be a razor-slim man with a short, dark beard, hooded eyes and skin the color of tea. HIM sat very erect on a chair wearing the uniform of a British Field Marshal, as befitted a graduate of the French Military Academy, Saint-Cyr. He was surrounded by Swiss-trained Imperial bodyguards and a multitude of pages, aides, and advisors. The deposed ruler studied his visitor insipidly through hooded eyes that seemed to hang permanently at half mast.

He acknowledged Major Randal's snappy salute with a slow, lazy, expressionless nod, watching the young American all the time like a sleepy hawk. His Imperial Majesty seemed serene. The meeting had a dream-like quality to it.

The drill was that HIM spoke in Amharic to Major Chapman-Andrews, his British Political Liaison Officer, who then translated what he said into English.

"Greetings and welcome to you, Major."

"Good evening, sir."

"The Emperor says that he has followed your military exploits with great interest while he resided in the United Kingdom. He prays you will enjoy as much success against the Italians as you have against the Germans."

"Tell His Imperial Majesty I intend do my best."

"The Emperor is curious to know what the Americans called themselves during your American Revolution. He is greatly troubled by his forces constantly being made reference to as 'rebel bandits' by the Italians and even the British press."

"I believe the Continental Army generally referred to their troops as 'Patriots.'"

A light glowed behind the Emperor's dark hooded eyes though a slight pinched lip nod of approval was his only reaction to the answer. HIM spoke a few soft words and the Imperial bodyguards, pages, aides, advisors, etc. vanished – including Major Chapman-Andrews – as if he had waved a magic wand.

When they were alone, Emperor Haile Selassie said in flawless English, speaking very carefully in a small voice, "Major Randal, I have a new military advisor, Major Orde Wingate. Do you by chance know this officer?"

"No sir, I do not."

"Major Wingate has let it be known that he is in possession of a private letter from Prime Minister Churchill giving him extraordinary powers. No one has ever seen this letter and in fact, I do not believe that such a letter exists.

"However, it has come to my attention that you *do* have correspondence from His Royal Highness, the King of England. Would you produce it for me that I may bear out this report?"

"Sir, I do not have such a letter."

The drowsy, cobra eyes studied him without the slightest change of expression. "You do have some document from your sovereign authorizing direct communication with him. I have this on best authority."

"Yes sir, I do."

"Please show it to me, Major." The Emperor was not making a request, it was an imperial command.

Major Randal produced his leather pigskin credentials case and extracted a simple card emblazoned with the Royal coat of arms. There was a single code word written on it and a series of numbers. He handed the card to HIM without explanation.

"DEAD EAGLES," the Emperor read softly, then politely handed the card back.

The private audience was over.

After the American left, His Imperial Majesty Emperor Haile Selassie I, the King of Kings, Lion of Judah and claimant as direct descendent of Solomon – the 111th in the line to be exact – speaking in Amharic – remarked to Maj. Edwin Chapman-Andrews, "You British send me a mad man and a boy to liberate my country. Why is it you choose to go about the serious affairs of state in such a cavalier fashion?"

"I am afraid I cannot say, Your Most Exalted Highness," the Political Liaison Officer admitted ruefully. "Historically, we British tend to trust to luck, confident we can always muddle our way through somehow. We always have."

In the car, Maj. Gen. James "Baldie" Taylor inquired, "How did it go in there, John?"

"I have no idea."

9
TREASON

MAJ. GEN. JAMES "BALDIE" TAYLOR ARRIVED EARLY THE NEXT morning. He was wearing a grin from ear to ear. "Whatever you said to the Emperor, it worked like a charm."

"I hardly said anything, General."

"Well, Major, you must have done something. The Emperor has cabled Prime Minister Churchill, The Lord Privy Seal, Secretary of War Anthony Eden and General Wavell endorsing you for the mission and requesting that effective most immediately all resisters, rebels and bandits in Abyssinia henceforth be referred to as 'Patriots' by imperial decree on your recommendation."

"Reading the Emperor's mail?"

"If I were – and I never would – I should never tell you," Major General Taylor said sanctimoniously. "The Prime Minister has cabled back express orders to General Platt to ensure the word 'Patriots' is used exclusively and is holding him personally responsible to make certain that they are never called rebels, bandits or shifta in any future memos, orders, or statements made to the press or in official communiqués released to the public.

"What did you do in there, John?"

"All I said was…"

"The Emperor had the cheek to send me a hand-carried imperial directive demanding, can you believe – *demanding*, that I provide you all possible support on a priority basis. And get this… the Lion of Judah, Elect of God informed me he is going to personally hand-pick an interpreter to jump in with you when you deploy. As if I were going to send you in without one – though to be perfectly honest I had no idea who it was going to be. Qualified interpreters are hard to find."

"General…"

"I bet Orde is seething this morning. 'Wingnut' can be petty about things like access. He tries to monopolize all of the Emperor's attention. You sure you did not bow a few times? Sounds to me like you must have bloody well low-crawled up to the throne, slithered around and licked Highly Salacious' passive-aggressive boot!"

"I barely said anything."

"General Platt has blown a gasket about the Emperor going over his head with the personal communications. That is not his idea of how chain of command is supposed to work. He is, after all, *the Kaid*, which means 'Leader of the Army.' In his mind that makes him a virtual Pharaoh."

"I only answered the man's questions."

"Well, HIM has signed off on you most publicly. You are his personal emissary as of now," Major General Taylor laughed, slapping Maj. John Randal on the back. "We're off to a great start."

RM Butch Hoolihan departed to inspect a shipment of 20,000 United States Rifle Model 1903 A-1 .30-caliber Springfield rifles that had been provided by the United States to Great Britain for the Home Guard. The rifles had been diverted to the Middle East specifically for the purpose of liberating Abyssinia.

At a time when the Home Guard was standing on English beaches armed with shotguns, pitchforks and golf clubs in the belief that invasion was imminent, the rifles represented a major commitment by the British government to see OPERATION CANVASS succeed.

An advisory team of U.S. Army tech sergeants led by a warrant officer from the Ordinance Corps had arrived in Khartoum to provide familiarization training to the personnel who would be arming the Patriots. Royal Marine Hoolihan was a light infantry weapons specialist; however, he had never handled the U.S. M-1903 A-1 Springfield. He was looking forward to this day's work.

Major General Taylor and Major Randal returned to the briefing room for the first of what would be a series of intensive sessions on OPERATIONS CANVASS and ROMAN CANDLE. The SOE Station Chief Khartoum acted as briefing officer.

"Everything I am going to tell you is classified – it cannot leave this room. The story you are about to hear is a sordid tale. Not one I am proud to relate. But you need to hear it in order to have a working knowledge of the actions that have taken place up to this point that may have an effect on your mission. You will not repeat a word of it to anyone, is that clear?"

"Roger."

"The Italian-occupied colonies and territories bordering the Red Sea are of central importance to the war's big picture. So vital are they that we are doing everything in our power to play down their true significance. No good can come from confirming to the other side how valuable we consider certain territory.

"The military situation is simple and easy to understand. In order for the Middle Eastern Command to receive vital Lend Lease supplies shipped directly here from the United States, the Red Sea Shipping Zone has to be cleared of enemy forces. By that, the U.S. means no enemy surface or undersea craft can operate in or on it and no enemy aircraft are able to overfly it.

"As long as Italy occupies her present position in Italian East Africa, the Suez Canal is considered blockaded — Middle East Command does not qualify for Lend Lease."

Major General Taylor walked over to a three-legged stand with a map covered by a cheesecloth. He flipped over the cloth to reveal a map of Abyssinia marked with a series of red arrows.

Using his walking stick as a pointer, he began, "To clear Italian East Africa, the CANVASS plan is to attack into Abyssinia from two different directions with all available force. It will start with a diversion and then hammer the Blackshirts with a one-two punch. However, we will still be going up against staggering odds.

"The diversion will be Mission 101, with the Emperor in the van entering Abyssinia first. It will consist of two small, locally-raised battalions supported by a massive camel caravan. We want all eyes focused on the column. With approximately 25,000 camels it should travel at a snail's pace and give the Duke of Aosta plenty to think about.

"The first punch will be Maj. Gen. William Platt attacking out of the Sudan to the Port of Massawa on the Red Sea with the 4th 'Red Eagle' and 5th 'Ball of Fire' Indian Divisions. As we speak, the 'Ball of Fire' under Maj. Gen. Louis 'Piggy' Heath is in the process of deploying directly to the Sudan from India specifically for the operation. Piggy will be reinforced later with the veteran 'Red Eagle' as soon as it can be released from combat operations in the desert.

"Once the Blackshirts are focused on the Emperor's column bringing him in to regain his throne and fighting the Kaid, a mechanized three-division corps launched out of Kenya under the command of Maj. Gen. Alan Cunningham will lash out with the second punch and drive up the coast – initially toward Massawa – then pivot and attack up the rail line to the capital city of Addis Ababa. He will be commanding the first totally mechanized corps in history, consisting of the 11th and 12th African Divisions and the 1st South African Division mounted on mostly civilian trucks built in South Africa specifically for this operation.

"ROMAN CANDLE, meaning you, will be deployed roughly in the middle of the triangle of all three in south central Abyssinia. Your primary purpose is to raise a guerrilla army to operate against the Blackshirt interior lines of communication to prevent the Italians from being able to rapidly shift their forces from one front to another in order to concentrate them against either Platt or Cunningham. Your secondary mission is to create havoc throughout the Abyssinian countryside in order to make the Italians think the natives have risen against them.

"When General Platt attacks out of the Sudan, drives to the Red Sea and captures the Port of Massawa, your part in the operation will be concluded. We will pull you out of the country even though much of Abyssinia will still be under Italian control at that point. The objective is to secure the coastline of the Red Sea… not liberate the country. Is that clear, Major?"

"Perfectly."

"I do not want you arguing with me that there is still fighting to be done when I order you to stand down – the minute we clear the coast, the Abyssinian campaign becomes a sideshow."

"Understood, General."

"The advance party of Mission 101, commanded by Col. Dan Sanford, is already inside Abyssinia attempting to raise a guerrilla army for His Imperial Majesty Haile Selassie to command. In addition, one company of Sanford's troops is also in-country attempting to hack out a clandestine forward landing strip to use to fly in troops and supplies.

"Just between us, Sanford is not having much luck recruiting, and the advance company is encountering hard going at building an airstrip in that rough terrain with only hand-held tools – which is all they have to work with.

"Neither HIM, Colonel Sanford nor Maj. Orde Wingate is aware of the true nature of their mission. They have been led to believe that restoring the Emperor to the throne is the main goal. Make no mistake – it is NOT.

"To arrive at the point where British Forces have decided to go over to the attack, John, has been a journey highlighted by incredible stupidity, stick-your-head-in-the-sandism, pessimism, defeatism, passive collaboration with the enemy, outright cowardice, defeat in the field, passive obstructionism, obsolete equipment and not much of it, plus some rotten luck.

"The story goes back to 1935. The Kriegsmarine had been scrapped at the end of the last war, and it needed to be completely rebuilt, ship by ship. The Treaty of Locarno imposed a quota on German naval hardware. The Kriegsmarine was specifically prohibited from operating a submarine fleet."

"Before LOUNGE LIZARD, Terry briefed me about the Admiralty allowing the Nazis to build 80-plus U-boats so the Royal Navy could build more battleships," Major Randal said.

"Right, when Italy came in on the German side, she brought with her an additional 108 submarines. As you are well aware from the extensive briefings you received during OPERATION LOUNGE LIZARD, the U-boat fleet is winning the war single-handedly."

"Those extra subs are news," Major Randal said. "That can't be good."

"Commodore Seaborn has been astonishingly successful at hunting down and eliminating the Italian Red Sea submarines by a variety of means. Of the eight Eyetie subs known to be operating in it, he has sunk two, caused one to beach itself off Massawa where it was burned by its crew, and recently – after a surface action – he boarded and captured another, the *Galileo Galilei*.

"The Commodore towed the *Galileo Galilei* to Alexandria where it has been commissioned into the Royal Navy. A sure sign of how desperate the Navy is, we are flagging captured submarines and manning them with British sailors. Our old friend Dickey the Pirate has turned into a real fighting sailor."

"Good for him."

"Now the time has arrived for our Empire Forces to shut down enemy access to the Red Sea from the land side. Unfortunately, our ability to do that has been drastically complicated by the fact that we, meaning me, have not been allowed to spy on the Italians, so we are operating against them somewhat blind."

"You can't spy on the enemy again? Sounds like the Gold Coast all over again, General."

"A 'Gentlemen's Agreement' of 2 January 1937 between Chamberlain and Mussolini contained a clause discouraging activities that might 'impair relations between Britain and Italy' so we had no agents in place in Abyssinia when the war started. Can you believe that when I showed up in Khartoum nearly three years later the agreement was still being honored by the fools in the Sudan Civil Service?"

"That's crazy," Major Randal said.

"The Sudan Civil Service, unlike the sundowner scum we had to deal with in the Gold Coast, is an elite organization. Quite a few of the members are Eaton men like your pal Zorro, and an applicant is not allowed in unless he has won a Blue in either boxing or rowing. The SCS are scholar-athletes, the best and brightest England can produce.

"The trouble is – being smart, many of them believe Britain cannot win the war out here… no thinking man would."

"That's a problem."

"It is, and here's why. The Italians in Abyssinia are commanded by Amedeo Umberto Isabella Luigi Filippo Maria Giuseppe Giovanni, Prince of Savoy-Aosta, Duke of Apulia and Aosta – whom we will refer to henceforth as the 'Duke of Aosta.' Before the war, the popular polo-playing Duke of Aosta and his lovely wife socialized back and forth across the border with the senior members of the Sudan Civil Service. They all like each other.

"The Duke let it be known that, in the event of war, after the Italians conquered the Sudan, not to worry. He was going to see to it that everyone would keep their same jobs. Things would go back to business as usual – the SCS will merely report to Italy – not Great Britain.

"That being long-established, the brave hearties of SCS do not want me rocking the boat."

"Isn't that treating with the enemy?"

"I am glad you noticed," Major General Taylor said in disgust. "Now to complicate the situation, the subject of Abyssinians generally tends to cause the average SCS colonial officer to see blood red over his pink gin. Virtually no one out here likes them except for the small circle of Englishmen who currently advise the Emperor – and those men are self-serving political sycophants.

"Privately, most SCS officers believe the Abyssinian people are fortunate to have come under the firm hand of Italian colonial rule, though it is a pity the Wops had to soak them with all that poison gas – not to mention the wholesale slaughter of the religious and educated elite. One must break a few eggs to make an omelet, what?"

"Are those people crazy?"

"Not from their perspective. The Sudan Civil Service point of view is that Abyssinia is a wild land, chock full of warlords vying for power. They believe, and rightly enough, that the average Abyssinian always has and always will be an unrepentant killer of man or woman, an elephant poacher, gold smuggler, murderous bandit and slave-trader who deserves what he gets.

"Murder is indeed in the Abyssinian culture. In most tribes, the right of passage into manhood requires you to take out someone and show proof of the kill. Friend or foe, man or woman, in a fair fight or sound asleep – it does not matter. There are no bonus points for style or technique."

"Doesn't sound very sporting."

"In Abyssinia murder is sport – as long as a man can prove he did it, the kill goes on the scoreboard."

"Lovely."

"At the end of the day, the Sudan Civil Service bureaucrats believe it is distasteful for thugs like me to be concocting wild schemes with a bunch of Abyssinian killer bandits against their friend the Duke. More than a few of the SCS secretly tend to look upon him as their future employer. Almost makes me ashamed to be an Englishman."

"You said almost the exact same thing about the Gold Coast crew."

Major General Taylor produced a packet of Player's cigarettes and offered one to Major Randal who lit them with his battered Zippo lighter.

"Too true; our government seems to be having a great deal of trouble getting the political people out here in Africa on the same page as the military people in this war," the SOE Chief said unhappily. "Before we call it quits, John, I need to hear your impression of the Emperor – you never said last night."

"I thought he was stoned."

10
PET SNAKE

RM BUTCH HOOLIHAN HAD BEEN FAMILIARIZING MAJ. JOHN RANDAL at night with the various weapons they could expect to encounter in-country. Every Abyssinian male in the country carried a rifle worn on a sling over his shoulder and his chest was criss-crossed with bandoliers of ammunition exactly like Mexican banditos – only they were called *shifta* in Abyssinia.

Rifle notwithstanding, the primary weapon of choice was the spear. The men and many of the native women carried spears everywhere – all the time. Abyssinia was a dangerous country. The wise traveler did not go unarmed.

In practice, the rifles were for show, the spears for killing. The Abyssinians were miserable shots because they never practiced marksmanship. The average shifta seldom fired his weapon for the simple reason that ammunition was money. The three forms of currency in the countryside were Maria Theresa thalers (silver dollars) – aka *Fat Ladys* – salt and bullets. Touching off a round was the equivalent of lighting a cigar with a $20 bill.

The idea of target practice was never considered.

Royal Marine Hoolihan was taking his responsibility as the team light-weapons specialist seriously. He had joined the service to see the world, and it was fair to say the Royal Marines were living up to their part of the contract. Working one-on-one with Major Randal was his dream assignment.

"Sir, by all reports every kind of weapon known to man is floating around over there. The Abyssinian military has at one time or another been advised by Russians, Swiss, Belgians, the U.S. and even the British. The Germans have never been let in, but they sold arms to the Swiss and Belgians, which means we also have a wide variety of their rifles thrown in the mix."

"I'm confident you can get a handle on it, Butch."

"Trying to keep up with the different calibers is enough to cause a migraine, sir. To name only a handful, we have 7.92mm German Gewehr 98s, Lee-Enfield .303s, 8mm French Lebels and Berthiers, Italian Carcanos in 6.5 – plus now there's the '03 A-1 Springfield in .30-caliber which is also sometimes called 30-06. We both carry Colt .38 Supers and High Standard .22s. You have a 9mm Browning P-35 and an A-5 12-gauge shotgun while I am armed with my .45-caliber Thompson submachine gun."

"What do you reckon," Major Randal asked, "the shifta maintenance program is going to look like, Butch?"

Royal Marine Hoolihan rolled his eyes. He took his weapons seriously.

Working until the late hours every night, the two Commandos disassembled and reassembled various models of weapons until they could do them blindfolded. Not that they would ever need to assemble one blindfolded. But working to that level developed their skill to where they could do it by touch without even thinking. And that might come in handy at night or in a firefight when it's a good idea to keep your eyes up.

Little details in combat can spell the difference between life and death.

"Sir, I have serious concerns about the Hotchkiss guns. The weapons are not reliable and nothing I am going to be able to do will make them operate consistently under field conditions."

"Like the general said, they're all we're going to get, Butch."

"You need to know what to expect, sir. It's my job to advise you."

"Consider me advised."

The U.S. Springfield rifles came back from Holland & Holland delivered by Maj. Gen. James "Baldie" Taylor, who had taken a personal interest in the work. He had stopped by the shop several times over the last couple of days to make sure that it was being carried out according to instructions.

That the intelligence chief would take the time out of his busy eighteen-hour-a-day schedule to supervise such a minor aspect of the operation spoke volumes about the type of officer he was.

Major Randal racked the bolt of the U.S. Marine Corps model rifle with the No. 6 aperture sight. The action ran butter-smooth, the way the weapon would have worked if they had enjoyed the luxury of putting a couple of thousand rounds through it. The '03 A-1 Springfield was a handy infantry fighting rifle.

When Major Randal snapped the weapon to his shoulder, he discovered to his great surprise and pleasure that the front sight had a gold bead welded to it. The gold bead made the sight highly visible.

"I had them install the sights, John, exactly like the ones Captain McKoy put on your Colt .38 Supers and the Browning," Major General Taylor told him. "I also had the same trigger and action work performed on the other '03 Butch selected for you with the open sights, except I had an ivory front post installed on it for night work."

"Thanks, General," Major Randal said. "He had a fine set of battle rifles. Few soldiers ever went to war with better."

"Tomorrow, John, you have been summoned to a command performance with Maj. Orde Wingate, the senior staff officer for Mission 101 at his hotel," Major General Taylor announced, changing the subject. " 'Wingnut' has taken to holding press conferences and meeting with his staff officers in his hotel room while lying on his bed in the nude and brushing his body with a toothbrush. The press eats it up. We British do love our eccentric military men."

"You're kidding."

"About meeting with him… yes, I am. You do not ever have to meet with that pervert. With Col. Dan Sanford in-country leading the advance party, 'Wingnut' has basically usurped him as the commander of Mission 101. Major Wingate is not a man you would want to turn your back on; he is a self-serving, back-stabbing, empire builder loyal only to himself. He is openly claiming to be on a mission from God inferring divine intervention in his assignment – appointed by the Lord.

"I know the minute 'Wingnut' goes into Abyssinia that he is going to seize command. Old Colonel Sanford is not going to be able to handle him. And I also know as soon as he gets in-country I will lose my ability to control him. I am positive of that."

"You always have a plan, General."

"No need for one in this situation. Their mission is of zero importance other than to mystify, mislead and confuse the Italians. Sanford, Wingate and the Emperor have the mistaken idea they're the main event. And that is exactly what we want the Italians to believe too. Why else would we classify Mission 101 'Most Secret' and then allow 'Wingnut' to hold all those press conferences?"

"I was wondering about that."

"Now, having thoroughly trashed the man, the mad Major does have his own thoughts on how to conduct a guerrilla war, and they are worth listening to. According to Major Wingate, 'It is a bad idea to pass out arms and ammunition to the Patriots gratuitously.' He calls that the *Lawrence Method* and claims it's wrong – being expensive, wasteful and possibly even dangerous to be arming unruly and treacherous natives over whom you have little or no actual control.

"Orde believes it is best to have a small core of professional soldiers who do the actual fighting and let the Patriots tag along, surrounding this small force, creating a buffer of confusion and spreading rebellion throughout the countryside.

"He goes on to stipulate that the qualities of the guerrilla commander and men must be of the highest order; they must have unity of command and a mission vital to the overall success of the operation. They must be independent, possess adequate communications and operate with a supporting propaganda campaign designed to aid their purpose.

"What do you make of it, Major?"

"I'd say the man knows what he's talking about, General."

"While I hate to admit it, he's got the theory down cold. 'Wingnut's' crazy like a rabid fox. We are agreed then, you will incorporate his ideas into your operation, tailored to when and where they apply."

"Can do."

Major General Taylor glanced at his wristwatch, "Need to cut this short, Major, because we do have a command performance that you must attend today, for real. General Platt has invited us to his office. The Kaid wants to meet you."

On the drive over, Major General Taylor continued briefing nonstop, as was his habit. "Platt is an extremely capable officer put in an exceedingly difficult situation out here. He has been "*the Kaid*," for three years. The story is that his dark hair turned snow white overnight after the first year.

"The general is a combat veteran from the last war and saw a lot of action on the Northwest Frontier. All his experience has been put to the acid test keeping the Italians out of the Sudan. No one could have done a more brilliant job, though much of the credit for his success can be attributed to Dudley Clarke."

"Colonel Clarke?"

"Dudley is the mastermind behind a deception campaign that has kept the Duke of Aosta from launching an offensive into the Sudan that would be a walkover."

"How'd he do it?"

"Somehow, Dudley has managed to fool the Duke into believing the Kaid has a massive army hidden away, secretly lurking in ambush. What a joke!"

As they pulled up to the Headquarters Building, Major General Taylor said, "One last thing, the Kaid always carries a fly whisk instead of the regulation officer's stick, so do not act surprised when you see it."

"I thought the Sudan was famous for not having a single fly!"

"True," the SOE Chief of Station said. "Platt can be a strange one himself at times."

Maj. Gen. William Platt was not a happy Leader of the Army. The last thing the Kaid wanted was a freelance officer who was not required to report through his chain of command anywhere in the vicinity of his area of operations once the incursion into Abyssinia began. On the other hand, the General was familiar with Major Randal's fighting record.

Prone to be cantankerous from time to time, Major General Platt was also known to have a mean streak. One wit described the Kaid as a "pet snake... sooner or later he is going to bite you."

When Major General Taylor and Major Randal walked into his office, Major General Platt immediately launched a verbal strike before the introductions even began. It was one of his favorite techniques to keep people off balance, giving him a chance to gauge their reaction and judge how they react under pressure. "I suppose your idea is to be the next Lawrence, eh, Randal?"

"Sir?"

"The bane of this war is Lawrence in the last. My guess is you have memorized his book, eh, Major."

"Negative, sir."

"You shall be the only officer in my entire command able to say that. Most of them have perused it at least twice. *Seven Pillars of Wisdom* is more popular out here than the Bible."

"Never could get all the way thought it, sir."

"Why bloody not, Major?"

"Lawrence was political," Major Randal said. "I'm not interested in politics, sir."

"Who are you planning to emulate then?" the Kaid sneered nastily. "You cannot stand there and tell me you do not have someone in mind. Everyone wants to be someone else."

"John S. Mosby, sir."

"By the ghosts of the Great Pyramid, who pray tell is that?"

"Colonel," Major Randal said, "Confederate States of America, sir. Rangers."

"Bah, never heard of the man. Patriots be dammed, keep your bloody shifta guerrillas far away from my troops Major, and we shall get along fine. Should my men see armed Abyssinians to their front they will indeed *'Kill 'em all and let Allah sort 'em out!'* "

"Yes, sir."

"I read your book, and if you did not actually say that, you should have, for it is precisely what I have in mind," Major General Platt slapped his leg with his fly whisk. "My HQ shall issue that exact order, word for word."

After he dropped Maj. John Randal at his quarters, Maj. Gen. James "Baldie" Taylor ordered his agent to proceed to the Khartoum General Library by the most direct route in order to obtain every bit of information he could on the subject of Colonel John S. Mosby, CSA. An hour later the man returned empty-handed.

"There was only one book in the library on Mosby – *The Gray Ghost* – but it was already checked out, Chief."

"Well, get on the blower and have the Cairo office put a copy on the next plane headed this way. No, scratch that. Go back to the library, ascertain the name of the person who checked it out, locate him and commandeer the book forthwith."

"That could prove difficult, Chief."

"And why might that be?"

"*The Gray Ghost* was signed out to General Platt's aide five minutes before I arrived."

11
INVITATION TO A BATTLE

THE BLACK FORD POWERED THROUGH THE NIGHT. MAJ. GEN. JAMES "Baldie" Taylor rode in the back with Maj. John Randal. The SOE Chief's assistant drove. They were on their way to a battle.

Major General Taylor briefed Major Randal as the Ford cruised along. "Last week Anthony Eden, the Secretary of War, flew into Khartoum to conduct a 'Most Secret' high-level strategy session with the Kaid, General Platt. That is classified information – no one is to know he was here. General Cunningham, the General Officer Commanding East Africa Force, flew in from Kenya bringing with him South African Prime Minister Smuts, whose South African troops will make up the bulk of the southern pincer when the invasion of Abyssinia launches.

"I was present for the meeting, and I can tell you from the perspective of a first-hand participant, it was an unhappy symposium.

"The Kaid stepped off on the wrong foot immediately when he announced that he had secretly built up his army to 28,000 troops, being primarily the 5th Indian 'Ball of Fire' Division, some artillery, plus a handful of tanks. General Platt said that, for the first time, he felt like he could defend against any Italian incursion into the Sudan. Considering we are still outnumbered by more than ten to one and the Duke of Aosta has the advantage of being able to concentrate his Blackshirts at the point of attack while General Platt has to secure a long, porous border, I personally thought his statement was short of wildly optimistic.

"Secretary Eden did not see it the same way. Sent out by Prime Minister Churchill to put the whip to his generals, he did not want to hear about defending anything. He wanted General Platt to attack... and right now, action this day. The Secretary tore a strip off the Kaid, accusing him of lethargy, incompetence, failure to support the Abyssinian resistance and a few other things. Some true, most not.

"Next morning Secretary Eden flew off on a whirlwind surprise inspection of the RAF base at Gedaref. I accompanied him, and what we found were the skeletal remains of eight Wellesley and two Vincent bombers still smoking. The Italian Air Regina caught them on the ground and destroyed virtually our entire Bomber Command in a single air raid just before we arrived.

"The British gunners manning the anti-aircraft battery paraded in their short-sleeve shirts and shorts – all the rage these days. Their arms and legs were all scratched, swollen and bandaged. Poison thorn bushes abound, and the troops were paying a terrible price for fashion."

"Have every man reporting to my command arrive in-country wearing a long-sleeved shirt, long twill trousers and boots," Major Randal said. "No shorts, short sleeve shirts, shoes or desert sandals."

Major General Taylor nodded firm agreement, "I shall make it a court-martial offense if they do."

"Maj. Gen. Louis 'Piggy' Heath, the commander of the newly-arrived 5th Indian 'Ball of Fire' Division, showed up at the airfield swathed in bandages also," the SOE Chief continued. "Piggy had smashed himself up driving his staff car into a camel. Altogether, it is fair to say the inspection trip was less than inspiring."

"I can see why, General," Major Randal said. "When are you going to get to the part where you say 'but the good news is...'"

"Don't hold your breath," the SOE Chief responded dryly. "Anthony

Eden is a man of action. The day he returned to Khartoum, he formally ordered General Platt to attack straightaway. Then he cashiered the head of the Sudan Civil Service and ordered him home for being an Italian sympathizer, though that little blot will never appear on the man's record."

"The Secretary sounds like the 'right man, right job,'" Major Randal said quoting from his "Rules for Raiding."

"He is, and so is the Kaid. Given a direct order to go over to the offense, General Platt decided to conduct a tuning-up operation to recapture the tiny hilltop border frontier post at Gallabat. It actually sits on this side of the Sudanese border, and its twin town, Metemma, is immediately opposite on the Abyssinian side. That's where we are headed now, to observe the action. The attack starts at dawn."

"I've never watched a battle," Major Randal said, "I wasn't in."

"General Platt's idea," the SOE Chief explained, "is to select an easy objective, then smash it with overwhelming force. The victory will be a sham designed to get Prime Minister Churchill and Secretary Eden off his back, to build local confidence in our newly arrived fighting forces and to demonstrate to the Abyssinian people that the Italians can be beaten decisively on their home ground."

"Good thinking," Major Randal agreed, "that's what I'd do."

"Brig. William Slim's 10th Infantry Brigade has been given the assignment. Slim is a highly regarded Indian Army officer. This is his first combat command and the betting is he will do it right.

"Problem is the Italians have not exactly been idle. On Gallabat their 4th Colonial Brigade has surrounded the hilltop fort with a thick mud wall enclosed in concertina wire entanglements 600 yards long and 400 yards wide. Next door, twin city Metemma is manned by the 77th and 25th Colonial Battalions with a six-gun mountain battery sited to give mutual supporting artillery fire. So the Blackshirts have a small but well-thought-out defensive system in place."

"What's the 10th Brigade consist of, General?"

"Typically Indian Army brigades are made up of two Indian battalions and one British battalion. Over the long course of history that formula has proven to be an almost magical mix of men. Many knowledgeable authorities, me included, believe the Indian Army to field some of the best fighting units in the world.

"Slim's 10th has the 1st Battalion, Essex Regiment, as its British battalion with the Indian 4th Battalion, 10th Baluch Regiment and 3rd Battalion, Royal Garhwal Rifles as infantry, reinforced by a regiment of artillery and *get this*, Squadron B, 6th Royal Tank Regiment equipped with Matilda 'I' tanks."

" 'I' tank?" Major Randal said. "I never heard of it."

"Infantry Tank... the 'I' tank is a secret weapon in the Sudan – nothing the Italians have can knock out a Matilda. They are Slim's ace-in-the-hole. Everything possible has been done to conceal Squadron B's presence in theatre. Dudley Clarke even got into the act sending instructions out to have the crews refrain from wearing their signature black berets. An order which, I understand, the tankers only reluctantly agreed to comply with."

"Always helps to have an unstoppable weapon," Major Randal said. "10th Panzer Division taught us that at Calais."

"Slim's battle plan is to chop up the barbed wire with pre-planned artillery fire, send in the tanks at first light to knock down the mud walls, then have the infantry pour through and mop up. Repeat the process on Metemma as needed, call in the press and have a highly publicized celebration, medals all around. Victory is assured!"

"A set-piece battle by the book," Major Randal said. "Raiding Forces rehearse missions in detail too, but ours never turn out the way we thought."

"This morning should be instructive. According to the timetable we should be on our way back to Khartoum by tea time."

The Ford began passing troop carrier trucks pulled over on the side of the road and infantry forming up in the dark. Military Field Police with hooded flashlights directed the car off the road. Major General Taylor and Major Randal stepped out to be greeted by a staff captain. The officer was assigned to escort them to Brigadier Slim's command post located on a small hill in front of the Khor el Otrub, a deep-cut, dry river one and a half miles from the objective.

The three officers arrived at the brigade command post as the sky was turning to deep purple. In addition to the normal bevy of staff officers going about their appointed tasks, also present were the senior Royal

Air Force Wing Commander and the Colonel commanding the artillery regiment. The artillery had been firing steadily, the rounds making their *WHHHSSSSKKKKNNNGGG* sound as they passed overhead while Major General Taylor and Major Randal were making their way up to the CP. Detonations could be heard thundering on the hilltop in the distance, flashing golden in the beginning morning twilight.

No introductions were made. Major General Taylor merely said to Brigadier Slim, "I wanted the Major to see firsthand the caliber of the opposition he will be going up against when he parachutes into Abyssinia."

Brigadier Slim, a big, lantern-jawed man wearing a flat-brimmed bush hat, studied Major Randal briefly; but before he could make any comment, the RAF Wing Commander announced, "Aircraft will arrive on station in eight minutes."

"Be ready to shift your fires," Brigadier Slim ordered the artillery colonel who was studying the objective through a telescope he steadied against a six-foot spear for support. Major General Taylor looked at Major Randal and gave a slight shake of his head as if to say, *What is that fool doing with a spear?*

The battle plan was a tightly coordinated combined arms operation, and it kicked off right on schedule. Militarily it was a thing of beauty. The artillery fired on target, then shifted their fires from Gallabat to the secondary objective, the twin town Metemma. The planes swooped in and dropped their bombs right on target. The tanks rumbled forward. And then the Garhwali infantry stood up and advanced to attack on line.

Every man in the CP was cheering. The troops going in were a stirring sight. The attack was a textbook operation. There did not seem to be much opposition. Soon, red and green Very lights were signaling success in the sky over the objective.

In a conversational tone, Brigadier Slim commanded, "Gentlemen, if you will come with me." He led them to a nearby motor park where his staff vehicles were waiting. The officers climbed into two open-topped command cars and drove forward. Major General Taylor and Major Randal rode in the second car with the artillery colonel who was still clutching his spear.

At this point, the attack looked like a walkover.

Suddenly, the lead car halted for a small mine field. Out of nowhere, a young Italian officer covered in gold braid appeared as if by magic. Clearly he wished to surrender.

"A Wop general!" shouted the artillery colonel. He piled out of the staff car to make the capture with a Webly .455 revolver in one hand and his trusty spear in the other.

The first enemy officer was joined by another older, more senior officer decked out in full dress with even more tangles of gold braid. He was wearing a sword. Both appeared young to be generals; and, in fact, one was a major while the other was his lieutenant. Spear, sword and a Webly revolver designed in the 19th century, this battle really was a throwback to another time.

Brigadier Slim walked up to take the surrender. Major General Taylor and Major Randal dismounted their staff car to observe the little ceremony. The senior Italian officer proffered the sword, hilt first with his left hand while standing at a rigid position of attention with his right hand locked behind his back in the traditional pose that indicated he was surrendering and would not take blade in hand.

This was the moment every commander dreams about, right out of a storybook.

Suddenly a pair of pistol shots cracked, two tufts fluffed on the enemy officer's blouse. Eyes glazed, the Italian was dead before he hit the ground. He had a startled look on his face.

Brigadier Slim whipped around, glaring at Major Randal who was gripping his Colt .38 Super in both hands pointed at the younger officer standing petrified in horror.

"Drop it," Major Randal ordered through clenched teeth, "or I'll drop you."

The man dropped it, but in the haste of the moment he failed to put on safe the cocked Beretta 9mm Kurtz he was concealing behind his back. The pistol landed on its hammer, causing an accidental discharge that made every officer except Major Randal involuntarily duck. The Lieutenant jumped about a foot in surprise, afraid that he had accidentally shot himself. Luckily, no one was hit.

"Don't kill me," the young Italian called out in perfect English; he was on the verge of bursting into tears. "I capitulate, please."

"Bastard," sneered the artillery colonel, dropping his spear to grasp his Webly .455 revolver more securely in both hands. "Shoot him, Major or I will."

"Bloody hell," the Wing Commander cursed as he rolled the dead officer over on the ground and found another Beretta. "Blighter nearly shagged us, right enough."

Major General Taylor reached down, picked up the sword and handed it to Brigadier Slim.

"Where is your commander?" the SOE Chief demanded of the prisoner in an ominous tone that clearly implied much unhappiness ahead if there was not an immediate response.

"When the battle began," the Lieutenant quivered, "our commanding officer shouted 'to the walls, to the walls,' then he disappeared in the direction of Addis Ababa."

"Frog-march this would-be-assassin back for interrogation," Brigadier Slim gruffly ordered his aide. "Should the bounder give you any more trouble, any trouble at all, shoot him in some place that hurts. He's forfeited any protection coming under the Geneva Accords."

"Sir!"

"Pretty quick on the trigger," Brigadier Slim noted, "fortunate to have you with us today, Major."

As the party climbed back in their staff cars, Major General Taylor asked, "What tipped you off?"

"Lieutenant kept glancing over at the Major's back."

"Watching for his boss to make the first move," the SOE Chief mused. "Learn anything yet?"

"Yeah," Major Randal said, "don't trust Italians bearing swords."

"Probably recognized your badges and had second thoughts about surrendering to your 10th APB paratroopers," Major General Taylor chuckled. "Rather shoot it out than face those ugly prospects."

"Can you blame 'em?"

The follow-on attack was against the companion town Metemma, located across the border. In the early morning sunrise, it became apparent that the town somehow appeared to have all its buildings standing and the wire intact even after the artillery barrage and the air strikes. This was the point where the tanks were supposed to arrive, break in and exploit the enemy's confusion so the infantry could pour through and the slaughter begin.

On paper, Matilda tanks composed the perfect unit with the deadliest weapon, in the right place at the precise time to guarantee an Italian debacle. The British tanks were impervious to Italian fire. The tanks were the decisive weapon on the battlefield. Brigadier Slim had six of them.

In his words, the Matildas were "worth their weight in rubies."

However, much to everyone's surprise, they soon encountered four of the six Matilda 'I' tanks sitting, knocked out of action with their crews lying dead beside them. The tanks may have been impenetrable but they were not unstoppable. On closer inspection, it turned out that the Matilda's caterpillar tracks were made out of steel plates connected by hard rubber links.

Gallabat Hill was formed out of volcanic trachyte rock. Jagged edges of the rock were as razor sharp as the broken tops of beer bottles and a thousand times as hard. The shards sliced through the rubber connectors causing the tanks to throw their tracks.

"Price of rubies," Major General Taylor observed in an aside, "just took a hit."

"I hate it when that happens," Major Randal said.

To add injury to insult, the highly trained tank crewmen who had remained incognito right up until the moment the Matildas crossed the line of departure had clapped their beloved black berets back on their heads to ride into battle in style. When the tanks threw their treads, the tankers climbed down to inspect the damage. The Garhwali infantry, who had virtually no training in armor recognition and had never seen a Matilda 'I' before, mistook the tankers in their black headgear for Italians and promptly shot them dead.

Armor crews were virtually irreplaceable in Middle East Command.

Because of the double calamity of the cut tank treads – which can be replaced, and the blue-on-blue tanker casualties who could not, the second phase of the operation had to be postponed until afternoon. Instead of an immediate attack by the 1st Essex Battalion, which was waiting at their start line to step off for Metemma as planned to exploit the breakthrough, an artillery preparation had to be laid on to soften up the target, causing an additional delay.

The 6th RTR's Tank Recovery Vehicle was summoned to tow the four tanks back to a safe location to repair their tracks. Because it had been held well back in a position of safety, the recovery vehicle would not be able to arrive and begin recovery operations until the following morning.

While they waited for the artillery to get going, a loud droning was heard in the distance. Soon a fleet of Savoy bombers appeared in the sky escorted by at least 20 Fiat fighters. The enemy aircraft winged over and toggled their bombs on Gallabat, unopposed.

"Our fighters," the Wing Commander explained, "have strict orders to attack en masse only when all of them are on station. That requirement has not been met yet, so there will be no RAF interference with the Italian Air Force."

No sooner had he said that than two desert-tan Royal Air Force Gloucester Gladiator bi-planes swooped in to attack in direct contravention of their orders – and were promptly shot down in flames. In ones and twos, the RAF fighters continued to arrive over Gallabat going into the attack piecemeal, and the Italians shot them down as they came. The Wing Commander was beside himself with anger… so frustrated that tears ran down his cheeks.

The air attack was a disaster. Virtually the entire remnant of the Royal Air Force Fighter Command in the Sudan was downed in a matter of minutes.

Through it all, Brigadier Slim was stoic, completely unflappable. He showed no signs of panic. The man was a rock. The thinking at the CP was that the infantry should have been all right through the air attack. All was not lost.

"Stout fellows, the Essex," the Brigadier commented idly. "Only regiment in the Army allowed to drink their toast to the King sitting down. The tradition stems from when they served as marines 200 years ago. Ship ceilings in the wardrooms were too low to stand up."

The command party set out to see how the infantry had fared. When they reached the traffic control point outside Gallabat, the Baluchi officer in charge came rushing up to the lead vehicle to report that British soldiers were driving through his checkpoint in disorder, claiming the Italians were coming. "The troops say the order has been given to fall back!"

"Nonsense," snorted Brigadier Slim, "those must be empties coming back from the front."

The Jemadar pointed to another truck crammed full of 1st Essex men racing down the hill full bore with no intention of stopping despite all signals to halt from the traffic control personnel.

"The Wops are right behind us!" the panic-stricken troops yelled as the truck careened past. "Run for it!"

Clearly, they were not empties.

The command party dismounted their cars and continued up the road to the fort to investigate. Brigadier Slim was livid, but he was not saying much, maintaining his composure. Shortly, another group of stragglers appeared. Although in retreat, these soldiers were not in the same state of panic as the last bunch.

They took the time to stop and describe how the battle had dissolved into vicious hand-to-hand combat during the Italian counterattack. Their colonel was killed in action. The Essex had fought like lions, naturally, but had been simply overwhelmed.

One of the privates blurted out the shocking news, "Brigadier Slim's been killed too."

The 10th Brigade's Commander cooked off like a volcano. The air turned blue with highly-creative cursing. In short order Brigadier Slim convinced the shocked Essex trooper the reports of his demise had been premature. The Brigadier ordered the men to turn around straight away and escort the party back to the objective so he could see firsthand what was taking place.

When the group arrived at Gallabat, they found chaos. The 1st Essex Battalion had fragmented and ceased to exist as a fighting organization. The troops were completely demoralized. However, there had been no last stands, no hand-to-hand combat and no dead battalion commander. The Italians had never even advanced out of Metemma to counterattack, which was a pity for them because the Blackshirts could have retaken the town virtually unopposed if they had.

Night fell before Brigadier Slim could restore order.

Back at the Ford, Major General Taylor and Major Randal settled in to await the attack on Metemma the next day. Major General Taylor observed, "Total Essex casualties out of the entire 800-man battalion were three dead and two wounded. Hardly what you would call a last-ditch fight. I understand you had something like 70 percent casualties at Calais and never gave up."

"Swamp Fox Force lost over ten times more men in 72 hours," Major Randal said, "than Raiding Forces has in all its operations since."

"Heads will roll for this," Major General Taylor predicted.

Next morning, the attack was filled with promise. The Essex officers voiced determination to take their objective. Then the Italians fired smoke rounds from Metemma to mark Gallabat for a Regina Aeronca air strike. The smoke sent the poor, bloody Essex into another panic, screaming "*gas, gas, gas!*" They fled down the hill again in their lorries – nearly crashing into Major General Heath, the commander of the 5th Indian "Ball of Fire" Division, who had the bad timing to drive up at that exact moment to see how his troops were faring.

His staff car ended up in a ditch.

"Take my advice," Major General Taylor recommended. "Never ride with Piggy – there is no telling what will hammer him next."

"Roger that."

A final bit of bad luck occurred. One piece of equipment on the battlefield was even more precious than a Matilda – the Tank Recovery Vehicle. The 6th Royal Tank Regiment had only one. The nearest replacement was in Cairo.

This priceless asset arrived on the battlefield to retrieve one of the broken down Matildas at the exact moment a lone Italian Savoy bomber swanned over. RAF's last surviving Gladiator dived in gamely to attack, guns blazing. The Italian pilot panicked, took evasive action, jettisoned his bombs to lighten his plane and curled away, trailing smoke.

Major General Taylor and Major Randal watched in awe as a single bomb screamed down with unerring precision and scored a direct bull's-eye on the TRV – blowing it to smithereens. The odds against that hit were astronomical. Nevertheless, it brought the attack to a screeching halt. The battle of Gallabat was over, *finito*!

As they walked down to the Ford to return to Khartoum, Major General Taylor said, "There is another version of that story about the Essex drinking their toast to the King sitting down on board those ships."

"What might that be?"

"Some say the troops were too drunk to stand up."

On the trip back the mood in the car was black. The SOE Chief summed up the operation sourly, "Gallabat highlights that no matter how bad Italian troops may be, our officers and men are even worse. British technological advantage failed. Our battalion commanders were unable to control their troops. The Royal Air Force did not follow its battle plan. And Brigadier Slim botched an attack on a weak Italian position even though he had an overwhelming advantage in numbers and was supported by a combined arms team.

"What we witnessed was a disgrace."

Left unsaid was that these same troops would be in the van of the army attacking into Abyssinia when the balloon went up on OPERATION COMPASS. And that Major Randal and his guerrilla army would be counting on them to fight their way through a vastly superior Italian force to come to their relief.

12
GUERRILLA TACTICS

THE MORNING AFTER THEY RETURNED FROM THE GALLABAT fiasco, RM Butch Hoolihan trekked off to a familiarization course on the Hotchkiss light machine gun, then to the rifle range to fire the M-1903 Springfield. Maj. Gen. James "Baldie" Taylor and Maj. John Randal retired to their improvised briefing room for another briefing.

"John, we have completed your background briefing here in Khartoum on the military situation in Italian East Africa and you have observed a conventional East African battle – unhappy though it was. Now I want to turn to how guerrilla war functions in conjunction with conventional operations and in particular how we intend for you to operate in Abyssinia."

Major Randal had been waiting for General Taylor to get around to this subject since the series of intensive pre-mission briefings had started.

"The British Empire, it has been said, is a nation of irregulars. But, in my opinion, you Americans set the gold standard with men like Robert Rogers, Daniel Morgan and Francis Marion to name a few, all three described as 'Rangers.' As I recall, you named your command at Calais 'Swamp Fox Force' in honor of Marion."

Major Randal nodded silently, not interrupting. Military protocol is not to interrupt a briefer's train of thought until he has finished. Questions are noted and saved until the end.

"Guerrilla warfare is as old as war itself – irregulars were the first type of fighting forces long before the advent of full-time, paid, professional standing armies. That said, for reasons known only to the Great Pooh-Bah the subject of irregular war is little-studied by military scholars and virtually never taught in military academies.

"Special Operations Executive is, as far as I am aware, the first state-sponsored, national-level organization in world history specifically chartered to organize, equip and lead guerrilla forces. As you know from your own experience, SOE is highly distrusted by the professional services. MI-6, the Army, Navy and Royal Air Force basically detest it.

"Regulars like to keep things uniform and tidy. Conventional soldiers tend to loath guerrillas. The primary reason for their prejudice is because irregulars fail to follow the accepted rules of land warfare. Guerrillas do not wear uniforms and they will shoot you in the back or blow you up while you are asleep. Irregular's idea of a battle is to fight briefly – usually from ambush – then run away to do it all again tomorrow. They are here, there, everywhere... and then gone.

"Most line officers believe there is no mission a guerrilla force can perform that a regular conventional unit cannot accomplish as well or better if given the task and the freedom of maneuver. After every war, some staff swot always produces a case study claiming to prove it would have been more cost-manpower-and/or resource-effective not to have supported guerrilla operations. Exactly like the General Staff claimed in a study of Lawrence of Arabia's irregulars long after the shooting stopped in the Great War – which is pure bunk. Lawrence was very cost-effective.

"The truth is, no conventional commander relishes the idea of an independent force he has no control over running around in his area of operations. However, even the most by-the-book, button-down, conventional-minded general is forced to admit that it is militarily desirable to have clouds of armed, angry locals constantly harassing the rear areas, disrupting the lines of communications and threatening the unguarded flanks of his main opponent.

"Guerrilla fighters can upset the enemy's flow of operations, distract him from his main objective, kill his troops, deny him supplies, disrupt his communications and degrade his freedom of movement. More importantly, they cause the enemy commander to divert scarce assets to hunt them down and/or tie up valuable troops guarding fixed installations. And finally, an active guerrilla threat that can strike anywhere, anytime, unannounced is hard on your enemy troop's morale.

"So much for background. Now, let's turn to OPERATION ROMAN CANDLE; specifically, how you and I are going to conduct our own private war.

"Sandhurst, West Point and other noted military academies all teach it is axiomatic that irregular action in the field should always be ancillary to parallel regular action – what you would expect them to say considering their predisposition against guerrillas. However, the military schools are right. As far as I have been able to determine, there is not a single recorded example of an insurrectionist campaign that ultimately proved to be successful without the support of regular conventional forces which came in and conquered the country after the rebels softened it up. Guerrilla raiding alone will not win a war.

"With that in mind, our goal in Abyssinia is to pave the way for OPERATION CANVASS. So we are going to be doing it by the book, even though there is no book.

Major Randal lit up a Player's, focused on the recital.

"Two little guerrilla wars virtually unknown outside the professional military sphere of studies teach lessons that should be instructive on how you can operate in Abyssinia.

"In the Southern Atlas from 1912 until 1935 the French had 35,000 men in the field against 3,000 Berber rebels. The cagey Berbers proved so familiar with the tactics of the French Army it was virtually impossible to subdue them.

"Why? It was discovered the tribesmen had approximately 20 deserters from the Foreign Legion serving as military advisors. The Berber Insurrection is the premier example of what a handful of highly trained military personnel employed as "stiffeners" can do to improve the performance of a ragtag army. High-grade leadership in a guerrilla army can achieve great things – all out of proportion to its actual size.

"That's what you bring to the mission, Major – leadership.

"Another case, the Dagestan Revolt, during the winter of 1921-22 is instructive because it is a classic example of how NOT to fight a guerrilla war. The revolution was started by tiny bands of a few dozen men who infiltrated into Soviet territory across the border of the independent Georgian Republic. At the height of the insurgency, a force of approximately 3,500 rebels was in the field fighting against over 100,000 Red Army regulars. They were extremely successful in the beginning, but over time, they made two fatal mistakes.

"After the war, the victorious Soviet commander analyzed the blunders made by the rebel leaders. First, the Russian general noted the insurgent forces' ill-advised decision to 'advance out of the rugged mountains into open country' gave the Red Army the chance 'to locate the insurrectionists, pin them down and to deploy superior artillery and armored vehicles against them.'

"The lesson learned is that the wise guerrilla leader never allows his command to be drawn into terrain that allows the opposition to marshal its strength against him. Is that clear?"

"Perfectly."

"Second, the Russian commander pointed out that 'the decision of the rebels to defend fixed positions from time to time,' in this case always some village, 'deprived the insurrectionists of the guerrilla advantage of mobility and forfeited the golden opportunity to choose the time and place to do battle.'

"The result was that the Dagestan irregulars allowed the Red Army to force a final decisive action under siege conditions because they elected to fight a last-ditch defensive action protecting a fixed location rather than disperse into the countryside and disappear."

"Sounds like the Alamo," Major Randal said. "Col. William B. Travis failed to follow his orders to destroy the fort, stood and fought, and a lot of good men died."

"Precisely. Travis failed to 'run away to fight again another day' and that proved fatal. Major, I am ordering you to never defend a fixed position. Is that clear?"

"Absolutely, sir."

"Guerrilla soldiers recruited locally have a natural reluctance to abandon their villages to the enemy in the interests of a higher strategy or national purpose. They either insist on defending them or desert.

"If this ever happens to you, Major, ride out with your British personnel and leave the bloody natives to it. Never allow yourself to be drawn into a last stand under any circumstances. That is a direct order."

"Don't worry, General," Major Randal said, stubbing out his cigarette. "Raiding Forces was created specifically to hit and run. It's how we fight."

"Excellent! Mobility is the advantage which you must retain at all times. Mobility favors surprise, and the element of surprise is the basis of all guerrilla tactics. Mobility and surprise allow you to retain the initiative even though vastly outnumbered by a superior enemy force. Being mobile while maintaining the element of surprise magnifies the shock effect of your violence of action. Never give up your mobility, never do anything unless you have the element of surprise in your favor and never lose the initiative... attack, attack, attack.

"Stay in the mountains, raid the valleys, avoid the lowlands as much as you can. Do not move into the towns in any strength. I want you to constantly harass the Italians, drive off their animals, conduct sneak raids on their remote installations at night, ambush the roads, take out their wire communications and cut the railroad in a hundred places.

"The purpose of the exercise is to make the Blackshirts believe the entire countryside has risen against them."

"The Chinese," Major Randal said, "call it 'death by a thousand cuts.'"

"Exactly. Now, let's discuss the composition of troops under your command. I promised to bring out Raiding Forces personnel. Even if we are able to bring out the entire Force, which won't happen because it is currently committed to some other high-value operations in Europe, you would still need at least 50 additional officers and at least four times that many noncommissioned officers to be your 'stiffeners.'

"Our only option is to recruit locally from the adventurers, mystics, crazies, misfits and frontier riff-raff that inhabit this part of the world –

plus volunteers from the Cavalry Division."

"Those men can make good unconventional soldiers," Major Randal said, "as long as you handle 'em right."

"Let's hope so because they are all you have to work with. You have an interesting leadership challenge ahead of you."

"Try to screen out the totally crazy."

"We will do our best, but do not expect miracles. Now, when it comes to the indigenous troops you recruit, always bear in mind the Abyssinians respond to strong men, what they call 'big shots' – *tillik sau*. The natives will follow a hard man who can lead them to the loot, but you better always sleep with one eye open.

"The various bands of outlaws you encounter out there will all have their own private agendas. Quite probably you will find it difficult, if not impossible, to forge them into any large-scale unified fighting force. My recommendation is not to even try.

"Little bands attacking all over the country will serve our purpose nicely. Small, highly mobile guerrilla units led by aggressive British junior officers and NCOs roving at will should be extremely challenging for the Italians to pin down and virtually impossible to destroy. Lots of small units striking here and there will give the impression that you have a much larger, stronger force in the field than you actually do.

"You have two main goals. The first is to keep the Italians from being able to shift their forces at will. The other is to draw off more and more Italian regular troops from the borders and tie them down in the interior of the country."

"I get it, General," Major Randal said. "We take out the rail lines and ambush the roads. The Italians will react by coming after us. Blackshirts busy chasing us won't be available to repel the invasion coming out of the Sudan and Kenya."

"In a nutshell now, one last thing... discipline in a guerrilla force is the law of the pirate ships, not the Kings Royal Rifle Corp, Raiding Forces or the U.S. Army you are used to. The men never eat first, you do. Paid mercenaries and professional outlaws only respect the man who can demand their loyalty by strength of character and skill at arms. They expect their leader to command with an iron fist.

"If, by necessity, you have to shoot the odd man or two... or fifty – shoot them and be quick about it. No one will ever second-guess your decisions or hold you to account. A commander of Kings Royal Riflemen *commands*, a commander of Commandos *leads*, but a commander of mercenary bandits *rules*."

Major General Taylor paused for dramatic effect; then in a formal command tone, he ordered, "Major Randal, your mission is to effect entry into the nation of Abyssinia, raise a guerrilla army, interdict Italian lines of communication in the interior, raid military and government installations countrywide and divert enemy troops from their primary duties by means of your own choosing in anticipation of an overland invasion by Imperial Forces at an unspecified time.

"Do you have any questions?"

"No, sir!"

Despite a confused military scenario complicated by vast distances, badly mapped terrain, shortages of everything, poor communications, evil politics, untrustworthy allies, a murderous populace, rampant disease, man-eating animals and a vastly superior enemy, Major General Taylor managed to lay out for Major Randal a clear, simple mission statement he could easily understand: go in-country, take charge, raise a guerrilla army, attack in all directions, fight until relieved.

It does not get any better than that.

13
STAND BY READY

MAJ. JOHN RANDAL AND RM BUTCH HOOLIHAN WERE RESTING ON their parachutes in the shade of the wing of the ancient, single-engine, Royal Air Force Vickers Vincent bi-plane bomber that was going to transport them to their drop zone in Abyssinia. The two were going to jump in broad daylight so they could more easily recover the supply bundles the bomber would drop with them. Those bundles would include a dozen U.S. Springfield Model 1903 A-1 .30-caliber rifles, 10,000 rounds of .30-caliber ammunition, their radio and assorted other equipment.

The OPERATION ROMAN CANDLE plan called for them to cache the equipment until they could make contact with local tribesmen to purchase mules. Then the team would retrieve the bundles and pack the gear on the animals. Their mission was to travel around the countryside recruiting native irregular troops to serve in Patriot units to be led by Raiding Forces personnel, the temporary duty officers commissioned locally and volunteers for special service from the Cavalry Division in Egypt who would arrive later.

As Major Randal recruited Patriots, the officers and NCOs to lead them would be parachuted in with additional Springfield rifles, ammunition, etc. The goal was to organize at least three muleborne raiding battalions able to operate country-wide. Operational Centers (OC) would come in later to raise additional regional Patriot guerrilla units to support the battalions.

The two British Commandos were going in behind the Italian lines to start a classic guerrilla insurgency. The concept of the operation was to find one recruit, then another, and another until they built an army. Major Randal planned to raise at least 1,000 native soldiers who he would arm, equip and pay – by Abyssinian rules they would then be loyal directly to him.

The one pre-condition OPERATION ROMAN CANDLE had going for it (and it was the only one), was a common border between the Sudan and Abyssinia; supplies could be infiltrated by mule train and camel caravan across the border to arm and equip the Patriot Forces – once there were some. This advantage was offset by the fact that they would be operating far from the Sudan border. Overland, re-supply would be a long, arduous trek fraught with danger from tribal warlords, random bands of shifta and wild animals. Rugged terrain and patches of heavy jungle crossing the Riff Valley – a canyon on the scale of the Grand Canyon that is 3,000 feet deep in places – would also slow down the supply caravans, not to mention the Italian Air Force (which enjoyed total air supremacy) and the odd Italian-officered Abyssinian Cavalry squadron known to patrol the countryside.

The plan was to try, as much as possible, to supply Major Randal's team by air. This idea seemed overly-ambitious considering that one obsolete bomber squadron made up the entire Royal Air Force contingent in the Sudan. Since the Italians were the complete masters of the sky in Italian East Africa, any re-supplying aircraft would have to sneak in, trusting to luck – as the transport dropping them today was doing.

Both Major Randal and Royal Marine Hoolihan were wearing heavy money belts around their waists, each containing 250 Maria Theresa thalers, the ounce-weight floreate silver coin of preference in the Red Sea trade. An additional 500 Fat Ladys were packed in the bundles with the rifles and ammunition. The coins had been newly minted in Bombay under a special license granted to the Royal Treasury. Called the "Fat Lady", there were 250,000 of them in the vault in Khartoum and a second contingent of 500,000 en route from India, with many more to follow. Major Randal had been promised a steady flow to run his private war. In Abyssinia, the man with guns, ammunition and Fat Ladys was a king.

Maj. Gen. James "Baldie"Taylor was pacing back and forth like a caged tiger as they waited for the arrival of the interpreter that the Emperor had promised. The team could not go without him. Neither Major Randal nor Royal Marine Hoolihan spoke any of Abyssinia's 84 languages.

"You are going to be parachuting into Galla territory," Major General Taylor said, going over the plan one more time, working hard not to sound as anxious as he felt.

"They compose the most warlike Abyssinian tribe and are not overly loyal to the Emperor. The Galla want their own separate country, so it is debatable how much good royal decrees from him will have." (Twelve such decrees, written on canvas with the Lion of Judah Seal, were stashed in a watertight folder inside Major Randal's jungle-green battle dress uniform).

"The Galla people are a temperamental group of mountaineers, given to alternating feelings of intense excitement, happiness, depression, courage and cowardice. They respect leadership, and it has been said they swarm around a strong *tillik sau* like ants to a honey pot. I am reliably informed the Galla always think they know better than anyone else. There is not a single word for 'thank you' in any of those 84 languages the professor briefed you on, but especially not among the Galla. They are a tribe of know-it-alls.

"Every adult male carries a rifle but has little skill in using one, can be vain, restless, and has beautiful manners. Though bound in a rigid feudal system, the tribesmen can be great individualists. Legend has it the Galla invented coffee."

"I that a fact?" Major Randal said. At this particular point, the last thing he cared about was who discovered the coffee bean.

"Well, the Galla claim one of their sheepherders from Caffa, thus the name 'coffee', noticed how red berries growing in a certain pasture affected his sheep. The animals became hyperactive after eating the 'cherries.'

"He tried a few and became as hyperactive as his flock. A Coptic monk happened by and scolded him for eating the 'devil's fruit' but took a few of the beans along home to the monastery and showed them to his master. The head monk threw them into the fire, which resulted in two things happening. One, the monks immediately became addicted to the aroma produced by the roasted beans. And secondly, after munching a few on the idea that they probably ought to test them before condemning something that smelled so marvelous, the monks found out they could stay up a lot longer to pray."

"No kidding," Major Randal said. "Did you know that, Butch?"

"Now, unlike the monks, the Galla did not utilize coffee beans to make into a drink or to increase their praying power," Major General Taylor continued. "No sir, they merely wrapped the coffee bean in animal fat and used it as rations for their long-range raiding parties when they traveled out on slaving expeditions."

"Let's get this straight," Major Randal said, reclining on his chute. "The Emperor's the direct descendent of a one-night stand between Solomon and Sheba, the Ark of the Covenant is hidden somewhere in-country, and now we learn Abyssinia is the birthplace of coffee. For a nation I couldn't have pinpointed on a map for a million dollars last week, it sure seems like the cultural, culinary and religious center of the universe."

"Don't forget, sir, the ancient Greeks believed the Fountain of Youth was there somewhere," Royal Marine Hoolihan added.

"Sorry, John," Major General Taylor offered with a grin of embarrassment. "Guess I got carried away with the local color.

"There is something I do want to mention that we have not talked about," the SOE Chief added, choosing his words carefully. What he was about to say was of vital importance to the mission, but since the two men going on it were in peril of being captured and interrogated, he needed to be careful not to provide them with information they might reveal to the enemy under torture.

"We have reason to believe that the Italians have a key man in Kenya, a master spy. If this spy learns the fact there will be an attack coming out of Kenya and can provide the Italians with the date of that attack, the Blackshirts will be able to move troops into position to counter it. If that happens, the entire operation to retake Abyssinia might fail.

"While you are in-country, if perchance you should come across any information as to the identity of the spy, send it out – top priority. Locating and eliminating the Italians' man in Kenya is of paramount importance."

"Will do, General."

"Let's run over your instructions to me one more time. We will bring Raiding Forces personnel out from England with a priority to your communications NCO, Lovat Scout snipers, officers or men from Cavalry regiments to handle the mules, anyone who has previously served in Africa and Lieutenant Karen Montgomery, the commander of your rigger section, to take charge of parachute packing and supply-drop rigging. After that, Raiding Forces personnel who volunteer to serve in Abyssinia are going to be parachuted in to you in the field to lead the Patriot Forces you will be raising."

"Roger."

"I am to signal your pilot, Squadron Leader Paddy Wilcox, to cut short his recruiting trip to Canada where he is currently enlisting bush pilots for a Special Duties Squadron and have him report directly to me in Khartoum."

"The quicker you can get him out here the better," Major Randal said. "Put the Squadron Leader in charge of our aerial supply, sign off on what he recommends and back him to the hilt."

"Consider it done. Next, you want me to contact Political Warfare Executive and have an officer sent out from England to serve as your political warfare advisor. PWE is a hush-hush organization, possessed of a higher priority than SOE. How is it you happen to know so much about them?"

"They carry out joint operations with Raiding Forces."

"Anything else you want me to do?"

"Give this to Brandy Seaborn for me," Major Randal said, pitching him the richly-engraved M-1935 Beretta .32 ACP he had captured from Admiral Count Emmanuel Lombardi. "Tell her I said to put it in her purse and keep it there; Cairo's a rough town."

"She's with A-Force, I shall have it hand-carried to her," Major General Taylor promised. "What else?"

"Keep the guns and money coming."

"Count on it. Now, I have one last item of importance to discuss with you," Major General Taylor said. "You are going to be operating way out there in the middle of nowhere – on your own hook. The last thing you will want is interference from long distance. I also know – because I have been there – it will be only natural for you to question and/or resent tactical instructions or orders to carry out a specific task that originates back here in Khartoum."

"Try not to send me very many."

"Major, you need to expect that from time to time I will radio you specific instructions to perform a certain task or carry out an assignment that may not sound important or even make sense to you. When I do, you need to have faith I have a reason and not simply ignore the orders."

"Like you do, General?"

"We have worked together and trust each other. That is likely going to prove of critical importance to the success of this mission." the SOE Chief ignored the remark both men knew to be true. "However, simply having faith in my judgment is not enough. I want you to be absolutely confident I know exactly what I'm doing when I send you certain specific pieces of information or instructions to act on."

"I see."

"No, Major, you don't. But here is how we need to handle certain situations – give me a code word I can use as a prefix to special messages. When you receive a radiogram with the code word identifier you will automatically understand to respond to the information it contains explicitly. Execute the instructions unhesitatingly, to the letter, without question in the time frame ordered, no questions asked."

"I can do that."

"What word do you want to use?"

"Frogspawn."

"Good clear identifier you won't confuse, perfect. Now, I have your first verbal 'frogspawn.'"

Major Randal clicked on.

"Go for the tires. The Italians have done a yeoman's job of establishing supply dumps of fuel, ammunition, etc. – enough to last for years. Problem is, some idiot in the Fascist's supply system forgot tires. The Italian Army does not have a reserve of spares in Abyssinia and no way to bring in any."

"We'll make it a point to remind 'em of the oversight."

"You do that," the SOE Chief said. "Can you think of anything we might have overlooked?"

"There is this one little thing, sir."

"Oh?"

"I don't see any reason why I should have to parachute into a remote foreign country, charged with specifically impressing the locals that I'm a big shot, having a mere Royal Marine private serving as my aide."

"I can see how that might pose a problem," Major General Taylor agreed, looking off into the distance. "Particularly after all the trouble we have gone to turn you into a *tillik sau*. Definitely would not do for you to go in under-aided; it always pays to use enough gun."

"You bring those trinkets I requested, General?"

"I did, Major," Major General Taylor responded with a big grin, tossing him a little blue box.

Major Randal caught it with one hand and struggled off the parachute he had been resting on. "Royal Marine Hoolihan, on your feet! Front and center, Private."

The husky young Marine jumped up with a questioning look on his face. He had been following every word of the exchange closely and was wondering what kind of trouble he had gotten himself into now.

"Stand at attention there, Marine," Major Randal ordered sternly. "By the authority of whoever the powers may be that are responsible for this kind of thing out here in the wild blue on the other side of nowhere…"

"That would be me," Major General Taylor interrupted with a serious demeanor.

"You are hereby promoted to the rank of Bimbashi, forthwith making you by official decree, a temporary officer and gentleman," Major Randal said, opening the box and taking out the rank insignia inside. "Congratulations, Butch."

Bimbashi Butch Hoolihan was so stunned he nearly hyperventilated. Major Randal pinned the badge of rank on the epaulets of his jungle green BDU blouse.

"Sir, what exactly is a Bimbashi?"

"The lowest commissioned rank in the Sudan Defense Force, but don't feel bad... it's higher than a colonel in the Egyptian Army. You outrank any national officer in the Abyssinian Forces except the Emperor, but are lower on the totem pole than a British second lieutenant."

"Major Randal," the young Royal Marine queried uncertainly, "are you sure about this, sir?"

"You wouldn't want me to look bad, would you, Butch?"

"No, sir!"

An open-topped black Rolls Royce Shooting Brake arrived at the airstrip with six passengers onboard. One was easily identifiable as His Imperial Majesty Haile Selassie I by the ornate, multicolored umbrella his slave riding on the running board was holding to protect the Lion of Judah from the harmful rays of the midday sun. This was the Official State Umbrella – HIM being the only head of state on the planet to have an officially designated one. Sitting next to the Emperor in the back wearing a scruffy beard, rumpled uniform and an old-fashioned Colonel Blimp-style pith helmet that appeared to be three sizes too large for his head was Maj. Orde Wingate. Maj. Edwin Chapman-Andrews, political advisor to His Imperial Majesty, rode in the front seat next to the chauffeur. Seated between the political advisor and the chauffeur was a smooth-cheeked youth in a beautifully-tailored jungle-green BDU wearing a sidearm in a highly-polished brown flap holster.

"So much for bloody Highly Salacious remaining incognito," Maj. Gen. James "Baldie" Taylor groused in disgust. "Time for you to link up with your interpreter, John. Better late than never."

They walked over to the Rolls Royce. Maj. John Randal gave a crisp salute, which the Emperor acknowledged with a limp-wristed semi-wave. Major Wingate glared piercingly from a pair of deep sunken eyes but did not offer any acknowledgment.

Major Chapman-Andrews introduced the smooth-faced youth wearing the sidearm, a Smith & Wesson .38 Special Military and Police Model.

"Gentlemen, this is Kaldi, the Emperor's wife's cousin. Because you will be operating in areas where that relationship may not always be something that is desirable to advertise, for this operation he will be going by his first name only.

"Kaldi completed a little over two years at the French Military Academy, Saint-Cyr before the Nazi blitzkrieg forced him to flee to England.

"By selecting a member of his own family to accompany your mission, the Emperor hopes to emphasize the great importance he places on your success. HIM wishes you Godspeed and good hunting, Major."

The effeminate-looking Kaldi got out of the automobile, went around to the trunk of the car and retrieved a heavy pack and a U.S. Springfield .30-caliber rifle Model 1903 A-1.

Walking back on the way to the Vincent bomber, Major Randal inquired, "Made many jumps, Kaldi?"

"No, sire. Today will be my first."

"Do much training to make one?"

"I spent an entire afternoon mastering the art of the parachute landing fall, sire."

"Outstanding, this jump should be a piece of cake," Major Randal lied, remembering how difficult "mastering" the PLF had been for him at No. 1 British Parachute School.

"I like cake, sire."

"Then you're going to love jumping from an aircraft in flight."

"I am quite looking forward to the experience. Have you many parachutings, sire?"

"One or two."

The Royal Air Force Vickers Vincent was a single-engine bi-plane with three open cupolas. The pilot rode in the front cockpit, Major Randal rode in the second cupola with the bombardier, and he put Kaldi and Bimbashi Butch Hoolihan in the third open cupola.

"When I give you the order to 'GO,' Kaldi exits first, then you go," Major Randal ordered Bimbashi Hoolihan in private. "No matter what happens, he's jumping today, Butch."

"Yes, sir."

Major Randal said to Kaldi, "You do everything Bimbashi Hoolihan tells you and you'll be just fine. He's a seasoned veteran at this stuff."

"Yes, sire."

Bimbashi Hoolihan had never heard himself described as a "seasoned veteran" of anything before and decided he liked the sound of it, though it came as something of a surprise to realize maybe it was true.

The pilot strolled up, did a quick walk-around inspection of the antique airplane that seemed more show than substance, then climbed into the cockpit and cranked the engine up without bothering to introduce himself. Clearly, the faster he got today's flight over with, the better.

He was not interested in making new acquaintances. Why bother? It was widely known what happened to aviators who went down over Abyssinia. The same would surely apply to parachuting Commandos. Had anyone thought about that?

Today the Vincent would be operating at the absolute extreme of its range, making for a high-risk day of flying.

"John, Abyssinians assume any parachutist floating down to be Italian so they kill them out of hand and if they make a mistake, oh well," General Taylor advised – as if reading the pilot's mind. "Wave that proclamation with the Lion of Judah seal if you encounter any natives on landing."

"I'll make sure to do that."

"By the way, what do you want to call your mission, since we plan to scratch the original name 'Mission 106?' We never got around to discussing a name," Major General Taylor said, thinking there was a lot of stuff they had not had time to address.

"Why not call it 'Force N?'"

"Good, short and simple. Now, there is this one last item the Emperor asked me to present on his behalf as a token of your command authority," the SOE Chief said, producing an ivory-handled riding whisk out of his briefcase.

"Aren't we carrying ivory handles a bit far, General?"

"No, in point of fact we are not, John. This is the kind of personal affectation a genuine *tillik sau* would adopt as a status symbol, like a Marshal's baton. Concealed inside the grip of this particular horse tickler is 14 inches of razor-sharp homogeneous steel. You may need to produce the blade as a surprise for some deserving recalcitrant. Carry it… that's an order.

"HIM wanted me to specifically advise you to never entirely trust the Galla. He said they are half men, half snakes, which is exactly what the Galla are officially on record as saying about Highly Salacious himself."

"Lovely."

Maj. John Randal climbed aboard the museum-quality aircraft, the pilot revved up its single-engine and the obsolete bomber lumbered down the grassy strip until it finally clawed its way into the air.

As they watched it fly out of sight, Maj. Gen. James "Baldie" Taylor's man asked, "What's wrong, Chief? I never saw you act this nervous at the start of an operation. You have been prattling on like a fussy old maid."

"That would be because Force N does not stand a Chinaman's chance in hell," the SOE Chief of Station said grimly. "We are throwing away the lives of two good men and one really stupid member of the Abyssinian Royal Family."

"Don't be so sure about that, Chief. I have been scanning the book you ordered, *Gray Ghost*. It came in on the Cairo plane this morning."

"Tell me."

"Colonel John Singleton Mosby, Confederate States of America, commanding the 43rd Battalion, Virginia Partisan Rangers, who operated as guerrillas for two years in the Shenandoah Valley behind Federal lines.

"The Rangers specialized in snatching Yankee generals out of their beds, cutting the rail lines, capturing Union payrolls and even raided into the outskirts of the U.S. capital. Nothing was safe from them. The Federals had to guard every fixed installation within 500 miles of the capital city.

"The interesting thing is the 43rd Virginia was not made up of elite soldiers. Mosby used what men were available, including wounded veterans discharged from service, and even Federal Army deserters and freed slaves."

"The American Civil War was not the same thing as Abyssinia."

"Maybe not, but there is one other detail to consider. Colonel Clarke stuck a note in the book for you. The Colonel penned that immediately following the first Commando raid, while they were in the hospital having his wound attended to, Randal told him a story to the effect that for 10 years, 1,000 Apache warriors tied down a third of the entire U.S. Army hunting for them in Arizona and New Mexico.

"It's the reason Colonel Clarke selected him to command the small independent pinprick outfit that became Raiding Forces – he says Randal has an 'innate understanding of the concept of guerrilla war.'"

"Raiding Forces has a list of rules," Major General Taylor mused, watching the speck of the RAF bomber disappear into the brilliant saffron sky. 'One of them is 'Right man, right job.'"

"Major Randal fits that bill, Chief – almost."

14
ROMAN CANDLE

THE VICKERS VINCENT FLEW INTO ITALIAN EAST AFRICAN AIRSPACE – and it flew… and it flew… and it flew. The ancient aircraft was so slow that when Maj. John Randal looked down at a terrain feature on the ground it did not move. The flight seemed to take forever.

To keep the Australian slouch hat he had been issued from blowing away, Major Randal tucked it inside the blouse of his lightweight jungle-green, battle dress uniform. Maj. Gen. James "Baldie" Taylor had commissioned the uniforms to be made by an Indian tailor he had brought to their quarters the first night they were in Khartoum. The faded jungle-green color was going to be better camouflage than khaki BDU once they got on the ground.

All troops coming in-country were to be issued traditional Aussie hats with the side pinned up in the hopes that it would mislead the Italians into believing that Australian soldiers were operating in the theatre. The idea was doubtless one of Lt. Col. Dudley Clarke's misinformation brainstorms. Why he might want the Blackshirts to think Australians were involved in Abyssinia was a mystery.

The hat was an excellent piece of headgear, only Major Randal could not quite get comfortable wearing the side pinned up even if it was almost identical to the slouch hat Col. John S. Mosby, the "*Gray Ghost*," had worn while leading his Rangers in the Civil War. The daring Mosby had sported a black ostrich plume from his.

Major Randal had tried unpinning the brim, but then the hat seemed too wide, so he took a pair of horse shears and trimmed it down to a smaller, much more manageable size. British Parachute Wings were pinned to the front on the traditional cream-colored gathered silk hat band. The notional 10th Abyssinian Parachute Battalion, 1st Special Air Services was headed into action again, scheduled to make its second-ever combat drop this very day.

Any native who saw Major Randal and reported the encounter to the Italians (there were no secrets in Abyssinia) would be sure to describe the hat and wings. The possibility of parachutists dropping in unannounced and unexpected at odd hours should give the Duke of Aosta and his toadies in Addis Ababa something to think about.

The ancient Vickers aircraft popped and crackled, making Major Randal flash back to the many times he had flown in Whitley bombers modified for use as troop transport. On every flight, he had thought the planes were going to fall apart around him. At least on this obsolete old aircraft the wings did not flap like a bird the way they were designed to do on the Whitley.

As he did going in on every mission, Major Randal mentally ran over the task list of things he had to do. Today the list was so short because of all the unknowns that he gave it up as a bad effort and curled up out of the wind on the bottom of the open turret and went to sleep on his parachute.

The Royal Air Force bombardier looked down at him and shook his head in wonder. It was a mystery to him how anyone could go to sleep on a mission where they would jump out of a perfectly good airplane over enemy territory. Particularly when Major Randal had to know all parachutists were routinely executed on the spot. Abyssinia was a dark, bloody land where it was widely known that the natives killed for social advancement; and dismemberment seemed to be the national sport. And there were lots and lots of wild animals down there with big teeth.

The pilot finally informed the bombardier over the voice tube that they were ten minutes out. The airman reached down to shake Major Randal awake, but the Commando's eyes flashed open before he was actually touched. "Ten minutes to the drop zone, sir."

Major Randal climbed back up into the open cupola and signaled Bimbashi Butch Hoolihan by holding up both hands with the fingers spread wide and mouthing the words, "TEN MINUTES!"

Bimbashi Hoolihan turned and gave his first order as an officer, "Ten minutes, Kaldi."

In both turrets, the next few minutes were spent getting equipment ready to exit the aircraft. The plan was for Kaldi to go over the side first, followed by Bimbashi Hoolihan and then Major Randal. When the bombardier saw the Major make his exit he would release the external bundles carried on the hard points mounted under the wings. They would be jumping at 1,000 feet.

"SIX MINUTES!" The bombardier announced. Major Randal passed the information to his two men in the rear turret, then hooked up his static line to a D-ring bolted to the side of the fuselage. He carefully threaded the safety wire through the hole in the snap link and bent it down on the far side before giving the line a sharp jerk to set the hook and make sure the D-ring was secure.

They would not be doing any hanging-out-the-side-on-rappel Hollywood stunts today with a novice, zero-jump paratrooper in the party. Upon receipt of the signal to 'GO,' all three jumpers would simply leap over the side of the airplane and trust to luck. Each man had his individual weapon disassembled in a parachute bag that was attached to his left ankle by a toggle rope. When they exited the aircraft, they would be holding the bag in their arms and would drop it once their chute opened.

There were a lot of things that could go wrong on an improvised jump like this.

The elderly Vickers Vincent droned steadily on toward the drop zone. The sky was clear and bright with excellent visibility. Down below, yellow hills and green valleys with thick patches of jungle and open swaths of savanna were visible. The Blue Nile glittered in the far distance.

"ONE MINUTE!"

Major Randal peered over the side of the open turret and saw that they were passing over a big, wide open savanna. He knew that they were not going to find any better spot so gave thumbs up to the bombardier who nodded in response.

"GO!" he shouted at Bimbashi Hoolihan.

At the signal to exit, the Royal Marine picked up Kaldi, who was peering wide-eyed over the side of the cupola, and pitched him overboard head first before the surprised interpreter realized what was happening. Apparently, Bimbashi Hoolihan had been doing some prior planning of his own; developing an estimate of the situation, he had made his first independent command decision, which was not to give the Royal Abyssinian a chance to balk at the last second – a wise choice.

The young Commando was getting off to a ripping good start as a combat officer.

The instant he saw Kaldi was clear of the aircraft, Bimbashi Hoolihan leaped over the side after him. Major Randal went over right on his heels. When his parachute cracked open, he could see the Vickers Vincent had released the external bundles as planned. Something whizzed past... one of the supply bundle parachutes streaming in, a complete malfunction giving new meaning to the name OPERATION ROMAN CANDLE. Oh, well.

Major Randal craned his neck to follow it down and saw a small group of horsemen galloping toward their drop zone below. They were not part of the plan. The other two supply parachutes deployed, and their loads, being heavier than the jumpers, drifted silently beneath him on their way down. The wind was minimal but enough to cause him to come in forward at a fair rate of speed.

Sailing in, Major Randal made a classic right front parachute landing fall – utilizing all five points of contact. Springing to his feet instantly, he saw a cluster of men less than 10 yards away with round shields, clutching long spears they were jabbing wildly at one of the parachute-shrouded weapons containers holding the M-1903 A-1 Springfield rifles. Apparently, the natives mistook the container for a prone paratrooper.

The wild-looking shifta were dressed in long, white, toga-like garments over jodhpurs with bullet-studded leather bandoliers criss-crossed on their chests and little round buffalo-hide shields on their left arms. The men had a variety of rifles of different makes slung over their shoulders. All five were wearing cone-topped, pearl grey, 1920s Tom Mix-style, ten-gallon hats. The group spotted Major Randal when he came to his feet facing them with his parachute billowing out over one shoulder.

Without a word of warning the five bandits charged instantly with their spears raised.

Major Randal was forced to make a decision. Hit the quick release on his parachute or produce one of his Colt .38 Super pistols to defend himself and risk being jerked off his feet and dragged cross country if the wind kicked up. There was not time to do both. Or, he could whip out the Emperor's proclamation and see how that worked.

Without hesitation he immediately drew one of his ivory-stocked Colt .38 Super automatics and shot all five charging shifta, rapid fire... *Blam, Blam, Blam...* so fast it was hard to distinguish between the individual rounds. Then he changed magazines, racked a round into the chamber and popped the quick release on his parachute harness.

"DON'T SHOOT, I'M AN AMERICAN HOSTAGE!" a voice screamed from the weeds in a gully some distance behind the crumpled pile of dead spearmen.

Bimbashi Hoolihan and Kaldi ran up with their pistols out. The effeminate, dreamy-eyed Abyssinian interpreter did not look quite as pretty as he had before the jump. He had apparently skidded in on his face and had a considerable amount of dirt and a grass stain on the front of his beautifully tailored jungle-green jacket. Generally, it takes more than one afternoon's training to get a handle on all the nuances of the parachute landing fall.

"Step out where I can see you right now," Major Randal ordered, "or you're going to be a dead American hostage."

"Don't shoot. I'm a non-belligerent."

A frail-looking white man with a snow-white beard and long white hair hobbled out of the brush with his arms raised. He was wearing tattered but clean khaki safari-style clothing but no hat.

"Hold your fire, I've got two native women with me – they're friendlies."

While Bimbashi Hoolihan and Kaldi covered the stranger, Major Randal reeled in the canvas bag on the toggle rope attached to his left leg; the bag held his disassembled M-1903 A-1 Springfield Rifle with the Marine Corps No. 6 aperture sight.

"Are you men Australians?"

"Who are you, and what are you doing here?" Major Randal demanded, fumbling with the rope attached to his ankle.

"Waldo Treywick's the name," the old man announced. "Until you emancipated me just now, I've been a slave goin' on five years now.

"Mister, you shot those shifta stiffer than a woodpecker's beak, faster than anythin' I ever did see. How'd you do that? Normally any man inside 10 yards with a pistol against a trained spear operator is dead meat, much less five of these bad boys. Was that some kind of machine pistol?"

"Who was holding you hostage?"

"Ras Abba Gada, a shifta bandit leader of some renown, a prolific raper of women, molester of small children, dealer in human flesh and general evil-doer. That would be the Ras himself lopin' his white mule up that tall hill over yonder."

In the distance a man wearing flowing white robes that were streaming out behind him could be seen spurring a white saddle-animal up a steep incline. Like the others, he was wearing a wide, cone-topped, Tom Mix-style cowboy hat. When the Ras reached the top of the hill, the rider reined in his mule and turned back to observe the proceedings from a safe distance.

"He as bad as you make him out?"

"I've seen worse. The Ras wasn't too awful terrible to me, seein' as how I could handle most of his business. I never made it past the sixth grade in Tupelo Junior High School back in Mississippi, but compared to these idiots I'm like a brain surgeon, rocket scientist, mechanical engineer, international financier, custom gunsmith all rolled into one," the old man rattled.

"To answer your question, the Ras is an all-around despicable human bein' by anybody's score. If I ever get my chance, I'll put him underground right quick with no regrets."

"How far would you make that hill?" Major Randal inquired, opening his parachute bag, taking out his M-1903 A-1 Springfield and beginning to assemble it.

"Altitude can be a little tricky, makes things look a lot closer than they are – I'd say 650… no, make that 700 yards. He's safe up there, and the smug bastard knows it."

Major Randal adjusted the battlesight zero on the rifle, then – taking his time – he rolled up his parachute using the straight-arm figure eight method taught at the No.1 British Parachute School and stuffed it into the parachute bag. When the bag was full, he carefully lined up all the snap buttons, popped them shut, then lay down behind it and rested the .30-caliber rifle over the top.

"Mister you're wastin' your time. You can't…."

KABOOOOOM!

The sound of the shot echoed across the savanna, rolling out lazily and thundering up into the hills. In the far distance, nothing happened; the little white-robed figure on mule back continued to calmly study the happenings below on the drop zone. Then the shifta wobbled slightly and tumbled off the back of the tall white mule in slow motion. Some time passed before the whack of a bullet striking home made its way back to the DZ.

Waldo shouted something in Galla, and two women in colorful turbans mounted on matching, blue saddle-mules burst out of the gully and raced in the direction of the hill. They both had Carcano carbines and bandoliers slung over their shoulders.

"Them's Lana Turner and Rita Hayworth, female slaves; and that is one shifta Ras who had sure better hope he is completely dead by the time the girls get to him."

"Lana Turner and Rita Hayworth?"

"Yeah, that's what I call 'em, you can't hardly tell 'em apart. One of 'em has amber eyes, and the other 'en has amber eyes too. I think maybe they was originally Egyptian. The girls was captured by an Abyssinian raidin' party when they was babies. Ras Gada kept them around as his personal body slaves to show off what a *tillik sau* he was.

"I been teachin' 'em English for the last five years cause I ain't had nobody else to talk it to, and the girls understand it real good only they won't talk it none themselves – mister, that was a hell of a shot!"

"Why would slaves have weapons?"

"Abyssinia is a dangerous place. I carry a Steyr-Mannlicher 8mm myself. I left it in the gully not wantin' to get myself shot, you thinkin' I was a combatant; you bein' so quick on the trigger," Waldo explained. "There's a lot of bad villainous people roamin' around this uncivilized country, and while we all hated Ras Gada's guts, they's plenty a' evil-doin' warlords out there that'd make him look like a benevolent Christian gentleman. The Ras knowed we knowed that, and he knowed we'd watch his back to protect our own interests 'cause out here to the victor goes the spoils, and we didn't want to be nobody's spoils."

"He let slaves carry weapons?"

"Every gun is added insurance," the old man explained.

"Major, take a look at these bandoliers," Bimbashi Hoolihan called as he and Kaldi were lining up the five dead shifta and searching the bodies. Young Kaldi may have looked like a sissy, but he did not seem much affected by his first parachute jump, subsequent close-range attack by cone-shaped, cowboy hat-wearing, shifta spearmen; and was not acting the least bit squeamish about handling dead men.

"The ammunition is a mixed lot of different calibers, and some of it does not match any of these rifles. This is awfully bloody strange."

"Don't matter none about caliber," Waldo explained. "Ammo is the coin of the realm 'round here, son. Hardly anyone ever fires any of it. Besides, they couldn't hit nothin' anyway. A bullet makes good money – only better 'cause you actually could shoot one if you had to in a pinch. Try shootin' a silver Fat Lady when the chips is down and see where it gets you."

"What's with the Tom Mix hats?"

"A fad, started out as a status deal, Major," Waldo explained. "Big-wig government officials kicked it off wearin' 'em as a mark of their rank, imported outta' Europe someplace after seeing 'em in the cowboy movies. Then the Ras wanted 'em as a sign of how they was rich enough to afford one. Eventually shifta bandit gangs started in with 'em, having stole theirs from some official or other. Now a' days it's a sign of how big a *tillik sau* the bandit chief is if all his men has 'em.

"Regular people make theirs out of straw, and all the government officials has done been executed, so if you see a man wearin' a felt Tom Mix, he's a bandit."

The two female slaves came trotting up, leading the white mule with the dead Ras strapped across the saddle. Waldo spoke to them in English to demonstrate his story about teaching them the language, "Go bring in the mules we was holdin' down in the gully, ladies."

Without hesitation, the slave girls dropped the reins of the white mule and loped off to carry out their next assignment. The animal was obviously well-trained; it stood quietly, rein tied with the dead body of its former master on its back.

"What was in the chute that Roman Candled?"

"You do not want to hear this report, sir."

"Butch..."

"The radio, Major... it's in a million tiny pieces."

"Maybe two million, sire," Kaldi added helpfully.

EXECUTION

15
PARACHUTE

"EXPECT THE UNEXPECTED" WAS A GUIDING TENET OF THE STRATEGIC Raiding Forces, one of Randal's Rules for Raiding. Or, at least had been until Maj. John Randal personally did away with it.

One of those feel-good military aphorisms that sounds really catchy in planning situations, it had proven to be practically worthless in the field. There is no way to "Expect the unexpected" because, as Major Randal had learned from hard experience, the unexpected was different every single time, and the only common denominator to the dictum was that the unexpected always turned out to be the worst possible news a commander could receive at any given time and place.

Major Randal had come to despise the phrase "Expect the unexpected." What idiot ever said that... *well gee sir, I believe it was you*!

Without a radio, the Force N team was cut off. They were surrounded by assorted enemies and unable to bring in the rifles, ammunition or money needed to attract recruits, purchase transport and sustain a guerrilla army, nor could they bring in additional officers and NCOs to command it. In fact, without communications they were unable to let anyone know that Force N was alive and well.

The broken radio represented absolute worst-case scenario. In fact, it was a death sentence. Without a way to communicate with Khartoum the advance party of Force N did not stand any chance of survival.

Not to worry, Major Randal was not considered the best unconventional warfare officer in the business without cause. Another of Randal's Rules for Raiding was "It's good to have a plan B," and it always is. He had one.

If the team for any reason was unable to transmit a situation report to Khartoum immediately upon landing, an RAF plane would over-fly the drop zone the following day. Force N could signal by light indicator or ground panel that they needed a replacement radio dropped in – there would be one pre-positioned onboard the aircraft to meet such a contingency.

The rest of the day was spent inspecting the 10 mules they had captured, the weapons that the shifta had been carrying and the equipment Force N had dropped in with. At this point, with the exception of the destroyed radio, things were looking fairly good.

Major Randal had been advised to expect a "low quality of horse and a high grade of mule" in Abyssinia. The animals they had captured certainly lived up to that piece of intelligence information. Ras Gada's white saddle-mount was definitely a prize.

The mule was a tall young animal with a graceful-looking, horse-shaped head sporting big pointed ears. Well-trained and well-cared for, apparently by Lana and Rita, he was outfitted with an ornate saddle. The rifle bucket contained an Italian military issue 6.5x52mm M-1891 Mannlicher-Carcano infantry rifle that was well-maintained in perfect working condition, courtesy of Mr. Waldo Treywick.

The Mannlicher-Carcano was replaced by Major Randal's Springfield as he prepared to swing aboard the tall mule to take a test drive. Both sets of his grandparents owned farm and ranching operations in California, so he had grown up around horses, mules, donkeys, burros and cowboys. Also, he was a former cavalry officer, a graduate of the U.S. Cavalry School and had served in the U.S. 26th Cavalry Regiment.

Major Randal had not failed to note that the old ex-slave who had not quit talking from the minute he had been freed had gone silent the moment he began to make preparations to mount up. Waldo had not quit rattling his vocal cards since his rescue. Why pick now to go mute?

Growing up around working cowboys, Major Randal knew that when they went quiet as you were swinging aboard a saddle-mount not previously known to you, watch out – things were getting ready to get "western," and right now. Mr. Treywick was not a cowboy, but he knew this animal.

The white mule allowed Major Randal to seat himself in the saddle just long enough to lull him into thinking maybe he had been wrong; then the tall animal went totally berserk – crow hopping, switching ends, landing stiff-legged and fighting the reins to get his head down so he could do some serious, moon-shot, high-heel kicking.

The ride was like being on the inside of an explosion.

Major Randal fought to keep the mule's head up, but otherwise he let the white devil do his best work. The outburst did not last long but while it did, the animal's performance was truly inspiring. The mule settled down again shortly, acting as if nothing out of the ordinary had happened. Major Randal proceeded to put him through his paces. The mule reined well, was very responsive, stopped, backed, started, cut on a dime with the smoothest gait of any saddle-animal he had ever ridden.

"Does he do that every time?"

"Seems like," Waldo admitted, shaking his head and fighting back a grin. "I was just gettin' ready to…"

"Maybe you'd like to cool him for me, mornings, Mr. Treywick?"

"No thanks, Major. I ain't no bronco buster. That long-legged demon nearly killed Ras Gada a couple times, hated the man. Don't never think a mule ain't smart and don't have feelin's. They can flat-out hold a grudge."

"What's his name?"

"He don't have one I know of."

"I'll call him 'Parachute.'"

"Parachute? Ain't never heard of a' saddle-animal bein' called that before."

"Yeah, well climb on board this mule; you'll wish you were wearing one."

Upon examination, the dead shifta's rifles were a mixed bag consisting of a French Lebel, a Mannlicher-Carcano, a Martini-Henry, two Mausers and a Belgium-made .12-gauge single-barreled shotgun with a broken stock that had been wrapped in leather and wired tight to hold it together. The weapons were pitted and rusted.

"I fixed 'em up best I could when they broke, but I ain't responsible for the general low state of weapons maintenance in this outlaw outfit. You can't make a shifta clean his gun. The only ones in any shape at all is my Steyr-Mannlicher, the girls' two Carcano carbines and the big shot's Mannlicher-Carcano, and that's because I took special care of 'em personally, meaning daily.

"These are junk," Bimbashi Butch Hoolihan griped in disgust.

"Your average Abyssinian lets the rear sight rust in place, clinches both eyes shut, trusts to luck and jerks the trigger," Waldo explained. "And, he don't like recoil one little bit, no sir. Long range to your local native shooter is anythin' over six feet or so. Shifta tend to use a rifle like a spear and don't pull the trigger until the muzzle's nearly touchin' the target."

"Why even bother to carry them?"

"Natives look on guns as a symbol of manhood and in time of desperate peril they rely on volley fire at point-blank range as a last resort, like if a rhino rears up and charges 'em unexpectedly," Waldo explained.

"Maybe at night if they can creep up close enough on a sleepin' enemy they might pop off a round. I ain't never knowed shifta to ever engage in a sustained firefight."

Bimbashi Hoolihan and Kaldi unpacked the air-dropped supply bundles and inspected the equipment each contained. Out of all their meager supplies, the radio was the only thing damaged.

The recovered parachutes were used to make makeshift tents for the night. Lana Turner and Rita Hayworth took charge of setting up camp. The two slave girls were very efficient, and in no time at all they had a cozy little encampment organized that looked like a drawing out of a Baden-Powell's *Scouting for Boys* handbook.

As dusk was setting in, Major Randal and Waldo rode out and shot a small antelope for their evening meal. At the sound of the shot, Lana and Rita trotted up on their blue mules and immediately set about the task of field-dressing the animal.

"We need to gather in a lot of firewood," Waldo advised Major Randal as they rode back to camp. "Too much ain't enough, Major."

"Why?"

"Hyenas. They'll come callin' just as soon as it gets good and dark. Mule is prime rib to a spotted dog, and we have to watch out or they'll get at the livestock. A big fire will generally drive off hyena, but it don't always work for hungry leopard or lion. Which means, Major, we have to maintain a herd guard all night long."

"You want me to build a fire? We're in Italian East Africa, Mr. Treywick… enemy territory! Why not roll out a big spotlight and shine it on our camp and tell the bad guys where we are."

As a normal rule, Commandos do not infiltrate behind enemy lines and light bonfires during the hours of darkness. It was not a technique encouraged at the Special Warfare Center at Acknacarry, nor had it been in favor at the U.S. Cavalry School. A fire at night would have spelled disaster operating against the 10th Panzers at Calais or the Huks in the Philippine jungles.

"Major, there ain't any Italians goin' to be roamin' around out here in the middle of the night, but you can bet the bank the hyenas will be. They always are, and this is lion country too. The Blackshirts never leave their forts after sunset. If Wops are out on an extended patrol they stop, set up an overnight position and hunker down well before sundown. They burn bonfires themselves all night long."

"What about bandits?"

"The shifta own the night, Major, but even they don't get out much come last light. Africa ain't real safe after dark."

A fire sounded like sacrilege to Major Randal, and militarily it was. No disciplined soldier ever builds one in the field at night. Tonight would be the first time in his career – going all the way back to ROTC at UCLA – that he had ever even considered lighting a fire after last light when on a field maneuver, much less in a combat zone. The idea was going to take some getting used to.

Major Randal had one quality that set him apart from most other commanders: he was willing to listen. While it went against everything he held dear as a military professional, he put in motion plans to have enough firewood on hand to burn down the Empire State Building.

He need not have bothered. A thunderstorm of epic proportion rolled up the escarpment, bringing thunder and lightning all night long. The mules were tethered close to the tent, but no wild animals were out and about on such a stormy night, not even the dreaded hyenas.

The storm raged on all night and into the morning. Force N and the freed slaves rode it out snug in their parachute tents. Unfortunately, it continued all the next day. No Royal Air Force bomber would be overflying the drop zone in this inclement weather.

Now Plan B was down the tube. Not to worry. Major Randal really was the best in the business, and he had a Plan B for his Plan B. In the event they were unable to make contact for any reason when they attempted to execute the original Plan B, the final fallback plan called for an RAF bomber to fly over a pre-selected location 30 miles east of the drop zone on the fourth day after the insertion of Force N.

The rains stopped in plenty of time for the hyenas to arrive the second night. The bonfire was duly lit, and it kept the mule-killers at bay, but they were out there circling around – lime-green eyes glowing – snapping, coughing and cackling. The mules were uneasy, snorting and baying in fear. Major Randal's only experience with hyenas up to this point in his military career had been at the L.A. Zoo, but tonight it did not take him long to form a lasting impression.

"Will hyena eat one of their own?"

"They ain't particular, they'll eat anything and if you wound one the others will turn on it and kill it when it squeals."

Taking his flashlight, Major Randal stepped outside the tent and walked out to the edge of the circle of light from the fire Kaldi was tending. He flicked on the light and swung it in a sweeping arch immediately picking up a pair of lime-green eyes in the beam. Behind the eyes he could make out the grinning features of a large male hyena.

Boooom, the Colt .38 Special barked. The weapon of choice of such notables as Baby Face Nelson, John Dillinger, the FBI and Texas Rangers to name a few, it was capable of shooting completely through the engine block of a speeding automobile. The cartridge was never intended to penetrate the frontal lobe of an African scavenger who did not have the courtesy or patience to wait until its next meal was completely dead before chowing down.

Nevertheless, that particular spotted hyena was smacked down without a whimper.

Feeling a surge of satisfaction, Major Randal quickly spotlighted and shot two more of the scavengers before returning to the tent. For the rest of the night they could hear the pack dining on their dead companions. Hyenas sounded like messy eaters.

There were no more problems with the mules.

The next morning, Force N and its recent attachments stood to at sunrise and made ready to move cross-country to the location where they could rendezvous with the RAF bomber the following day. They hoped to make good time, and it was the perfect shakedown cruise to get acquainted with the mules inherited from the dead shifta. If things worked out as planned, they would be spending a lot of time with each other, and it was in everyone's best interest to get the kinks out of the relationship as early as possible.

Before they departed, Waldo informed Major Randal, "Don't do no good for you to go and shoot all those shifta if you ain't going to get any mileage out of it."

"Mileage?"

"If you go to the trouble to kill someone in Abyssinia you need to let everybody know you done it… makes the doer a certified *tillik sau*. Since you're here to liberate the entire country, Major, it's time you got started advertisin' that fact, don't ya' think?"

"How do we go about it?"

"Put their heads on a stick, that's how. Start getting' the word out there's a new sheriff in town."

"Kaldi?"

"Mr. Treywick is right, sire. The heads of your enemy will be a symbol to all who pass by that you are a strong man, a *tillik sau* not to be trifled with. I endorse the recommendation most highly."

"What do you think, Butch?"

"As long as I don't have to be the one to chop the heads off, sir. The bandits are dead anyway, what could it hurt?"

The U.S. Army Cavalry School teaches the concept of "mission before man." Major Randal seriously doubted cutting the heads off your dead enemy to enhance your personal reputation as a big shot was what the shool had in mind. Then again, maybe it applied.

"Go ahead, Mr. Treywick, hoist away."

When they rode out of camp, there were six heads grinning from the tops of 10-foot bamboo poles to keep the hyenas from getting at them. On the forehead of each one was the letter "N" written in charcoal. Major Randal had seen a human head on a stick before; the Huks liked to post a message of warning to anyone thinking about encroaching into their territory. But this was the first time he had ever been personally responsible for an enemy's head being put on one.

The truth was, and Major Randal would not have wanted anyone to know this, the experience was not all that bad. There was something strangely satisfying in the primeval gesture. He was announcing loud and clear to all Italian East Africa in terms everyone would understand, "I'm here, I plan to stay, go ahead… come and kill me if you dare – look what happened to the fools who tried!"

And that was OK by him.

Force N set up another camp when the party reached the vicinity of the over-flight area. That night Major Randal went out periodically, spotlighted and shot more hyena.

After he left the tent, Waldo turned to Bimbashi Hoolihan, "Let me make sure I got this straight. Your mission is to recruit shifta to fight the Italians for the British and the Emperor?"

"That is the plan, Mr. Treywick."

"Hell, Butch, it looks to me like the Major done went and shot your entire first batch of potential recruits. I hope you can figure out some way to sign 'em up faster than he can gun 'em down."

When Major Randal ducked back inside the tent the ex-slave informed him, "Major, this here scheme of yours to raise an army is worse than no plan at all."

"Why do you say that, Mr. Treywick?"

"Half the tribes out here are treatin' with the Wops, and the other half ain't loyal to anyone, much less the Emperor. The locals all have old scores to settle with each other. Blood feuds, cattle quarrels, water hole disputes, boundary disagreements, trouble over stole' women and what not.

"Out here is a feudal system to make the dark ages look like a well-oiled bureaucracy. There's the Emperor who's gone AWOL; a bunch of kings nobody recognizes; Rases, which is sorta' like your dukes, overlords, lords and warlords; and most important of all these days, local *tillik sau* – each one with his own posse of cutthroats.

"You arm and equip these worthless evil-doers, and all they'll do is war on each other settlin' old scores, not fight the Blackshirts. With the shifta, all fightin' is for profit. You give 'em one of your fine Springfield rifles and they'll simply trot out and sell their old gun to the Italians because the Wops got a firearms 'buyback program' hopin' to disarm the natives.

"Then at the first opportunity, they'll run off with your '03 A-1 and go back to bein' a bandit."

"Mr. Treywick, how would you like to sign on as my political advisor?" Major Randal said, "If not, consider yourself drafted."

"Sign on? I'm your slave, Major. That's how it works out here – you kill a slave's master and you take ownership of his property, then and there. You're responsible for 'em. Rita and Lana wanted me to ask you if you would consider not beating them too often, once a day ought to do right fine, maybe more if the situation demands."

"Beat?"

"Now me, I'm an American. You can't draft me. Like I said, I'm a non-belligerent – but that don't mean I ain't hostile. I hate Italians. They knowed I was a slave and wouldn't do nuthin' about it.

"You need an advisor, I'm your man! Sign me up, at least temporarily until we can get outta' here."

"You're on the payroll."

"Works for me, but I ain't kiddin' about the girls. You done flat-out own Rita and Lana, and that's a fact."

"They're free to go."

"Free? Go? Major, you got a lot to learn. They ain't free and they ain't goin' nowhere. You own yourself a couple of fancy, high-grade slave girls, Bwana, unless you sell 'em or trade 'em… that's all there is to it."

"You're kidding."

"No, I ain't," Waldo insisted. "That's the way it is – jungle rules."

Before they turned in for the night, Major Randal pulled Bimbashi Hoolihan aside and told him, "Butch, I'm putting you in charge of Mr. Treywick's health regime. He looks like he probably has every disease known to medical science. I want you to give him one of every pill in the medical kit at least twice a day."

"Does that include the horse pills the vet gave us, sir."

"Couldn't hurt."

"Sir, if you do not mind me asking," Bimbashi Hoolihan inquired, "What's it feel like being a slave master?"

"Really good, Butch. You ought to try it," Major Randal said. "I knew that whip the Emperor gave me was going to come in handy for something."

"I could not help wondering, sir, what do you reckon Lady Seaborn's reaction is going to be to you owning a pair of slave girls?"

"Jane is a married woman, Butch. Rita and Lana aren't any of her concern," Major Randal said. "Besides, it ain't like I bought 'em on the open market."

"Abyssinia is turning out like an open-air lunatic asylum, sir. Weirder than briefed," Bimbashi Hoolihan added. "I am almost positive slaveholding is against King's regulations."

The next morning Force N set up to wait for the Royal Air Force to arrive. Bimbashi Butch Hoolihan and Kaldi rehearsed laying out the signal panels in the correct pattern. The slave girls managed the livestock. Waldo napped in the warm sunlight. Unit morale was high.

At the appointed time, there was the sound of an approaching aircraft in the distance. Just as they were able to make out the distinctive silhouette of a Vickers Valentia, a tiny speck dived out of the sun, spitting fire, sending the RAF plane spiraling down in flames. There were no parachutes.

Force N and all attached parties stood transfixed, watching in open horror as the Plan B to Plan B slowly looped down, crashed, burned and then exploded. At this point, Maj. John Randal was fresh out of fallback plans. Force N was cut off behind the lines, out of contact, and with no hope of establishing communications.

And that meant they were fair and truly in big trouble.

"Major?" queried a seriously worried-sounding Bimbashi Hoolihan.

"What, Butch?"

"Sir, do you think we may have acted prematurely putting those heads up on the sticks?"

"You want to ride back over there and cut 'em down?"

16
BUTTERFLY

THE NEWS THAT MAJ. JOHN RANDAL WAS MISSING IN ABYSSINIA exploded like a blockbuster bomb at the Strategic Raiding Forces Headquarters, which was located at Seaborn House in the Restricted Zone 90 miles south of London. While there was no outright panic, the atmosphere could be described as "chaotic." Commando soldiers the caliber of the Raiding Forces personnel in this state of dismay was not a cheery sight.

The duty officer who received the encoded message was the glamorous socialite RM Lt. Penelope Honeycutt-Parker, the daughter of a brigadier formerly of the 10th Hussars, wife of a Royal Dragoon captain, friend of Mrs. Brandy Seaborn and her sailing partner during the rescue of troops off the beach at Dunkirk during Operation Dynamo aboard Brandy's houseboat. When the "Most Secret" encrypted message came into the Tactical Operations Center, she followed standard operating procedure and immediately sent for RM Sgt. Mickey Duggan, the Raiding Forces Chief of Signals, to decode it. Sergeant Duggan arrived in the TOC within minutes of being summoned and wasted no time in decrypting the message.

Lieutenant Honeycutt-Parker noticed the Chief of Signals turn pale as he completed his task. Sergeant Duggan had served with Major Randal in Swamp Fox Force in the heroic last stand by the Green Jacket Brigade at Calais, which had bought the Royal Navy enough time to evacuate the beleaguered army trapped at Dunkirk.

He was intensely loyal to his commanding officer.

"What is it, Sergeant?" Lieutenant Honeycutt-Parker asked, fighting a catch in her voice, knowing it took some doing to rattle Sergeant Duggan – a virtual living legend in Raiding Forces for being extraordinarily cool in a tight spot.

Unable or unwilling to read the message aloud, the Chief of Signals handed the flimsy to the Duty Officer.

> MAJOR J. RANDAL AND PARTY OF TWO PARACHUTED INTO ABYSSINIA FOUR DAYS PREVIOUS ON MISSION OF HIGHEST PRIORITY STOP NO CONTACT WITH PARTY AFTER DROP STOP RAF CREW REPORT FIRING ON DROP ZONE STOP TWO FOLLOWUP ATTEMPTS TO ESTABLISH CONTACT UNSUCCESSFUL STOP

Without hesitation, Lieutenant Honeycutt-Parker immediately swung into action. First she dispatched a runner to locate Capt. Jeb Pelham-Davies, MC, the acting Commander of Raiding Forces, and then she picked up the telephone and placed a priority call to Cap. the Lady Jane Seaborn.

Captain Pelham-Davies arrived in the TOC as Lieutenant Honeycutt-Parker was hanging up from a brief emotional conversation carried out in an edgy, makeshift code of sorts with Captain Lady Seaborn, who had been crying uncontrollably on the other end of the line.

He read the message stone-faced.

Captain Pelham-Davies, a triple-Military Cross recipient from the

Duke of Wellington's Regiment and a former instructor at the Special Warfare Center, immediately called a briefing for all the officers and NCOs on duty at Seaborn House.

The designated Raiding Forces personnel assembled in the briefing room in a high state of anxiety, the word having already gotten around that Major Randal and RM Butch Hoolihan had gone MIA. The men present made it clear that they wanted to stand down their current operations and go out to Africa immediately to launch a search-and-rescue mission.

Captain Pelham-Davies vetoed that suggestion on the spot. He had his orders from Major Randal before his departure for the Middle East Command, and he intended to follow them to the letter. The acting Raiding Forces Commander was a supremely talented combat officer handpicked by Major Randal to take command in his absence; although he hated not being able to agree to Raiding Forces folding their tent and riding to the sound of the guns, his hands were tied.

"We shall stand by, press on with our operations here and wait for the situation to firm up," Captain Pelham-Davies ordered decisively. "When more information becomes available, we can make an informed decision about what to do next. Until then, Raiding Forces will continue to march. Dismissed!"

Walking out of the room, Sgt. Mike "March or Die" Mikkalis pigeonholed Sgt. Maj. Maxwell Hicks. They stepped outside to have a private conversation. Sergeant Mikkalis had served five years in all the bad parts of Africa with the 13th Demi-Brigade of the French Foreign Legion before joining the Kings Royal Rifle Corps.

Because of his misspent youth, he spoke French and Arabic fluently.

Sergeant Mikkalis was not the type of man to hold any officer in any regard other than contempt. However, he had been the senior NCO in Swamp Fox Force at Calais and although he never said much about it – meaning he never mentioned it at all – he was willing to die for Major Randal.

Raiding Forces' missing Commander was the officer Sergeant Mikkalis had personally chosen to follow in this war. There was a bond between the two men that was thicker than blood, could not be bought with any amount of money and could be established only through shared experience and maintained by continued performance. Not one person in Raiding Forces suspected how deeply the tough-as-nails Sergeant felt, including Major Randal.

"Sarn't Major," the ex-Legionnaire said, "I'm bloody well not sitting around twiddling my bloody thumbs waiting for any bloody developments to bloody unfold to make a bloody 'informed decision.'"

"I would be disappointed if you did, young Sergeant."

"Will you square me going AWOL with Captain Pelham-Davies?"

"I shall inform the CO you were ordered out to Africa to carry out a forward reconnaissance on my authority," Sergeant Major Hicks said. "We cannot leave the Major lost to the fuzzie-wuzzies.

"Get out there fast, find out what you can, report back to me," Sergeant Major Hicks commanded. "I shall arrange for Captain Pelham-Davies to funnel people out to you when we do have more information.

"Remember lad, if you're on time, you're five minutes late."

Sergeant Major Hicks was the consummate professional soldier. A Grenadier Guardsman, his regiment was famous for their fidelity. He never broke rules and always followed orders to the precise letter – unless some rare exigency of war dictated it absolutely necessary not to.

Neither man had any doubt this was one of those occasions.

Sergeant Mikkalis proceeded directly to his quarters, secured his personal weapons and equipment, walked outside, stole Captain Pelham-Davies' racing green Jaguar and sped off to a Royal Air Force airfield on the outskirts of London. He traded a Luger pistol to the crew chief of a Lancaster bomber flying out to Cairo that evening and stowed his gear onboard. The crew chief agreed to leave a note with operations to call Captain Pelham-Davies after they took off to inform him where to find his car.

Upon arriving in Egypt, Sergeant Mikkalis hitched another ride on a Wellington headed to Khartoum. The Special Operations Executive operative monitoring all arrivals at the airfield recognized the Sergeant as a member of Strategic Raiding Forces as he walked off the tarmac and immediately put him in contact with Maj. Gen. James "Baldie" Taylor.

The SOE Chief-of-Station Khartoum briefed the Raiding Forces NCO on the situation. Major General Taylor was not optimistic about

Force N's advance party's prospects and neither was Sergeant Mikkalis. He knew from his Foreign Legion days the chaotic lawless state of conditions in Abyssinia.

After the briefing, Sergeant Mikkalis disappeared for a week. When he returned to Khartoum he had with him three hard-as-nails corporals who had been serving in the garrison in French Somaliland, deserting being an ancient tradition in the Legion and not without honor... provided you did not get caught. The newly ex-Legionnaires spoke French and Arabic (and quite possibly another major European language, though if they did they were not telling anybody), but they did not speak English.

The men were professional soldiers.

Sergeant Mikkalis reported back to Major General Taylor. The General did not ask any questions about where he had been or who the three tough-looking strangers were, but did promise to provide the Raiding Forces Sergeant ninety M-1903 A-1 Springfield rifles, three Hotchkiss machine guns, and a half a million rounds of ammunition, along with a pledge of a monthly allocation of Maria Theresa thalers to finance the freelance company of Arab mercenaries he proposed to raise.

Sergeant Mikkalis' intentions were to enter into Abyssinia on an off-the-books operation to re-establish contact with Force N.

Additionally, Major General Taylor outfitted Sergeant Mikkalis with mules, saddlery and two long-range radios.

Neither Sergeant Mikkalis nor the three corporals had ever fired the M-1903 A-1 Springfield, but they were well-satisfied with the rifles when they compared them to the Lebels all four had worked with in the Legion. None of the ex-Legionnaires was much impressed with the Hotchkiss light machine guns.

Within two weeks of arriving in theatre Sergeant Mikkalis raised, armed, equipped and moved across the Abyssinian border in command of a mule-mounted company of 90 Arab mercenaries. The men were a rough band of cutthroats and reliable as long as they got paid. To a man, they hated Abyssinians.

In accordance with Randal's Rules for Raiding to "Keep it short and simple," the plan was straightforward. March cross-country to the

Force N area of operations, link up with Major Randal, re-establish radio communications with Force N rear in Khartoum and continue the mission.

The next member of Raiding Forces to arrive in Khartoum was Lt. Jack Merritt MC, MM, Inns of Court Regiment.

Lieutenant Merritt, a former Life Guards Corporal, had been Maj. John Randal's wingman-in-training at Achnacarry and had been on every Raiding Forces operation the unit had ever conducted with the exception of two. Due to his having been away on a training course, he had missed the Gunfight at the Blue Duck and the MI-9 mission into enemy-occupied France in which the Major had recovered Capt. the Lady Jane Seaborn's husband.

Immediately following OPERATION LOUNGE LIZARD, Lieutenant Merritt had been given a direct commission and sent straight off to attend an Officers Training Course. When he received word that Major Randal was missing in action in Abyssinia, he was still in the mandatory course learning which fork to use. He requested emergency leave to travel to Africa from the school's commanding officer, a "Colonel Blimp" stereotype right out of a *Punch* cartoon. For his effort, Lieutenant Merritt was rewarded by being scoffed at.

He went AWOL the same day. Unlike with Sgt. Mike "March or Die" Mikkalis, everyone in Raiding Forces was fully aware of his intense devotion to his boss.

Maj. Gen. James "Baldie" Taylor was delighted to have such a talented young officer show up unannounced in his area of operations. He immediately assigned him the task of evaluating, training and equipping the men from the temporary officers commissioned locally and the junior officer and other ranks of volunteers for "special service" from the blue-blooded regular and clubby territorial regiments of the Cavalry Division.

Select volunteers would eventually be sent in to staff the Operational Centers and fill the command slots of the Patriot fighting battalions Force N was hopefully raising inside Abyssinia. Lieutenant Merritt's assignment was to press on, building Force N as originally planned until communication was re-established with Major Randal.

Or, if it was proven that the advance party was killed or captured, Major General Taylor could carry on the mission with different players.

An assignment in the rear was not exactly what the Raiding Forces Lieutenant had in mind when he came to Africa, but it would have to suffice for the time being. Lieutenant Merritt threw himself into the work with a will. The first thing he did was make a rough syllabus listing what skills the Force N officers and NCOs would need before they were dropped in to Abyssinia. His first draft resulted in: parachuting, demolitions, guerrilla tactics, aerial resupply, mule husbandry, anti-armor mine warfare, intelligence gathering, evaluation and dissemination, reception committee organization, map reading, field craft, enemy weapons, silent killing, and all the things covered in the Abyssinian country briefing that Major General Taylor put on for all newcomers. Lieutenant Merritt put an asterisk beside "medical" – he wanted the doctor to give every man going in the same briefing in the same way he had heard.

While making the first rough draft, aware he was leaving out subjects that would need to be covered, Lieutenant Merritt recognized that a first-class trainer was what was needed. One of the marks of a good leader is that he knows when to ask for help. Major General Taylor immediately agreed to send a cable to Raiding Forces HQ requesting Sgt. Roy "Mad Dog" Reupart by name to be flown to Khartoum on an immediate priority basis.

Sergeant Reupart was a former instructor at No.1 British Parachute School before volunteering for Raiding Forces. When the first contingent of Raiding Forces personnel went through jump school, he was their physical fitness instructor. When it came to training men, he was the best in the business.

Lieutenant Merritt had an idea that he would soon serve in combat with the people he selected for duty with Force N. So, it was in his best interest for them to be well-prepared. He intended to be painstaking when it came to sifting through the volunteers.

Lt. Harry Shelby, Sherwood Foresters, MC was the third Raiding Forces operator to arrive on the scene. His grandparents owned a farm in

Kenya where he had spent every summer for most of his life. He was a champion long-range rifle shot and a dedicated African big-game hunter who had been the sniping/reconnaissance officer commanding Raiding Forces Lovat Scout teams prior to his departure for Khartoum. Capt. Jeb Pelham-Davies had finally authorized his coming out to Africa after being ground down by Lieutenant Shelby's constant barrage of requests.

Besides, he did not have any desire to have his Jaguar stolen again.

When Raiding Forces was doubled in size on Major John Randal's orders before he departed for the Middle East, Lieutenant Shelby had gone to great effort to recruit a highly-touted Lovat Scout officer to be his replacement, being more interested in leading direct action missions than sniping or reconnaissance.

Lieutenant Shelby was by nature what was commonly called a "thruster." Long-range sniping was well and good, and he was, after all, a world-class rifle shot. But his idea of killing the enemy was to shoot them multiple times up close, then put a bayonet in their chest.

Snipers are not supposed to do that.

After a conversation with Maj. Gen. James "Baldie" Taylor he hopped a plane to Kenya to recruit two of his former hunting associates, who he had been granted authority to commission with the rank of Bimbashi. The SOE station chief also authorized him to recruit a company of Patriots from the Abyssinians who had deserted from the Italian Colonial battalions. The deserters were currently being used by the South African Army as manual labor for road construction.

Why the Abyssinian fighting men's talents were being wasted as construction workers was anybody's guess. It was almost as if someone was intentionally diverting them from performing the mission they could do best. The Kenyan government claimed the Geneva Convention prohibited deserters from being allowed to serve in combat units against the forces they had deserted from.

It was argued the Abyssinians could only be employed as pioneers, which was patently ridiculous.

Arriving in Kenya armed with documents that would have given the highest ranking official in the realm pause, Geneva Convention be damned – or more accurately, properly interpreted – Lieutenant Shelby quickly signed on his two friends. Both were currently assigned to guard small installations of little military value in remote parts of the colony.

Why the skills of two talented young Kenyans were being wasted was a mystery. Something was clearly wrong with the military machine in the colony. The local Colonial Office Secretary in charge of officer manpower assignments was Capt. the Lord Joss Hay, the 22nd Earl of Erroll. He was not amused when Lieutenant Shelby showed up unannounced with orders signed by Lt. Gen. Sir Archibald Percival Wavell, and the Earl did not go out of his way to be helpful.

Lieutenant Shelby and his two new Bimbashi quickly recruited the native Abyssinians needed to form a 90-man company. The men were all combat veterans; most had served in both the Emperor's Army and the Italian Army which defeated it before they deserted and fled to Kenya. Major General Taylor flew in M-1903 A-1 Springfield rifles augmented by Hotchkiss light machine guns to arm the troops. He provided communications gear and enough of the Fat Ladys to pay the men's wages for six months.

Then, in record time, Lieutenant Shelby marched out for Abyssinia. The company would have to go in by foot because they had to cross a tsetse fly zone that would spell certain death for any horse or mule that penetrated it. The little unit had a hard trek ahead of them through the worst terrain imaginable and across territory inhabited by some of the fiercest tribes in Africa.

And that was just to reach their jumping-off point on the far side of the Forbidden Zone.

Major General Taylor, an astute observer of all things military, was keenly interested to note that not one of the three Raiding Forces people had arrived in theatre with travel orders, vouchers or any kind of documentation authorizing them to be in the Middle East Command. They just did it, on their own initiative.

He was impressed.

Capt. the Lady Jane Seaborn landed in Cairo onboard the Flying Clipper, the very same aircraft that had carried the commander of Raiding Forces and his Errol Flynn movie-star look-alike deputy to the Gold Coast two months previously. The giant passenger plane splashed down in the Nile River and taxied up to the terminal. As Lady Jane was exiting, the extraordinary Clipper Girl "Red" (the woman responsible for getting Capt. Sir Terry "Zorro" Stone kicked out of England) reminded her for the third time to have Captain Stone get in touch.

"Tell Terry I fly out of Cairo now."

Captain Lady Seaborn was met at the dock by Brandy Seaborn and whisked to a suite in Shepard's Hotel. She barely had time for a hot bath and change of clothes before a private candle-lit dinner hosted by Lt. Gen. Sir Archibald Percival Wavell. The General's second daughter had been Lady Jane's roommate at school in Switzerland, and the General looked on her as a virtual member of his family.

Before dessert Lt. Col. Dudley Clarke casually mentioned that the 8th Queens Royal Lancers Colonel sitting across from her had been the military attaché to the Philippine Islands in the years 1937 and 1938.

"The view from the Army-Navy Club of the sun going down behind The Rock on Corregidor Island out in the bay," the Lancer volunteered, "is a sight some claim to be the eighth wonder of the world."

"Did you by chance happen know a Lieutenant John Randal of the 26th Cavalry?"

"Actually there was a young officer by that name attached to the Philippine Constabulary who commanded a Flying Squad operating against the Huk rebels," the Colonel replied. "I recall he had two sergeants who worked for him with the colorful nicknames, 'Hammerhead' and 'Tiger Stripe.'"

"How did you come to know him?"

"Randal's team was extraordinarily successful as bandit hunters. I used to see their after-action reports, which read like fiction. Haruuuump, military attachés have an interest in those sorts of details, don't you know."

"Lieutenant Randal… do you recall if he had a nickname like the other two?"

"Well, yes actually, I believe he did. At least he had a code name, an identifier… 'Butterfly.'"

Captain Lady Seaborn remembered John had a small butterfly engraved on his Zippo lighter, the one with the crossed sabers of the 26th Cavalry Regiment.

"Butterfly's team was given the assignment to trek deep into the jungle and bring out Huk bandits dead or alive, and they did. Hunting Huks is an intellectual exercise much like hunting man-eating leopards, only more dangerous. There are not many of them; the Huks operate in isolated, inaccessible places like the tops of remote mountains or deep in triple-canopy jungles. They are very elusive, absolute masters of their environment, difficult to take unawares, and like man-eating leopards, they will bite you.

"Virtually everyone who ever tried to bag them failed miserably, and not a few aspirants who went in after Huks were never, ever heard from again."

"Sounds frightfully dangerous," Captain Lady Seaborn said.

"Butterfly and his cohorts 'Hammerhead' and 'Tiger Stripe' would swan off into the jungle, float down a river on a log or swim across a lagoon at night with a small team of native Filipino Scouts and they would get their man time and again. Butterfly's team achieved minor cult celebrity status around Headquarters, at least our HQ."

"Would the U.S. Army not be equally impressed?"

"G-2 Intelligence typically chose not to believe the reports. The Butterfly team would nearly always come out with a man strapped to a pole, but it is hot in the jungle... takes days to walk out if you go in deep, and the decomposed body would often as not be unrecognizable by the time the starched khaki set from Manila could lay eyes on it.

"Instead of patting the boy on the back and sending him out to bring in more banditos, the desk wallopers accused him – behind his back of course – of merely killing the first native he came across and claiming it was a Huk. American officers can be incredibly pigheaded at times about letting petty jealousy cloud their judgment, and they are insidiously envious of each other's military prowess.

"Initially, this viciousness was whispered around the U.S. HQ, then somehow Butterfly, or as seems more likely, his sergeants, got wind of it."

"What happened?"

"Randal's team received the assignment to go after a particularly nasty Huk called Smiling Jack because of a mouthful of gold fillings and a big glittering smile he liked to display to various and sundry.

"No one expected much. Smiling Jack was a wily bandit who seldom left his lair deep in the jungle. Exactly where it was located was a mystery. No outsider stood a chance of getting anywhere near him undetected. None of the other patrols sent out had ever even gotten close, and a couple never came back.

"Then one day a box arrived in Manila addressed to the U.S. Army Chief of Intelligence G-2. Unfortunately, it ended up on the desk of the Assistant Advisor to the Philippine Army, a Lt. Col. Dwight Eisenhower. Inside, packed in salt, was the head of a man with a mouthful of gold teeth. No one ever inferred Lieutenant Randal was a liar again, though there was talk about court-marshaling him – the two secretaries who unpacked the crate were in the hospital from the shock."

"Sounds like John," Brandy quipped.

"Some claimed 'Hammerhead' and 'Tiger Stripe' sent Smiling Jack's head to G-2 without the Butterfly knowing about it. I never ascertained what actually transpired. The Lieutenant may have eventually been cashiered over it, the Yanks were ruddy unhappy about the incident at HQ."

"Colonel," Captain Lady Seaborn said with a faraway look in her sea-green eyes, "I am reliably informed the term 'butterfly' is one used by ladies of the evening in the Orient to describe certain of their clients who flit from flower to flower.

"Do you think it possible that may have had anything to do with Lieutenant Randal's nickname?"

"Haruuuuump, I may have heard something to that effect myself, actually," the QRL Colonel offered vaguely. "One would have to set some kind of Olympic record to earn that particular soubriquet permanently, considering the magnitude of womanizing by the U.S. Army in the islands. So I would tend to doubt that as the origin of Randal's identifier."

Lieutenant Colonel Clarke coughed discreetly behind his napkin, though it sounded more like a suppressed laugh, and the golden girl, Brandy Seaborn, cocked her head and furrowed her brow as if she were trying to do mental long division.

General Wavell sat silently studying the scene as was his normal manner – periods of ponderous silence followed by long stretches when he did not say anything at all being his stock in trade. He did not miss much though, and having spent time in the Orient himself, he was wondering if Lady Jane could possibly be as naive as she came across tonight.

Also, General Wavell was trying to remember where he had heard the name John Randal. When you are running a hot war in three different countries at the same time with a fourth and possibly a fifth likely to break out any minute, you hear a lot of names.

Sitting at the table was a stocky, middle-aged American lawyer, William "Wild Bill" Donovan, Medal of Honor recipient, veteran of the famous U.S. "Fighting 69th" Regiment in the last war to end all wars. He was on the Cairo leg of a fact-finding mission for President Franklin Delano Roosevelt.

Mr. Donovan was particularly interested in unconventional military units like the Commandos, SOE, and LRDG.

He was being escorted on this part of his tour by Lt. Cdr. Ian Fleming on behest of his boss, Admiral John Henry Godfrey, the Chief of the Naval Intelligence Division. The debonair naval intelligence officer found the butterfly story rather more than mildly amusing. During OPERATION RUTHLESS, he too had noticed the butterfly engraving on Major Randal's cigarette lighter.

Lieutenant Commander Fleming was working hard not to laugh out loud.

"Wild Bill" recognized John Randal as the name of a U.S. citizen serving as an officer in Combined Operations. A man he had on his list of people to interview but had failed to contact because the officer had been out of the country when he was in England.

"Do you know this Randal, Lady Seaborn? I attempted to make contact with an American officer by that name when I was in London, without success. Would it be possible to tell me how I might be able to get in touch with him?"

"Major Randal is on a classified mission," Captain Lady Seaborn answered in a tone that was the personification of absolute, icy calm. "Contacting him should prove rather difficult, Mr. Donavan.

"He has gone missing in action."

After the dinner Capt. the Lady Jane Seaborn met alone with her old family friend. The Commander in Chief, Middle East Command, was not pleased when he discovered the exact nature of the relationship between Major John Randal (now he remembered where he had heard the name) and Captain Lady Seaborn – for reasons he chose not to share with her. He did sympathize with the slim, green-eyed brunette. Lady Jane was one of his genuine favorites.

What the CIC also did was cause a coded message to be dispatched to the Long Range Desert Group Headquarters with the purpose of determining the exact whereabouts of Capt. Sir Terry "Zorro" Stone. When that fact was established, Lt. Gen. Sir Archibald Wavell ordered a follow-up message to the LRDG containing detailed instructions over his signature.

After Captain Lady Seaborn departed back to her hotel – having received his pledge of personal assistance in attempting to locate the missing American – Lieutenant General Wavell issued one more order.

Cdre. Richard "Dickey the Pirate" Seaborn was instructed to report to the CIC's headquarters forthwith.

Capt. Sir Terry "Zorro" Stone was laagered in a wadi in the middle of a great sand desert approximately 1,700 miles behind the Italian lines with a small patrol of rough and ready New Zealand troopers of the Long Range Desert Group conducting what was known as a "Road Watch." The night was crystal bright and the air cold, surprisingly so, since he was in a desert and deserts are generally thought to be hot.

A "Most Secret" signal arrived over the wireless.

The heavily-bearded New Zealand radio operator decoded the message while the rest of the men lay around on bedrolls beside their pink camouflaged gun trucks, sipping piping hot tea they had brewed to help keep warm. The orders were succinct. Captain Stone was to turn over command of the patrol to his number two and move to a precise location where he would be picked up by a twin-engine aircraft at 1000 hours the following morning.

Instructions on how to mark the landing strip were included.

Fair to say, the dashing Life Guards officer was more than mildly curious as to what the flap was all about. This was the first time in the collective experience of anyone in the Long Range Desert Group that anything like this had ever happened – a plane being dispatched to pick up an officer in the middle of a mission.

That sort of thing was simply not done.

"Someone on high wants you somewhere else ruddy fast, Zorro," The LRDG signalman drawled. "Who do you reckon you made mad this time, mate?"

Another LRDG trooper chimed in, "How well did you say you knew those daughters of General Wavell? Ain't something like that what caused you to be marooned out here in the first place?"

Yes, as a matter of fact it was.

17
ORGANIZING A RESCUE

CAPT. "GERONIMO" JOE MCKOY FLEW INTO KHARTOUM AND WAS picked up at the airfield by Maj. Gen. James "Baldie" Taylor. The two men had worked together previously in the Gold Coast on OPERATION LOUNGE LIZARD. Following the successful raid on San Pedro Harbor together with Lt. Col. Dudley Clarke and Lt. Cdr. Ian Fleming, they had crafted a cover story to the effect that the German and Italian sailors on the three ships Maj. John Randal and the men of Raiding Forces had cut out from the neutral Portuguese Protectorate of Rio Bonita had mutinied and sailed away on their own. The story had not fooled anyone, particularly not the Germans, Italians or the Portuguese, but the team had a lot of fun making it up.

Captain McKoy volunteered to organize and lead a mule train of military supplies to Force N. Because the silver-haired cowboy had done favors for Special Operations Executive from time to time and because age was not considered a limiting factor in the Abyssinian theatre of operations and because he was an experienced hand at managing mules, the offer was accepted on the spot.

The idea was for him to follow along in the wake of Sgt. Mike "March or Die" Mikkalis' mounted company of mercenaries with a train of 400 mules carrying 1,000 M-1903 A-1 Springfield rifles and 1 million rounds of .30-caliber ammunition. He would also be taking with him two additional long-range radios plus 900,000 Maria Theresa thalers and sundry other military stores.

When Lt. Jack Merritt learned of the mission, he immediately demanded permission to accompany it.

Major General Taylor did not want to release the talented former Life Guards corporal from his invaluable post of screening and training the volunteer officers for Force N – a task he considered of paramount importance to the future success of the operation. But he knew how close the newly-commissioned Lieutenant was to Major Randal. The General was reasonably certain that if he turned him down, Lieutenant Merritt would simply find some other way to slip into Abyssinia. Raiding Forces personnel simply did not play by conventional rules and did not seem to recognize any chain of command but their own. And they were dead-set on going in search of their commanding officer.

When Captain McKoy suggested the Lieutenant be assigned to raise a company of Sudanese mounted rifles to provide security for his mule train, Major General Taylor reluctantly agreed to the proposal.

The first thing Lieutenant Merritt did was to handpick two Bimbashi volunteers for Force N who spoke Arabic. One was a young adventurer – a former police advisor in the Sudan conducting anti-slavery patrols along the Abyssinian border before the war. The other, the son of a Kenyan planter, was a professional white hunter.

The ex-police officer recruited his former policemen, and the white hunter recruited his old hunting crew, and the initial recruits enlisted some of their friends and relatives. In a matter of days, Lieutenant Merritt had a crack company of experienced men, all ready to go. They were kitted-out in Australian bush hats with light infantry green and black checkered cummerbunds, it being a tradition in that part of the world for each separate unit to have its own distinctive cummerbund; Sergeant Mikkalis had outfitted his mercenaries in tasteful Cambridge Blue and black houndstooth.

The supply of mules was desperately short for two reasons. First, the Italians had confiscated all they could lay their hands on for their own forces across the border in Abyssinia, which had been the primary source of mules in the Sudan. Second, the Patriots hoarded as many of the remaining mules as they could hide, hoping to drive up the price.

The Abyssinian people had been beaten down and oppressed for five long years by the ruthless Italian occupiers, but they had not stopped trying to make a fat profit off the war when they saw the opportunity. No one who dealt with the Abyssinians much liked them. If it were not for the strategic Red Sea trade route, most British military commanders would have been happy to leave them to stew in their own juices.

The SOE Chief resolved the issue of mules quickly by making the command decision to divert the needed animals from Mission 101. This action caused an almost apoplectic Maj. Orde Wingate to throw a temper tantrum of gargantuan portion in Major General Taylor's office. The wolf-eyed officer was literally frothing at the mouth in anger.

"Another plot by you military apes to thwart me in my quest to liberate the oppressed Abyssinian people and place the rightful emperor back on his throne," he ranted. "I demand you return my mules, General, and I require all 400 of them be given back today, this very instant."

"Shut up, 'Wingnut,'" Major General Taylor barked. "Do not speak until you are spoken to. The total number of mules I am diverting is 600 not 400. Another word and I shall have you shipped home by slow boat back to that anti-aircraft battery you were manning before SOE brought you out here to hold the Emperor's hand. Shoot down many planes, did you?"

Major Wingate became deathly pale. Major General Taylor's threat had scored a bull's-eye – one-shot, one-kill. Obscurity was what Major Wingate feared the most. He was insanely ambitious.

Without a word, Major Wingate abruptly turned on his heel with his ridiculous alarm clock swinging from its blue ribbon, stalked out of the office and never, ever raised his voice to Major General Taylor again. In fact, from that point forward, he did his dead-level best to avoid all contact with the SOE Chief, terrified the General might actually follow through on his threat.

Back at his HQ, Major Wingate made plans to significantly increase the number of camels he needed to purchase in order to make up for the loss of the mules. The only problem – Major General Taylor controlled the money to buy them. He would have to go back to him, hat in hand, for the funds – not a prospect he relished.

For his part, there was no chance Major General Taylor was actually going to send Major Wingate home, though he could if he chose to. The SOE Chief needed every single man he could lay his hands on. In this theatre of operations, being crazy was not considered a fatal flaw in an officer.

Sgt. Roy "Mad Dog" Reupart arrived in Khartoum and was immediately briefed on his new assignment as Force N selection and training officer. To go with his responsibilities, Major General Taylor gave him the "local" rank of captain, which in the British Army meant he was captain only in the Sudan. Everywhere else he was still a sergeant.

Volunteers for duty with Force N were in for some rugged training.

A signal went out to Sgt. Mike "March or Die" Mikkalis informing him an armed mule-train would be traveling on his trail. Capt. "Geronimo" Joe McKoy's pack-mules and their handlers – escorted by Lt. Jack Merritt and his company of mounted Sudanese rifles called "Merritt's Marauders" – moved covertly across the border, headed into the great unknown.

For his part, the old Arizona Ranger was having the time of his life. He was riding a long-legged, blue-black mule he christened "Georgie" – named after a squeaky-voiced West Point lieutenant he had served with while working as the chief of scouts for Major General John "Black Jack" Pershing during the punitive expedition to punish the bandit Pancho Villa.

"Who was this chap, Georgie Patton?" Lieutenant Merritt inquired as they rode into what Captain McKoy cheerfully referred to as "Injun' country."

"The dumbest sombitch to ever strap on a uniform."

In the dead center of nowhere, what the LRDG men called "out in the blue," Capt. Sir Terry "Zorro" Stone was sitting in his pink gun truck beside a clearly marked landing ground laid out in exact accordance with the coded instructions he had received from Long Range Desert Group HQ. The day was hot, and the sky was immense. It was only possible to view the horizon like this in the desert or at sea. The effect was so powerful you could almost feel the enormity of the sky suck you up. The vastness and isolation drove some men crazy, yet caused others to blossom and thrive.

Captain Stone could take it or leave it.

In the distance, a speck appeared in the sky, and after a time a twin-engine Royal Air Force Hudson roared over, rocking its wings; it then came around and lined up to shoot a landing. The Hudson was no run-of-the-mill bomber – that was clear from its hand-waxed fuselage. And the pilot was clearly no ordinary pilot. The Hudson greased down on the hard desert surface effortlessly. Only a highly skilled flying officer could have made such a tricky landing look that easy.

The door opened, and Captain Stone quickly tossed in his gear, hopped up and swung aboard. Before the door slammed shut, the Hudson was already taxiing, picking up speed then roaring off into the brilliant China-blue sky.

"You reckon General bloody Wavell himself was on board that airplane?" commented a heavily bearded New Zealand LRDG trooper who was resting his forearms the size of hams over the gun truck's steering wheel.

"Negative mate, even Zorro couldn't get into that much trouble."

"Never underestimate the man."

When sun-bronzed Captain Stone hoisted himself on board, he landed in the back of a bomber that had been converted into a plush VIP passenger carrier. Capt. the Lady Jane Seaborn was sitting in one of the overstuffed chairs. She was the only passenger. The green-eyed brunette flashed him a smile, but there was not much in the way of sunshine and happiness behind it.

"This airplane belong to who I think it does?"

"The Hudson is General Wavell's personal aircraft," Captain Lady Seaborn said. "His Majesty the King has one exactly like it."

"What a relief; I was rather hoping His Majesty was not on board,"

Captain Stone said with a rueful grin. "What is the occasion, Jane? By the way, it is so nice to see you too."

"Sorry, Terry; it's John. He has gone MIA. He parachuted into Abyssinia with Butch Hoolihan and an interpreter, then simply vanished."

"When?"

"Over three weeks ago. All attempts to establish contact with his team have failed."

"Abyssinia's a vile country, Jane. Not somewhere one would choose to go missing," Captain Stone said grimly. "What, pray tell, was your former fiancé doing parachuting into a place like that?"

"Jim Taylor dispatched him to raise a rebellion of the native tribes against the Italians," Captain Lady Seaborn explained angrily. "The mission was a suicide job."

"Better give me the full briefing," Captain Stone ordered, tight-faced. "I do not much like the sound of this, but we should not write the lad off yet. John has a knack of making it out of tight places; seems like all your men do."

The look she gave him would have burned a hole through the armor plate on the frontal area of a German Mark III main battle tank. "Here, this is the file. Read it for yourself."

Captain Stone opened the folder and started at the beginning. He took his time and was very thorough. The file contained more information than he had ever wanted to know about a country that he had virtually no knowledge of. Most of what he read did not encourage any real desire to ever visit there.

When the legendary lothario came to the medical report, he simply stopped and looked up and asked in wonderment, "You are expecting me to go into a country on a search and rescue mission with an 80 percent syphilis rate – have you lost your mind? Bloody right it was suicide. You must have driven John completely over the edge to accept this assignment."

Captain Stone had known Captain Lady Seaborn for years. Both their families were members of the Six Hundred – the wealthy, prominent all-powerful families who controlled the British Empire. They were both also members of the Beaufort Hunt – the most politically influential social organization in all England. Her father and her uncle, Col. John Henry Bevins, MC, had been members of the ultra-exclusive boy's club, Pop at Eaton, as had Captain Stone.

Also, he knew rather more than a few of her girlfriends.

But what happened next came as a complete and total surprise to him. Captain Lady Seaborn burst into uncontrollable tears. Considering her background, training and station in life, a public display of emotion was something simply not done – even if they were the only two present in the passenger compartment of the airplane.

She was so beautiful and crying so hard that his heart went out to her, even though he had been accused of not having one when it came to women – an accusation made mostly by other women who were crying uncontrollably at the time. However, this outburst was over a mutual friend, not a failed relationship, and the degree of her angst shook him.

Although Captain Stone had been exposed to quite a lot of weeping women, he did not have much practice in consoling them. Most of his experience had been limited to trying to figure out how to remove himself to some distant place once the tears commenced.

To be perfectly honest, he did not feel so great himself right at this moment. And he partially blamed Lady Jane for the situation, though in truth it was hard to see what exactly she had done.

"And the Gestapo," Captain Lady Seaborn sobbed, "has issued a shoot on sight order. If John should ever be captured, the Italians will execute him summarily."

"What are you sniveling about?"

"John gunned down two high-ranking German Abwehr operatives in Istanbul." She was hyperventilating between sobs. "The secret services are not supposed to kill each other's agents in neutral cities – it's an unwritten code among spies."

"When is this supposed to have happened?"

Unable to talk through her tears, the beautiful Royal Marine shoved a second thin file at him. Inside was a five-paragraph description of events and two 8x10 glossy, black and white photos of the dead agents – taken before their demise.

Captain Stone read the report incredulously. "Well, you have gone and done it now, Jane. No man in his right mind ever shoots a woman that good-looking. It's simply not done. You did, you drove him completely round the bend."

While Captain Lady Seaborn sobbed, Captain Stone laid it on even thicker. "Now, I want to tell you something and you to pay close attention. I never let it offend me when you called me a 'lounge lizard.' Not even after John rubbed it in by naming the raid on Rio Bonita OPERATION LOUNGE LIZARD.

"But, I never liked your prissy, narcissistic Royal Navy husband, Mallory... not ever! And that is a royal bloody fact!"

In Cairo at Grey Pillars, Cdre. Richard "Dickey the Pirate" Seaborn was ushered into Gen. Sir Archibald Percival Wavell's office. The Commodore had absolutely no idea why he had been summoned to meet with the C-in-C. When he was sent for, he had been visiting his fabulous wife, Brandy, taking a well-earned respite after his successful operation against Italian submarines in the Red Sea.

General Wavell was sitting like a mute statue carved in granite behind his huge desk. He did not smile when the Commodore came in. The General was a very unhappy Commander in Chief. That much was abundantly clear.

"Commodore, you recommended Major Randal for the Abyssinian assignment. I endorsed him for the mission based on your counsel," General Wavell began what, for him, was a painfully long speech. "Now I learn the Major has a personal relationship with the wife of your resurrected-from-the-dead cousin, Mallory. I shall not tolerate any David and Bathsheba scenarios in my command. The implication is you wanted him out of the way – or even worse, dead."

Commodore Seaborn was literally shocked speechless by the accusation. His ears were ringing, his face crimson and he had the same full-body slam sensation he felt that time he had been standing on the deck of the HMS *Hood* when her main battery fired unexpectedly.

"Sir, I..."

"Major Randal is Missing in Action," General Wavell continued, cutting him short. "Lady Jane is out here now attempting to organize a rescue mission. My advice is to get yourself to Khartoum and make sure everything humanly possible is being done to locate the man and bring him out alive."

"Sir!"

"Seaborn, if anything should happen to Major Randal I shall have to send you home."

General Wavell had laid down the worst threat a commanding officer can possibly make to a subordinate, particularly one of Commodore Seaborn's pedigree – public disgrace.

18

THE BEAUTIFUL ONE HAS ARRIVED

THE HUDSON ROLLED TO A STOP AT KHARTOUM AIRPORT. BEFORE Capt. Sir Terry "Zorro" Stone and Capt. the Lady Jane Seaborn made their way off the airplane, she turned to him and asked, "Did John ever mention me?"

"Only once," Captain Stone lied, feeling more than a little guilty for taking his anger out on her earlier. None of this was her fault. "We were taking the tour of the pyramids and when the guide mentioned Queen Nefertiti he gave us the English translation of her name. John said to me 'I think that every time Jane walks into a room.'"

"Nefertiti?"

"The beautiful one has arrived."

"Oh!"

The truth was, Maj. John Randal never said that. He may have thought it – in fact, he probably did think it – but he had never discussed Captain Lady Seaborn except in passing.

But, it not being true that Captain Stone was completely heartless, he could not see any harm in telling her a white lie at this stage. It did not look like there was any chance of ever being found out. Going MIA in Abyssinia sounded more or less permanent.

"Thanks, Terry. I shall always cherish the thought. You telling me means a great deal."

"Well, you have to promise to never let John know," Captain Stone ordered sternly. "No good would come of it if it ever got back to him that I revealed a personal confidence."

"On my honor," Captain Lady Seaborn agreed, managing one of her patented heart-attack smiles, though there were tears in her eyes. "You are a gallant knight, Sir Terry."

Well, if his old friend had not actually said that about Queen Nefertiti he should have, Captain Stone rationalized as they started down the stairs. Quite justifiably he considered himself something of an international expert on the subject of beautiful women. Queen Nefertiti, no matter how good-looking she had been, could not have held a candle to Lady Jane.

Suddenly, Captain Lady Seaborn remembered, "Your red-headed Clipper Girl asked me to inform you she is stationed in Cairo these days. She wants you to call."

"Safer for me in Abyssinia," Captain Stone moaned. "Surely you did not tell her where to find me!"

"Call her, Terry."

The pilot was standing at the foot of the stairs. He saluted Captain Lady Seaborn. "I shall have your bags transferred to the Great Western Hotel, Lady Seaborn. General Wavell has issued orders for me to keep the Hudson at your disposal until your mission is completed."

On the edge of the tarmac they could see a tousled RM Pamala Plum-Martin standing by a pile of her luggage reading the riot act to the Special Operations Executive Chief of Station who, to his credit, was taking the storm of abuse stoically, displaying admirable decorum and restraint considering he was kitted out in the uniform of an army major general.

The snow-blond Royal Marine was blowing her stack.

"Make sure Marine Plum-Martin's luggage goes to the hotel with mine, Flight Leader," Captain Lady Seaborn instructed the Hudson pilot.

"I should take pains if I were you, Johnson," Captain Stone drawled.

"That is one mad Royal Marine. Wonder what set her off like that?"

"I would not care to find out," the pilot replied ruefully, not entirely sure he actually believed what he was witnessing – a marine private locking the heels of a major general.

From the moment he had been ordered to pick up a passenger 1,700 miles behind the Italian lines in General Wavell's personal aircraft, a surreal quality had hung over this assignment. Shooting a desert landing behind enemy lines on an improvised airstrip in the General's hand-waxed Hudson was not the kind of mission he had expected to fly when he was handpicked to be the Commander in Chief's personal pilot.

Hanging out with the country club set in the fleshpots of the various capitals of the Middle East was how he had pictured the assignment.

As they approached, Royal Marine Plum-Martin was heard to shout, "You knew bloody well John had not recovered from his wound. How could you send him on a mission into a hell-hole like Abyssinia knowing he was not at his best? That's a bloody crime, Baldie, and you are a criminally negligent fool!"

"I admit to both," Maj. Gen. James "Baldie" Taylor retorted through gritted teeth. "General Wavell sent him out to me, the Major wanted to go, and I was desperate. I still am."

"Any news, Jim?" Captain Lady Seaborn called out as they walked up.

"No, Lady Seaborn," the SOE Chief answered, bracing for another onslaught. "Nothing of significance."

"I would appreciate a full briefing on the situation," Captain Lady Seaborn commanded. "At your earliest convenience, please."

"Commodore Seaborn is flying in shortly. Why not go to your hotel, get refreshed from your travels, and I will brief everyone from top to bottom at the same time," Major General Taylor suggested.

"The short version of what you are going to hear is that there is no new news to report. John's team went in by parachute and all attempts at communication with the team after the jump have failed. We are working to re-establish contact, but that could take weeks, or even months."

"Why should it take so long?"

"Here on the frontier, communications travel at a snail's pace. The civilized world really is flat, and we are standing on the precipice of where it falls off. Out there be dragons."

Reports on people missing in action do not get much worse.

Across the border in Abyssinia, the mule train led by Capt. "Geronimo" Joe McKoy pulled up to take an afternoon "*siesta.*" They had made fairly good time and were beginning to get the animals trail-broken. The initial shakedown phase had gone reasonably well. It was a time of men getting to know the animals and of the animals learning what was expected of them. The process can be painful to man and beast.

In a military caravan, the needs of the livestock are secondary to the mission. The mules have to shape up quickly or pay the price. In time of war, the universal rule is "mission over man." The same applies to animals.

If this were a trade caravan, the pack-mules would be pampered and allowed their individual idiosyncrasies because the cargo they carried could be converted into money. Profit was the purpose of the exercise. But because it was a military operation, a problem animal that held up the column or one who balked or could not be counted on to respond quickly in time of emergency was not to be tolerated. Captain McKoy cut out two pack-mules he identified as obstinate, unrepentant troublemakers and shot them with one of his ivory-stocked Colt .45 Peacemakers in plain sight of the other animals.

The pace picked up after that.

Shooting valuable mules sent a message that was not lost on the indigenous personnel. This was a serious enterprise. Not that the troops needed to be reminded. The Sudanese volunteers already knew full well that the Abyssinians were outlaws and brigands who killed for sport and collected body parts of their victims as trophies.

Most of them had fought against Abyssinian raiders for years. Now they were going in to liberate the Abyssinian people from Italian occupation, which to some degree had suppressed the cross-border shifta trouble. If the men felt any incongruity in that, none of them mentioned it.

Merritt's Marauders were fighting men, not politicians.

As soldiers from warlike tribes, the men quickly recognized Captain McKoy, Lt. Jack Merritt and the two troop leaders for the professionals they were. The Sudanese quickly became forged into a happy band of warriors. They were on campaign sharing a dangerous mission, serving officers they respected and getting paid for it. They could not have asked for more.

Captain McKoy was in high spirits. He was wearing his old, flat-brimmed Smokey Bear campaign hat and was armed with his favorite Colt .45 single-action revolvers and a Colt .38 Super in a shoulder holster. This expedition was like reliving his youth.

He called Lieutenant Merritt and his two platoon leaders – Bimbashi George Peak, the former policeman, and Bimbashi Lionel Teasdale, the professional white hunter – to a little command pow-wow. Captain McKoy, the ex-Arizona Ranger, Medal of Honor recipient, veteran of the Rough Rider charge up San Juan Hill, took a small stick and diagramed in the dirt how he wanted Merritt's Marauders to respond if the caravan met up with hostiles, whether a squadron of Italian-led Abyssinians or shifta bandits.

The caravan would eventually make contact with one or the other... it was only a matter of time.

"Now, Jack, here's how I want you to deploy your two platoons. I want one platoon to serve as the advance guard with the other platoon providing rear security. The rear security will also act in the role of strike element – ready to respond immediately. When they initiate their movement to contact, Jack, you as the Commander will always arrange to travel with the maneuvering element and lead 'em into battle."

"Sir!"

"The advance guard platoon will provide a point element and both left and right flank security. In the event the point element runs into something, they'll fix the hostiles in place by bluff or fire.

"The flank security details stick with the mule train like glue while I move it into a secure location and circle 'em up.

"While that's happening, the rear security platoon will immediately transition into our strike element and sweep around to the left or right in a wide looping movement – depending on the circumstances and the terrain – flank the opposition and hit 'em hard on their flank. Or, if the opportunity presents itself, Jack, loop around and take 'em from behind.

"Immediate action drills have to be executed fast with violence of action. Every move has to be choreographed and rehearsed and rehearsed and rehearsed. Then rehearsed some more so when the fight commences, your maneuver goes down as smooth as sippin' whisky," Captain McKoy concluded, gunfighter cool. "Get the picture, boys?"

"Yes, sir."

Lieutenant Merritt had been a corporal in the Life Guards, one of the world's premier cavalry regiments. The tactical moves drawn out in the dirt were not unknown to him, though he had never imagined performing any of them in actual battle, it having been long known that the Life Guards would be converted into an armored car regiment in the event of war.

Cavalry charges were supposed to be a thing of the past.

The former corporal was living a fantasy. Even in his wildest imagination, he had never dreamed he would be commanding a mounted company operating freelance on a long-range penetration mission deep behind enemy lines somewhere in darkest Africa. He had to pinch himself to actually believe it was happening.

They were marching into enemy-occupied territory against incredible odds with the primary mission to locate Maj. John Randal's team. Failing that, they were to raise and arm the rebellion, continuing Force N's original mission. If any training officer had ever laid out this scenario in a field exercise before the war, Lieutenant Merritt would have cracked up laughing.

"Keep conducting rehearsals, too much practice ain't enough – repetition, repetition, repetition," Captain McKoy ordered. "You'll fight the way you train. Train hard, boys.

"When we do this dance, and as sure as we're a' sittin' here, we will, I don't want to hear any man a' asking what he's supposed to do! I just want to see mule's tails, dust trails and dead bad guys a' layin' on the ground, quick."

Only one thing was certain on this entire mission.... Captain McKoy was a leader of men, the real deal. He knew exactly what he was doing. Every officer and trooper realized it. The old cowboy made them feel confident.

Merritt's Marauders drilled and drilled and drilled and drilled. Then they drilled some more. Having been on the Life Guards polo team before the war, Lieutenant Merritt trained the Marauders to Olympic-class standards. Sudanese make excellent soldiers and are natural cavalry troopers. The men worked without complaint. Over time, as they continued to march and continued to drill, the command became welded into a potent fighting force.

Eventually even Captain McKoy seemed satisfied.

Every evening the caravan of mules was forced to stop and make camp well before sundown. The troops of the security company and the mule handlers all had to pitch in and chop brush. The brush was piled up to form a tall, thorn boma corral to keep out the hyenas that constantly lurked, hoping for an opportunity to rush in and gut a mule.

The death dealers were always out there. They never completely went away. The brush boma was the only thing keeping them at bay.

However, the boma was not 100 percent guaranteed against leopard or lion. Bonfires had to be built around the outside of the perimeter in an effort to discourage the large cats. Men patrolled the bonfires on foot armed with hand torches and rifles. The combination of thorn brush boma, bonfires and patrols proved effective in guarding the caravan's livestock – at a cost.

Captain McKoy was a seasoned campaigner who did not like to advertise his presence, particularly at night when he was sneaking into Injun' country. He saw the bonfires and hand-held lights as a trade-off of all unhappy options. The fires were a direct invitation for any enemy to sneak up in the dark and shoot into the camp or launch a small raid.

On the other hand, if he did not illuminate the boma, the hyenas, leopards and lions would have eaten him out of mules before the end of the first week. Africa is like that. There is no school solution for every military problem. A commander has to make his choices and take his chances. Sometimes the most perfect by-the-book tactic will get you or your men killed, and sometimes the most egregious violation of military doctrine carries the day.

Soldiering in the Abyssinian bush is strictly for professionals.

19
MAN-EATER

THE NIGHT WAS DARK. MAJ. JOHN RANDAL WAS SITTING ON A TINY board stand in the top of a gnarled flat-topped acacia tree. Vampire mosquitoes were dive-bombing him like miniature Stukas with their tiny dive sirens screaming, and he could do nothing about it, especially not swat at them. He had his sleeves rolled down, the top button on his faded green battle dress uniform jacket buttoned, the collar turned up and the cut-down brim of his Australian slouch hat pulled low on his forehead. His shoulders hunched in a futile effort to keep out the blood-thirsty insects.

In the clearing to Major Randal's immediate front, a small donkey was staked out – at least it had been. Hyenas had gutted it early on, and now it lay dying as they circled, ready to commence eating their supper. Hungry hyenas had not been part of the plan. And there was no Plan B.

The idea had been for Major Randal to sit over the donkey using it as bait, and kill the man-eating lion that had been terrorizing the small village located 75 yards to his rear. What Major Randal did not know about hunting man-eating lions would fill up an entire book on the subject. The most important thing he did not yet know is that the instant you go into the African bush to hunt a man-eating lion, the man-eater is already hunting you.

When he was growing up, both sets of his grandparents owned agribusiness and ranching operations. From junior high school through college, Major Randal's weekend and summer job was to keep the predator population under control. During the Great Depression, when people were starving, domestic livestock was far too valuable to lose to wild animals. In California, predator control meant shooting a lot of coyotes, fox, bobcats and the occasional calf-killing cougar.

However, although they may be distant relatives, bobcats and cougars are not anything at all like African lions, so tonight was a different proposition altogether. An accomplished man-eating cat was prowling out there in the dark somewhere, and he was hungry. For months the great lion – or possibly lions; the rattled locals were not clear about how many there were – had been dining on the citizenry of the first clan of natives Force N had encountered after leaving the scene of the failed final attempt to establish communications with Khartoum.

The Abyssinian village was only about a dozen or so mud and straw mushroom-shaped huts, and the villagers were living in unremitting terror. Major Randal had never dreamed anything like this village existed, even in his wildest imagination. If anyone had ever told him there was such a place, he probably would not have believed them.

The village was a real-life horror show.

Every night the frightened natives forted up in their individual hooches, afraid to go outside. Nightly, the man-eating lion would prowl the area, break into the huts at leisure and cart off one or more of the inhabitants. Sometimes the hungry cat was impatient, or maybe just lazy, and did not carry his meal very far. When that happened, the locals were forced to listen to the sounds of the lion crunching the bones of family members or friends out in the street.

Anyone caught by the lion was strictly on his or her own. There was no civic organization to call for help; no one was going to sally forth on a rescue mission. When the man-eater came calling, it was every man, woman and child for themselves.

The pattern of people cringing in their huts, lion showing up, eating someone and facing no consequences had been going on for some time. Because no one was willing to stand guard duty on the domestic animals at night, almost all of the villagers' livestock had been slaughtered by hyenas and other predators. The crops were all gone because no one was brave enough to go out and work the fields.

The population of the tribe was in decline. No newcomers were moving in, and anyone with an ounce of common sense was long gone. Social organization had gone completely down the tube when the lion ate the head man.

And no one was stepping up even though, Major Randal noted when they rode in, the locals were heavily-armed with an assortment of large-caliber rifles. Every Abyssinian adult male carried one. The people should have been able to defend themselves.

Men had blazed away at the lion in the past, but no one ever hit it because no one ever practiced marksmanship. In time, the shooters abandoned hope of killing the marauder. Now they no longer even made an effort.

Besides, there was the real possibility the man-eating lion was a phantom. Everyone knows a spirit cannot be killed by a lead bullet. Why, the locals reasoned, waste perfectly good bullets trying to kill a supernatural apparition? Life can be complicated in the African bush.

The village witch doctor speculated that it might be possible to kill a spirit lion with a silver bullet. The problem was no one had a silver bullet and there was a general reluctance to take the financial risk of melting down perfectly good Fat Ladys to make any on the off-chance they *might* do the trick. In the end, no one was willing to invest the hard cash to find out.

Major Randal was sitting in the tree tonight because Waldo was of the opinion that if they could stop the lion from terrorizing the village the people would be in their debt, and it might then be possible to recruit a few of the men for the guerrilla army he was tasked with building. Why Force N would want to recruit any of these cowards was open to question, but they had to start somewhere.

Kaldi, the interpreter, agreed with the old African hand's assessment,

"What have we to lose by trying, sire?"

The eager young interpreter had clearly never hunted man-eating lion before either, or he would have realized exactly what was at stake.

"No problem," Major Randal said. "Let's do it."

But so far tonight, the only thing that had died was one more animal from the village's dwindling herd, which was not going to win Force N any hearts and minds or gain recruits.

Hunting man-eating lions may sound terribly exciting, and it probably is as a stand-alone enterprise. However, Major Randal was doing it 600 or so miles behind Italian lines surrounded by approximately 350,000 enemy combatants and who knew how many Abyssinian bandits – all of whom would cheerfully kill him. So he had distracters that took away from the thrill of the experience.

Sitting all alone in the acacia tree in the middle of the night clutching a U.S. Springfield .30-caliber rifle Model 1903 A-1 with an ivory post front sight to help him aim in the dark was long, lonely, hot work and about as exciting as watching paint dry.

Major Randal glanced at the luminous green hands on his Rolex. Looking at the watch made him think about Capt. the Lady Jane Seaborn, something he did not want to do. He was not surprised to see the hands had not moved, well maybe just a little, from the last time he checked. A blood-thirsty mosquito with teeth the size of a barracuda's zapped him on his bare wrist before he could get the faded green sleeve of his soft battle dress uniform-style bush jacket back down.

The bite stung like fire.

Now that the hyenas had made their move, Major Randal did not believe the cat would show up. And to be perfectly honest, he was having a hard time believing he was actually sitting in a tree somewhere in Africa waiting for a lion to walk out so he could shoot it.

This disbelief effect is not unusual when attempting something dangerous for the first time, like jumping out of an airplane (or hunting for a lion that likes to eat people). On his first-ever parachute jump Major Randal had never honestly believed he was actually going to jump out of a perfectly good airplane – even as he was in the act of flinging himself out.

The lesson learned from his experience at No.1 Parachute School should have been a hint that he had a lot more to be worried about right now than mosquito bites, boredom and his ex-fiancée. Ignorance is stupidity; whoever said it is "bliss" had never been engaged in an actual life-or-death enterprise. For sure they have never ever hunted a man-eating African lion all alone in the dark of the night.

If Major Randal had known anything at all about hunting lions gone bad, he would have been pounding for the safety of the village right this minute and firing off a shot every time his left foot hit the ground, hoping to scare off any big hungry cats working his immediate area.

However, since he did not, he sat tight.

When Major Randal had said "No problem…" he had never even seen an African lion in the wild. And, unlike jumping out of airplanes, he had never been afraid of cats. Also, he was probably a little overconfident in his hunting abilities.

Down below, the hyenas drifted away. The fact that the spotted scavengers were not munching on what to them was the equivalent of a T-bone steak did not cause him any sense of alarm or put him on any heightened degree of alert. Major Randal "clicked on" in tactical situations, even in training, and had a situational awareness that was uncanny. But apparently that sixth sense did not extend to hunting man-eating lions, at least not at this stage of his career.

Bimbashi Hoolihan had wanted to sit up in the stand with him, and even Kaldi had volunteered, but the small board was not big enough to support two men. Waldo had been too sick from the daily medicine he was taking – which was one of everything in the medical kit – to come down and inspect the set-up or even offer much advice, which was unfortunate.

The rickety plank Major Randal was perched on was about seven feet off the ground.

Among the many things he did not know was that on its worst day any lion can leap flat-footed more than seven feet – straight up. Most big cats could probably leap that high with a broken leg. Unwittingly, Major Randal had baited the hook to catch a hungry man-eating lion with himself.

Strange things happen in Africa. Some say it is witchcraft; others simply write off certain events to the great unknown and unexplained. The rat-cheese-colored moon came out full, and visibility improved. Now Major Randal could observe the donkey lying dead on the ground. Better yet, he could make out the ivory post front night sight on his rifle.

He should have seen the giant 600-pound cat pad across the clearing, but maybe a cloud passed across the moon, or he maybe he glanced away.

The first indication Major Randal had that the man-eating King of the Jungle had arrived was when the monster appeared unexpected and unannounced right in his face – eyeball to eyeball. The lion was seemingly standing on its tail in mid-air, suspended in space at a range that could be measured in inches. Surprise!

The giant cat took a swat at him with an enormous claw, knocking the M-1903 A-1 Springfield rifle spinning into the night like a toy. The ferocious animal let out a roar that seared through the night, simultaneously blasting the worst case of cat-breath in his face that anyone has ever breathed and lived to tell the tale. It sucked the wind right out of him.

Lions are silent hunters; they do not roar when they attack. Major Randal did not know that, but Waldo sure did. When he heard the lion's terrifying bellow from his pallet, he shouted, 'Get your gun, Butch, the Major's in real bad trouble!"

The horrifying soul-shattering scream of the angry man-eating killer was the kind of piercing sound that shattered the night. The big cat's awful howl tore through the jungle. And though it was just one long, high-pitched roar, it seemed to go on forever and ever.

Major Randal was left paralyzed on the plank, scared stiff, empty-handed, with no rifle, wondering if he was ever going to start breathing again. No one had ever suggested he wear a gas mask on a lion hunt. The giant cat's horrible breath had nearly suffocated him.

There was a Mills bomb in his pocket that he could have taken out and dropped on the man-eater right that very second, but the idea never occurred to him, which simply goes to show how green he was at fighting a hungry man-eating lion.

Raiding Forces' Rules for Raiding, which he wrote, stated "The first rule is there ain't no rules." If rule No.1 had ever applied to anything, now was the time and place.

What he should have done was to break out a flamethrower, had one been readily available, and hose down the big monster then and there. This was a no-holds-barred alley fight to the finish, not a sporting trophy hunt conducted by the rules of fair chase.

Also, Major Randal had not realized it yet, but when the cat swiped at him, the lion's razor-sharp claws had actually made contact. He was bleeding profusely from four evenly-spaced claw marks that ran from the top of his left shoulder down to the center of his chest. The claws had only just missed scooping out his heart. Additionally, there was a single, long slash down his left cheek. The Springfield rifle had saved him from major damage, but it had been a near miss.

Suddenly, the tree started shaking violently as the furious man-eater stood up on his hind legs to rattle it as hard and fast as he could. The vicious cat was trying to shake Major Randal loose from his perch. The monster attacked the tree with a vengeance.

The man-eater became quiet, but the silent anger was even more terrible. Determined to knock his prey to the ground, the savage animal was demonstrating how extraordinarily powerful he was. The acacia tree was no more than a reed to the 600-pound killer.

Major Randal was being whipped back and forth like a rag doll. So desperate was he to hang on, he actually bit one of the limbs with his teeth. My, that hurt! He realized that had been a really *bad* idea.

At this point Major Randal did remember the hand grenade in his pocket, but it was too late, he had no way to get it out and pull the pin. The violent shaking went on for what seemed like a long time but might have only been seconds. Realistically, holding on against the onslaught was not going to happen.

He never stood a chance.

Suddenly, Major Randal found himself flying through space in what seemed like slow motion. He realized he was going to get eaten up by an African lion. How could this have happened?

Whaaaaam! Things suddenly speeded up really fast, and he slammed into the ground 15 feet from the tree so hard he bounced – exactly like coming in for a parachute landing fall. Now that really did hurt.

Behind him, unaware Major Randal was no longer in the tree, the angry lion continued to rattle the acacia in a violent fit of rage. The infuriated animal did not realize what had happened until Major Randal coughed when he sat up, struggling to get his wind back. He was still suffering the effects of the horrible blast of cat breath and on the verge of passing out.

The man-eater instantly let go of the tree, leapt straight up, twisted around in mid-air, landed on all fours that were already moving and came for Major Randal at a dead run. The cat was throwing up clods of dirt with each bound, pounding so hard and fast his feet nearly flew out from under him.

The ivory-handled Colt .38 Super came up from Major Randal's waist holster, and he cranked out 10 rounds that made one sound. Before that weapon ran dry, the Browning P-35 that had served so well in Istanbul came out of its skeletal holster in the back from under his faded green bush jacket, and he emptied 13 .9mm rounds down range as fast as he could work the weapon left-handed.

While still in the act of firing the Browning, he was reaching for the second Colt .38 Super, wrestling it out in time to empty it into the angry face that was within bad-breath distance for the second terrible time tonight. This part of the attack seemed to be taking place in slow motion (a sensation he had experienced in combat a time or two), but in fact it was happening very, very fast. Incredibly fast!

Major Randal was sitting on the ground, legs outstretched with three empty pistols. The 600-pound man-eating lion, shot as full of holes as a cheese shredder, was inches away, still digging the dirt spasmodically with his giant hind legs trying to get to him. The monster was staring him straight in the eyes with flaming neon-yellow orbs blazing hate. The burning hate in the eyes was incredibly intense.

Why was the cat so mad?

Another thing Major Randal did not know about the gentle sport of lion hunting was that you should never to make direct eye contact with a lion. Eye contact infuriates them, and this man-eater did not need any extra motivation.

Making things seem even worse for Major Randal, the big cat had bared really large teeth. The gleaming fangs looked like they could bite off the barrel of a German Mark III. This was not good.

He knew he had hit the animal multiple times in what should have been fatal places, but the enraged animal kept on coming. Nothing he did to kill it worked; the cat seemed bulletproof – or maybe it really was a spirit. By now a Tyrannosaurus Rex would have succumbed to the volume of fire he had pumped into it.

There is more than one way to break eye-to-eye contact. Desperately, Major Randal levered his High Standard .22 out of his shoulder holster and punched the puny-caliber weapon at the huge, ugly face of the furious cat, then tried his best to shoot both the lion's golden glowing eyeballs into jelly.

This fight had grown intensely personal, gone beyond winning the hearts and minds of some cowardly natives or a military necessity to recruit troops. Now, all Major Randal wanted was to hammer this big ugly cat as hard and often as he could before it killed him.

And he wanted the lion to hurt – bad.

Tambourines and drums banged in the distance while flashlight beams pierced the night. Bimbashi Butch Hoolihan, Waldo, Kaldi, Lana and Rita and even the local denizens were coming to the rescue. The natives were not volunteers, at least not in the true sense of the word. Bimbashi Hoolihan had threatened to shoot every last one of them on the spot with his Thompson submachine gun if they did not join in the parade as noisemakers to help drive away the big cat.

The rescue party set out with Waldo limping quickly along being supported by Kaldi. "Lions ain't supposed to roar when they're on the hunt," Waldo remarked. "They's somethin' real bad wrong with this 'un. Prowlin' cat don't never make any noise at all… they be silent killers."

When the rescue party timorously arrived at the scene of the battle, they found the largest lion that anyone, including Waldo, had ever personally put eyes on lying dead with its head resting on Major John Randal's canvas-topped raiding boots. A gleaming Fairbairn fighting knife was buried to the hilt between the mush where the cat's eyes had been before they had each been shot out with a half dozen .22-caliber bullets. The signs of a terrific battle were clear in the flickering torch light.

In the end, it had been hand-to-hand.

The commander of Force N was unconscious, bleeding from his chest, face leaning forward, his upper body resting on the dead lion's gigantic head.

More natives who had managed to dodge parade duty arrived when the drums pounded out the message that the devil was dead. A murmur went up when the crowd saw the gleaming silver hilt of the Fairbairn knife buried between the lion's eyes. Everyone in the village had heard the fusillade but since they had all known it's not possible to kill a spirit lion with a bullet, they had not expected much in the way of tangible results.

No Abyssinian present had ever heard tell of a man attempting to kill a lion with a dagger. This was a first. The community was suitably impressed.

The natives pulled the dead lion off the fallen officer, and some of the men carried him back to the village, while another party lashed the monster to a long, thick pole and carried it home to keep the hyenas from getting at it. Eight men were required to lift the heavy cat.

"Would you look at that?" Waldo marveled. "There's a sliver of rusty metal, looks like a railroad spike, rammed through that lion's paw and its swoll' up, stuck tighter'n a tick. My guess is the lion hit the Major's rifle with his hurt paw by accident when he swatted him out of the tree yonder and that's why the cat screamed so loud like that. The kitty must a' been in some serious mean pain when that happened. A hell of a fight – might near an African epic.

"My old huntin' partner P.J. Pretorius would sure get a kick out a' seein' this."

Sometime later Maj. John Randal came to and thought he heard Capt. the Lady Jane Seaborn whisper "Draw on this pipe, John." Then he faded out again. The next time he swam into consciousness, it seemed as if he had awakened on the set of a voodoo movie. Or maybe he had been captured by a coven of witches.

Was he about to be the star in a real-life human sacrifice?

Drums were pounding, symbols clashing and two beautiful women with high cheekbones and long, thick, black waist-length hair dressed in shoulder-baring sarongs were dancing wildly, waving swords in one hand and drinking what looked like alcohol straight out of the bottle in their other. Was it Lana and Rita?

The girls were Muslims and not supposed to touch alcohol. One of the two women, whose skin was the golden color of weak tea, spit her drink into the fire and it flamed up. So it definitely was high-proof. Her golden-skinned dancing partner did the same, and Major Randal woozily recognized that it was, in fact, the two ex-slave girls.

As far as he could determine in his condition neither Bimbashi Butch Hoolihan, Waldo Treywick nor Kaldi were in the hut. In fact, the only men present were four worried-looking locals glistening in sweat, standing around the walls pounding large drums.

One or the other of the two golden, crazy-haired girls occasionally danced over and took a swipe at one of them with the flat of her sword. The drums beat a frenzy of sound, and other native women joined in the wild, exotic dance, occasionally sallying over to slap at and harass the men pounding on the drums. The clearly-frightened drummers never slacked up the beat. The hut was rocking.

Major Randal looked down in a detached state and noticed that he was shirtless and wrapped in a swath of clean white bandages. He wondered why. One of the ex-slave girls – *was it Lana or was it Rita*? – danced over and placed a lit pipe in his mouth. He seemed to understand he was supposed to inhale.

The two girls definitely did not look or act the same as they had out in the bush where they dressed in multi-colored turbans, short canvas jackets and loose, flowing pantaloons tucked into tall, soft antelope-skin riding boots. These dancing wild women looked more like the razor-boned semi-anorexic sado-masochist models in a men's magazine who did the tying up – not the ones that got tied up.

When he absently reached up to touch his left cheek, he found it too was covered in a bandage. Strange? Then before he had a chance to cipher out what was happening, Major Randal checked out again, unconscious.

20
CAT FIGHT

THE BRIEFING BEGAN AT 1800 HOURS AT MAJ. GEN. JAMES "BALDIE" Taylor's safe house. Present were Capt. the Lady Jane Seaborn, Capt. Sir Terry "Zorro" Stone, Sgt. Mickey Duggan, who had just flown in from Raiding Forces HQ at Seaborn House, RM Pamala Plum-Martin and a late arrival, Cdre. Richard "Dickey the Pirate" Seaborn who appeared to be suffering from either the onset of an advanced state of depression or a hangover.

Before the meeting began, Major General Taylor had a private conference with Captain Stone, late of the Long Range Desert Group.

"Before he left, the Major provided me detailed instructions. I am directed to offer you the position of either Deputy Mission Commander or the command of one of the battalions of mule cavalry he intends to raise, whichever you prefer, as soon as I can release you here."

"Now that is an offer I should have a rather difficult time deciding between," Captain Stone replied sardonically. "Deputy Commander of a mission that has vanished or command of a battalion that does not exist

– *Alice Through the Looking Glass*, old stick – it really is always darkest before pitch black."

"I do not recollect Alice ever saying anything quite like that, Sir Terry, but those are my instructions," Major General Taylor replied. "What I would like to see happen is for you to take the position of Deputy Mission Commander and in the event John and his team are dead or captured you continue to march and assume the mantle of Mission Commander. This show is going to go on Captain, regardless. And I need you in the wings as a stand-in ready to take center stage."

"As John would say, 'I see.'"

"We both know the Major always said that when he did not have a clue. In this case I am confident you know exactly what I am talking about."

"Quite right," Captain Stone replied. "I do. I simply do not like the sound of it. My preference would be to have John in command with me raising a battalion of mule cavalry. Now that sounds like my line of work. Whatever would the gentlemen of the 2nd Life Guards have to say about me riding a mule?"

"What I hear is that your old regiment is not having much of anything to say about you at all these days. The story going round is they would not let you back in once you arrived out here to the Middle East – something about absconding with the polo team?"

"One would have supposed the lads would have had the magnanimity to have overlooked that by now," Captain Stone admitted. "Those polo players made marvelous Commando raiders. I have always tended to look back on having had the vision to recruit the squads as inspired."

"I need you, Terry. We worked well together on OPERATION LOUNGE LIZARD – made a great team. I supplied the intelligence and support, and you planned the mission. That is exactly the way I want to run it out here," Major General Taylor said, putting an end to the small talk. "There is no one I would rather have. On top of which, you are all that's available."

"One condition, General – if we locate John, you release me to command that mule battalion. Now that is a dream assignment I would dearly love."

"You have my word."

Major General Taylor began the briefing by making a short speech that started out not unlike a eulogy.

"We have all gathered here under unpleasant circumstances. However, I have a couple of happy duties to perform before we get down to the nuts and bolts of what we are going to do next about the situation in Abyssinia.

"Captain Stone, will you please come forward?"

When the desert-bronzed officer obeyed, Major General Taylor continued, "In accordance with my instructions from Maj. John Randal, acting in his role as Mission Commander, Force N, I am pleased to announce your promotion to the rank of major, Sir Terry – congratulations, Major."

There was polite applause from the small group gathered in the safe house. The movie star-handsome Life Guards officer looked pleased though not overjoyed. It was both sweet and bitter to consider that his best friend had gone to the effort to advance his military career even while departing for a mission that he must have known was likely to be his last.

"Sergeant Duggan, front and center!"

"Sir!

"Also acting in accordance to Major Randal's instructions, you are hereby directly commissioned as a second lieutenant, Royal Marines."

The Sergeant looked like he was going to have a dizzy spell. He had never expected anything like this. In the pre-war Royal Marines, rankers were almost never commissioned.

"However, having given the matter serious thought," Major General Taylor continued, "I have come to the inescapable conclusion the Major did not adequately have the time to fully consider all the implications of naming a second lieutenant the Mission Signals Officer.

"The assignment is a considerable job. As the size and scope of the Force grows in order to carry out its various tasks, the Chief of Signals position will become one of immense importance and responsibility. One which will require the officer in charge to make many far-reaching decisions and deal with a myriad of strong personalities over long distances while husbanding precious few resources.

"A second lieutenant simply does not carry the rank to be up to the task. Therefore, I have concluded the best thing under the circumstances is to promote you to the temporary grade of Captain, Chief of Signals,

Force N, effective this date. Few men have ever been promoted three grades in one day. Congratulations, Captain Duggan."

The new Captain was one surprised Royal Marine. Everyone in the room came up to slap him on the back and shake his hand. To a social lion like Major Stone, military rank was a subject of indifference. He cared little for it and in the Household Cavalry – shot through as it was with millionaires and officers with hereditary titles – military rank was not as important as social standing.

To Capt. Mickey Duggan, the hero signaler who had saved Swamp Fox Force at Calais, it was everything. He had been swept up by a shooting star. And he owed it all to a man who was missing in action.

The rest of the briefing was far from pleasant. Major General Taylor did not have a great deal more to tell the group than the brief sketch he had painted at the airport.

"Force N parachuted into Abyssinia south of the capital, Addis Ababa, across the Great Rift Valley short of the Mendebo Mountains. One of the wing-mounted bundle chutes failed to deploy when it dropped. The pilot of the jump aircraft reported seeing a small party of cavalry on the drop zone, however he admitted it might have been a herd of wild zebras.

"Both the pilot and the dispatcher believe that they heard the sound of gunfire on the ground. The aircraft received no signal of any kind before it returned to base. The troop transport did not hang around to do a fly-by because it was running low on fuel.

"The plan called for a second aircraft to be dispatched the following day to overfly the drop zone in the event that communications had not been established after the drop. However, inclement weather conditions prevented this mission from flying.

"The second fallback plan called for a third flight to be dispatched to a predetermined location at a certain time and place to rendezvous with Force N in order to drop in a spare radio. This aircraft was duly dispatched but failed to return to its base. The mission did not result in radio contact being established."

The room filled with the sounds of disappointment.

"Sgt. Mike 'March or Die' Mikkalis arrived in theatre, induced three Foreign Legion corporals to desert their Vichy unit across the border, recruited them, and signed on a company of cutthroat Arab mercenaries. They entered Abyssinia on mules south of the Blue Nile. Mikkalis' Mercs are currently making a forced march to the area where Force N was dropped in an attempt to physically link up with Major Randal and his team.

"A 400-mule caravan carrying military stores led by Capt. "Geronimo" Joe McKoy and a company of Sudanese volunteers commanded by Lt. Jack Merritt set out two weeks behind Mikkalis' Mercs. With any luck. it should take four to six weeks for them to reach Force N.

"And, that is the sum of all that I can tell you at this time because it is everything I know. What are your questions?"

"What does the 'N' in Force N stand for?" Royal Marine Plum-Martin inquired. She knew from long association that Major Randal always had a reason for christening his operations. His names were never randomly selected, though they had been. on occasion, capricious. The code name might provide some clue to what the Major was thinking before he went in.

"Not sure why the Major chose that designator for the mission," Major General Taylor answered. "He failed to say."

Major Stone locked eyes with Captain Seaborn and mouthed the word "*Nefertiti.*" She showed no outward sign of expression, but her eyes were glistening.

Somewhere in Abyssinia, Maj. John Randal regained consciousness. He was lying on a soft, sheepskin pallet in a mud and straw mushroom-shaped hooch. Waldo was sitting in a canvas hunting chair next to the bed reading the paperback *Jump on Bela* by the light of a kerosene lamp. He had his 8mm Steyr-Mannlicher rifle lying across his knees.

"Butch gave me your book, the first one I have read in near five years. It's real good. I bet P.J. Pretorius would really get a kick out of it. Ole' P.J. liked to read when we was in camp.

"Now do you want to explain to me how a blood and guts fightin' man like the one they describe in this here book could just sit there armed to the teeth and let a full-growed lion walk right up to his tree stand and slap him out of it like that?"

"I never saw it."

"Major, you nearly got yourself ate. Did you know he had his two lady friends with him? I went out and doped it out in daylight and the sign is real clear. Overconfidence is a bitch, huh?"

"By the time I saw the lion, Mr. Treywick, the fight was on."

"Probably we ought to figure out some way to display your ripped-up jungle jacket, hang it out on a rack to play up your credentials as a *tillik sau*. You got blood on your jump wings – now that's real macho."

"I had a weird dream."

"Wasn't no dream, Major. After Butch packed your scratches with sulphur, Rita and Lana stitched 'em up; then they wanted to take a shot at curin' you 'Zar Cult' style so I told 'em to go ahead it couldn't hurt none. When them claw scars heal you're goin' to be a real conversation stopper around the pool at the Officer's Club."

"Zar Cult?"

"Sorta' an extortion racket, it's a woman deal," Waldo said. "The Zar Cult started in Egypt and spread around various parts of Africa and the girls maybe bein' Egyptian probably learned it as children. The idea generally is, the Zar priestess identifies and drives out your evil spirits. And here's the kicker… for a nominal monthly fee they'll keep 'em drove out.

"Don't worry, the girls ain't gonna' charge you, Major."

"I see."

"The Zar women go into a trance, act like men, drink hard liquor, wave swords around and harass any males in the vicinity, though the only men allowed in to one of their ceremonies are those bein' cured or those needed to beat the drums. I ain't never actually seen the show myself. Me and Butch wasn't invited in last night."

"For a minute I thought maybe I was getting ready to be a human sacrifice," Major Randal said. "What was in that pipe?"

"Khat," Waldo replied. "The local narcotic of choice, only I think they probably popped you with somethin' a little stronger. The girls say you acquitted yourself well. Only, accordin' to them, you got some real nasty demons holed up in your closet.

"You had a rough life, Major?"

"Had its moments," Major Randal said. "What about those other lions?"

"Man-eaters generally operate in packs. I guess I may have not gotten around to tellin' you about that. I been a little woozy myself from all the pills Butch has been stuffin' down my gullet.

"You killed ole' big boy, but his two girlfriends is out there right now prowlin' through the village as we speak, shoppin' for supper.

"Like I done mentioned, we went out and walked over the scene of the battle this mornin' and it dopes out like you violated every known principle of African lion huntin'. The only thing you done right is shoot off more ammunition than Wyatt Earp and the Clanton gang at the OK Corral combined.

"I policed up a total of 48 shell casings of three different calibers."

"Ran out of bullets at the end."

"Yeah, I saw that. We skinned out your lion, he's a genuine 10-footer with a little extra thrown in. Me, Butch and Kaldi has a plan for the skin. We're going to make a sorta' unit flag out of it, though it looks like a cheese shredder. I lost track of all the bullet holes. They's a lot of entries and exits, so it's hard to tell exactly how many times you tagged him. Sure don't look like you missed very many, which is real impressive pistol shootin', considerin' the state of conditions you was operatin' under."

"It was close work."

"From the looks of it, you just sat up there on that plank with your boots danglin' almost down to the ground and let ole' big boy mosey up and slap you off your perch, at least that's what the tracks say. Didn't anybody ever bother to tell you the reason they call 'em man-eaters is because the lions that particular moniker is applied to eat people?"

"I never saw the cat until it was too late."

"Well, ole' Simba saw you. The only savin' grace was how quick you went to work with those fancy handguns a' yours. And I thought you was shootin' fast when you lit up those five shifta spear chuckers. Those pistol shots was timed fire compared to the ones I heard last night.

"Your barrage must'a scared the two girlfriend lions bad enough they lost their appetite."

"I wouldn't know."

"Major, from the looks of the sign you just may be the worst lion hunter in the history of the sport, but you sure can shoot."

"It's easy when you're saving yourself."

"How'd it feel to be runnin' out a' bullets with ole Simba nibblin' at your boots? Is that when you went for the knife?"

"Knife?"

"Yeah, it looks like you finished 'im off by stabbin' the bad boy right between the blinkers with that silver pig-sticker a' yours. Did you do the knife work while he was still alive to polish him off or after he was already dead and you was just a' makin' sure – gettin' a little payback?"

"I don't remember stabbing anything."

"Well, don't tell anybody; the locals is real impressed. They think you killed the lion in mortal combat, hand-to-hand with a dinky little knife. Everyone knows there ain't no way to kill a spirit lion with a bullet."

"I don't …"

"Ain't nobody ever heard of anyone killin' a spirit with a hand-held knife before either, Major. That man-eater is as dead as world peace, and you're a *tillik sau* for sure. Nice goin'."

From outside, panicked people suddenly started screaming hysterically.

"What's happening?"

"Those two girlfriend lions of deceased ole' big boy are here in the village prowlin' for supper, actin' like maybe they want a little payback of their own. Butch and Kaldi are next door guardin' Lana and Rita, though those big cats better watch out if the girls go to work on 'em with their Carcano six-point fives, and I'm a' here a' guardin' you," Waldo explained. "I hope you're feelin' a lot better, Major, because we're gonna' need to pull out right quick come daylight."

"What's the rush?"

"Well, you done went from bein' the king of lion killers to the village goat," Waldo explained. "The locals are gonna' think you made the two female lions madder than they already was by killin' their consort. They'll blame you for the attack tonight."

"What are you talking about?"

"Abyssinians are like that, they ain't got a long memory for gratitude. They'll believe the lions is out for revenge. We're gonna' need to be movin' on right smart come first light or the villagers may turn on us."

"Those cowards?"

"Natives can be bold in a crowd; it don't pay to underestimate 'em. This bunch is Coptic Christians, but that don't mean that they ain't real superstitious and they done forgot about that commandment in the Bible, 'Thou shall not kill' a long time ago."

Major Randal struggled to his feet, "Get my rifle, Mr. Treywick, the one with the open sights and bring me my pack."

"Your weapons and the rest of your gear is right over there, Major. I cleaned 'em for you. Surely you ain't thinkin' about going out tonight! Ain't you had enough lion huntin' to last a lifetime?"

After rustling through his pack, Major Randal located a six-cell flashlight. He took out a roll of green tape and taped the flashlight to the left side of the full-length stock on his M-1903 A-1 Springfield rifle at the muzzle.

"Ever spotlighted a lion, Mr. Treywick?"

"Spotlight? Are you crazy? You're goin' to walk out there in the dark with two hungry man-eaters on the prowl a' plannin' to turn on a flashlight and illuminate yourself? You hit your head when you fell out of that tree, Major?"

"Most animals are dazzled when you shine a light in their eyes," Major Randal explained as he buckled his pistols on over his bandages.

"Well, there ain't no guarantees on that."

"I'm going to kill those two lions, Mr. Treywick," Major Randal said, gritting his teeth as the pain kicked in, "or they can kill me. But I'm not hiding in here like a scared mouse."

"Major, I never heard of anyone huntin' anythin' in Africa at night, except by sittin' in a stand," Waldo said anxiously. "It's dangerous out there in the dark."

"I need someone to cover my back."

"Cover your back… what's that mean?"

Someone behind me with a flashlight to make sure one of those man-eaters doesn't sneak up on my blind side – you coming with me, Mr. Treywick?"

"Major, can't you see I'm all bunged up, I'm practically a cripple. Besides, I'm sick."

"Well so am I – you coming?"

"Hell, I was better off when I was a slave," Waldo grumbled truculently, struggling to his feet. "The Ras always thought I was way too valuable to risk lettin' a lion gobble me. I'm tellin' you, we go out there we're goin' to get ate up."

Major Randal taped a second flashlight to Waldo's Steyr-Mannlicher then handed it back. "You see one, shoot it."

"You don't have to worry about that none," Waldo said. "I see anythin' move I'll thump it till its dead, and I ain't callin' out 'halt who goes there.'"

Major Randal switched on his flashlight and eased his way carefully out of the hut with his Springfield rifle to his shoulder. The night was dark as the bottom of an ink bottle, the moon not having come up yet. He scanned the gloom with the light-mounted rifle, experimenting with the changed balance of the weapon.

"OK, let's do it."

Waldo limped out behind him, walking backwards with his back touching Major Randal's. The night air was thick and hot. The two men worked their way slowly and carefully toward the sound of the terrified screaming coming from one of the huts, about 30 yards distant.

"Listen to them poor people goin' off their rockers. It ever occur to you, Major," Waldo complained, "if you can keep your head while everyone else is losin' theirs maybe you just don't understand the situation?"

"I have a friend who likes to say 'It's always darkest before pitch black.'"

"He ain't entirely wrong!"

Suddenly a female lion appeared in the circle of light walking away from them on the path less than 15 feet away. She did not seem to notice the two men or the light and walked purposefully in the direction of the screaming natives, her pads making a strange whispering sound on the hard-packed ground with each stride.

Major Randal placed the ivory post squarely between her shoulder blades and took up the slack in the two-stage trigger.

Boooooom. The Springfield bucked back against his shoulder, and he cycled the bolt rapidly before the rifle came back down from the recoil. The 157 grain .30-caliber slug slapped down the unsuspecting lioness in mid-step. She never knew what hit her.

Tippy-toeing five cautious steps forward, Major Randal placed the barrel of the rifle against the back of the cat's head and fired again. After his first lion hunting adventure, he was in no mood for taking prisoners.

"Nice goin', Major," Waldo said, sounding shaky as they inched past the sprawled carcass, with his Steyr-Mannlicher to his shoulder sweeping the trail behind them. He kept his back touching against Major Randal's. He was not in any mood for taking chances either.

The old African hand did not mind admitting he had never been more afraid in his entire life – and he had been in some tight spots, particularly in his army scouting days with P.J. Pretorius. He was really hoping what had happened, killing the lioness like that, was not a freak accident. Maybe they were on to something with this idea of walking around spotlighting. Then again, maybe not – he would have thought he should have heard about the technique before now but he never had.

He was willing to bet this was one story P.J. Pretorius was never going to believe.

The two men continued to inch their way carefully toward the source of the screaming. The night was muggy and sticky, the mosquitoes were active, and the tension was as thick as ground fog. Eventually Major Randal limped far enough so that the hooch where the shrieks were coming from was at the very edge of the limit of his light beam.

He played the circle of light all around the mud hut, sweeping every corner of every shadow, investigating carefully – nothing. Then Major Randal beamed the circle of light up onto the roof of the hooch and saw a lioness attempting to break through the thatch. The man-eater turned her head lazily and stared yellow-eyed into the beam.

The moment had a dreamy quality about it.

The ivory post of the Springfield came to rest under the lioness's chin, and he touched the trigger. The big rifle boomed, and the lioness crumpled, rolling off the roof, stone dead, at Major Randal's feet. He cycled the glass-smooth action, honed to perfection and fired one more round into the cat's brain, point-blank, to make absolutely certain.

Then, to be on the safe side, the two men carefully worked their way through the rest of the village, shining their lights into every nook and cranny, checking for other lions.

Like Waldo had predicted from reading the spoor, there had only been the two. The hunters did not find another living thing moving. The cats were dead, and the people still cowering in their hooches.

When Waldo called out the "all clear," relieved natives poured from their huts, and a jubilant celebration erupted on the spot. The people were almost delirious in their joy. The drums pounded out the happy message into the sweltering African night. The killer lions were dead.

The announcement was drummed from village to village by the age-old bush telegraph. With other man-eaters most likely out and about, no one was going to hand-deliver any messages in the traditional cleft of a forked stick until morning.

Besides, there were a number of blood feuds currently in progress between the villages in the neighborhood, the odd unresolved property dispute, and more than a few single young men needing to score their first kill in order to qualify for a marriage contract, so there was never a lot of casual commuting.

Runners carrying messages in the fork of a stick were generally accorded safe passage, but not always. So, a letter had to be important to be sent. It took a brave (or really stupid) runner to carry one.

The next day, messengers arrived from three different villages. The communiqués were virtually identical, "Come sire, at once please, to kill the demon lions in our village."

Major Randal had stumbled into a growth industry… killing man-eating lions. And from the looks of things, he had a complete monopoly. Knocking off man-eaters might turn out to be the ticket to building his army. Then again, maybe not.

As a recruiting method, the strategy carried high risk with its reward.

21
LION SCHOOL

MAJ. JOHN RANDAL CALLED BIMBASHI BUTCH HOOLIHAN AND KALDI into his hut the morning after the night of lion spotlighting. When they arrived, he was sitting on a canvas folding chair smoking a Player's cigarette. Other than the long bandage taped to the left side of his face covering his claw wound, he looked none the worse for wear.

"Butch, I have a mission for you," Major Randal announced without fanfare, "Are you prepared to copy?"

This was the traditional statement a commander makes to one of his junior leaders prior to issuing him orders, and it was the first time the words had ever been spoken to Bimbashi Hoolihan in his capacity as an officer.

A thrill ran down his spine.

The former Royal Marine private had been astonished to be promoted. He believed the promotion was merely window dressing to make Major Randal look important to the Abyssinian natives, having an aide who was the equivalent to a colonel in the Egyptian Army. At this point in his young military career, he had not gotten around to actually thinking about himself as being a real officer; in fact, Royal Marine Hoolihan was not expecting to function as one – he saw himself as a glorified batman.

Major Randal did not see things that way.

"Bimbashi Hoolihan, you are to raise, train, and command the Force N headquarters security platoon, which is initially to consist of a dozen picked men. Be prepared to expand the platoon to a full-strength, mule-mounted rifle company once we are able to re-establish contact with Force N Rear and have more '03s dropped in to us or obtain enough Italian military rifles locally to fill our needs."

"Sir!"

"Kaldi, you are assigned to be Bimbashi Hoolihan's personal assistant with corresponding military rank and privileges commensurate with your responsibility.

"What are your questions?"

"Where do I find troops, sir?"

"That's your problem Bimbashi – recruit some."

"The men will want to know about allowances, sir," Bimbashi Hoolihan heard himself ask as if in a dream, sounding as if he actually knew what he was talking about.

"You can promise them a Fat Lady per day."

"Sire, you will make them enormously rich men!" Kaldi exclaimed. "They will be like millionaires."

"We can't pay until we get the money – make that clear."

"Are you sure about this, sir?" Bimbashi Hoolihan pressed, thinking maybe the Major was playing a joke. "I never expected a troop command. I thought my promotion was purely symbolic."

"I've got a lot of confidence in you, stud," Major Randal said. "Now you men move out, get the job done. By the way, Butch, if you have a spare Royal Marine cap badge I could use it."

Waldo came in as the two were leaving. He was freshly outfitted in one of Major Randal's extra sets of olive green BDUs wearing an Australian bush hat Bimbashi Hoolihan had given him.

"We're pulling out this afternoon, Mr. Treywick."

"Where we headed, Major?"

"To the nearest one of those villages that dispatched a messenger asking us to come and kill their lions."

"Why in the world would you ever want to do that?"

"So I can kill their lion."

"Major, like I done told you," Waldo complained, "you're about the worst big cat hunter in the history of the Dark Continent. You ain't got no natural aptitude for it at all. Spotlightin' those two bad actors was a neat trick, but I ain't real confident it'll work on a regular basis; and with lions it's only got to not work once."

"We're moving out shortly."

"Last night could a' been chance luck," the ex-ivory poacher persisted. "You need to stick to soldierin', Major. I hear you're real good at that."

"I don't have any other option, Mr. Treywick. My mission is to raise an insurrection," Major Randal said. "To do that, I need an army of guerrillas. We've lost our communications, which means there won't be any money, weapons or reinforcements dropped to us. Without money or rifles, there's no incentive for men to sign on."

"Yeah, so what's that got to do with huntin' man-eatin' Simba?"

"You said if we killed the lions, people will be grateful. We did like you suggested; now the local natives want us to stay here, take wives and settle down."

"They'll make you head man if you do," Waldo said in a studied tone. "You ought to give it some thought, Major. We could hole up here in the mountains until somebody shows up to rescue us."

"I've assigned Butch to recruiting," Major Randal said. "He can take his pick of volunteers. If we travel from village to village cleaning up their lion problem, my guess is we can sign up the troops we need along the way."

"Maybe, but you ain't goin' to do anybody any good ate up – especially me. I want to get the blue blazes out of this heathen country now that I done been freed from servitude." Waldo added, "I intend to put you in for a life-savin' medal first chance I get, and the life you saved is my own."

"Killing man-eaters was your idea, Mr. Treywick," Major Randal said. "You have a better plan now?"

"Well, no. Your idea, or maybe it might a' been mine, ain't half bad,

Major; but if you're expectin' me to go back-to-back with you on a regular basis fightin' big hungry cats at night with a puny flashlight strapped on my trusty 8mm rifle gun, you can flat out forget it," the ex-army scout stated unhesitatingly. "I'm over the hill for that line a' work.

"Tell you what I'll do – Lion School. I'll teach you everythin' you need to know to hunt 'em but I'm too crippled up to go after 'em with you. How's that sound?"

"Fair enough; let's do it."

"Major, I don't guess it hurts none to point out the last time I heard you say virtually them exact same words you nearly got yourself munched. Try not to be so eager; you just might live a little longer."

"Point taken, Mr. Treywick."

The first thing that the old ivory poacher did was to lead Major Randal outside and show him the three carcasses of the lions he had killed. The animals had already been skinned. Lana and Rita were busy stretching and curing the tawny hides.

"Now, the most important thing to remember about lion huntin' is that the purpose of the exercise is to kill the lion. It's a flat-out flunk if you end up being the Blue Plate Special on any given hunt."

"I've heard words to that effect before."

"Well, it's somethin' people who hunt lion say a lot – don't you never forget, it's rule number one."

"I'll remember."

"You do that, Major. Now, the most important thing to remember about huntin' cat is that the African lion is a big, tough animal with a lot of muscles in his chest. When he comes at you, he is all pumped up with a lot of adrenalin goin' through his veins, so you got to shoot him with a gun firin' a bullet that is big, heavy and tough enough to penetrate all that muscle and get way in there and go to work on the vitals. You always want to shoot your lion in the chest, through the shoulders or under the chin like you done the one up on the roof.

"Neck shots on lion always work good, remember that."

"Roger."

"Now a male lion has a mane that can be deceiving; it creates an optical illusion makin' his head look real big, so the most important thing to remember is, never shoot a lion in the head.

"*Why not*, you ask. Well, sir, because the brain is only a tiny part of it, mounted low in the skull protected by the face bones," Waldo pointed to one of the dead cat's exposed skull. "If you hit any other part of the head area like the jaw, or just graze the skull, you're only gonna' make him mad.

"And as you done already know from firsthand, up-close, personal experience, when a lion comes after you they're already plenty mad enough; so there ain't no call to go out of your way to antagonize one of 'em. Now, repeat after me Major – 'never take a head shot on a lion.'"

"No head shots, Mr. Treywick."

For an hour, the two of them went over the bodies of the three dead lions with the old African hunter dissecting the carcasses to show Major Randal the vital areas so that he would know how the organs were arranged when he was setting up his shot.

"As you can see on the real big one that nearly ate you, your .38 Supers were through and throughs, while the 9mms all penetrated but failed to exit," the old hunter carefully pointed out. "The problem is, Major, these two calibers are such puny-sized cartridges it took a lot of them to bring this bad boy down; the cat nearly got you."

"I tried to shoot him in all the right places."

"And you did, too, real quick. But little fast bullets don't do hardly any damage at all unless they hit a major artery or a big bone. Unless they do, the lion don't even know he's been shot in most cases.

"Now, when you spotlighted that second one and shot her dead-center between the shoulder blades with your '03 Springfield, the 157 grain .30-caliber ball broke her spine, and your third lion's neck snapped when you shot her under the chin, causing instant death.

"That was real good, exactly how you want to do it from here on out. One shot – one dead cat. Thirty-ought-six is good lion medicine. The most important thing to remember about huntin' lion is to kill it dead first shot, and to do that you have got to use a big enough gun. Your Springfield is plenty of rifle for most things up to and includin' elephant, provided you allow yourself time to place your shot. However, it is not what we call a 'stopper.'

"If ya' ever have to go in after a lion in heavy brush, you need a double rifle of a reliable make – .450-caliber or bigger – for a fast, follow-up shot at close quarters to knock 'em down when they come at you. The problem is, we ain't got one of those, and there ain't a chance we're ever goin' to… so you'll have to make do.

"Call your shots real careful, Major. Kill 'em dead. You don't want to be followin' up wounded cats in pain that is real angry and will try to eat ya' at the end on the trail."

"Roger that."

"Now the most important thing to remember when you are a' huntin' a big hungry cat that is in the act of attemptin' to turn you into a tasty snack is to never get down out of your stand while the fight is in progress. You purely violated that principle first night, Major."

"Wasn't my idea," Major Randal said. "The lion had something to do with it."

"Major, excuses don't cut it out here in Africa. Huntin' the bad ones ain't somethin' where you can just alibi away things that don't go your way. In fact, you violated the two most important principles there is at the same time. The second one's a no-brainer, which is – when huntin' a big cat that wants to eat you, don't never get separated from your rifle."

"That's not exactly the way it went down, Mr. Treywick."

"The hell you say, the most important thing to remember…"

"Wait a minute," Major Randal protested. "That's the eighth, or possibly ninth, most important thing you've said to remember. I've lost count."

The old big game hunter gave him a withering look. "Let me tell you something, soldier boy. You ain't takin' this serious enough. Am I borin' you? Now, probably you think the worst can happen to you if it all goes wrong is to get killed and eaten by a lion, right?"

"Yeah, I'd say so."

"Well, no it ain't," Waldo said. "What you can never let yourself forget, because nothing you'll ever do is anythin' remotely like huntin' man-eatin' kitty-cats, is that from the second you start out to hunt them, they're already huntin' you. The contest begins the instant you set foot into the bush.

"Worst-case scenario is to be attacked by a lion, carried off and eaten later while you're still alive, watchin' it goin' on," Waldo added. "Happened to a friend of mine, pretty gruesome."

"I can see how it would be."

"They's a lot of things to remember in the man-eater huntin' business, and they're all 'the most important.' Forget any one of 'em, and you just might find yourself drug off, leisurely observin' yourself gettin' ate. Try that, and see how you like it!"

Major Randal said, "I get the picture."

"You think you're gonna' come out here to Africa and be a big-time king of the jungle, killer cat slayer all of a sudden?" Waldo sneered. "A lot of men ended up the Blue Plate Special who thought they'd show us old-timers how the close work's done."

"I didn't mean..."

"Now where was I, oh yeah… the most important thing for a certified lion killer is to have you a 'Big Cat Down Shoot Again Procedure' – your BCDSAP. Now, some cat hunters say 'Please' instead of 'Procedure,' but I'm a' former army scout, performin' reconnaissance duty like I may have mentioned to you with P.J. Pretorius in the last big scrap, so I'm a 'Procedure' man.

"Besides, when it comes to engagin' man-eatin' lions up close and personal, I ain't in to 'please' and 'thank you.'"

"BCDSAP," Major Randal said, memorizing the acronym. "Got it."

"The thing is, you done real good last night Major, pumpin' a second round into each of them cats once they was already down. That's the way to do it every single time, no exceptions – follow your BCDSAP. Always pop 'em again."

"Can do."

"On your BCDSAP follow-up shot, feel free to cap him in the head if you want to from a range of about two inches like you did last night."

"My policy is going to be BCDSAP – ASAP."

"What's ASAP mean?"

"As Soon As Possible," Major Randal said. "In Raiding Forces, we say 'as soon as possible – if not sooner.'"

"Yeah, I like that," Waldo reflected. "You're gettin' into the spirit of it, Major. I may make a lion tamer outta' you yet.

"Now the most important thing to remember…"

Bimbashi Butch Hoolihan called a formation of potential candidates for his platoon. Kaldi had spread the word about the pay scale, and every man in the village plus the three messengers who had arrived with the cleft sticks eagerly showed up to volunteer. This translated into a total of 11 men wanting to join Force N.

Kaldi explained to them that – if selected – they would be called "Patriots" and that they would be serving His Imperial Majesty, the Emperor. The volunteers did not seem particularly impressed. They were not very patriotic. Not one of them could even name the colors in the Abyssinian national flag, it having been banned for five years.

Clearly these lads were in it strictly for the Fat Ladys.

The local volunteers were as motley a crew as have ever stepped forth to march off to war. The men wore straw imitation Tom Mix-style cowboy hats, which they were hoping to trade up for the read deal; sported bouffant beehive hairdos that obviously required a great deal of care and maintenance; wore white, Roman-like togas over their jodhpur pants; had bandoliers of mismatched ammunition criss-crossed on their chests; carried spears and little round buffalo-hide shields; and were armed with a Mauser, two Mannlichers, two Lebels, a Lee-Medford, two Mannlicher-Carcanos, one Vetterlis, a Le Gras and a Martini-Henry with the front sight broken off.

To a man they were barefooted.

Looking over the rabble, Bimbashi Hoolihan had to make a command decision. He had no way to know which men would make the best soldiers, though personally he was not prepared to be impressed with any man from the village. They had cowered inside their hooches – heavily armed – while man-eating lions feasted on their families and friends.

Not recruits a Royal Marine would normally care to share a foxhole with.

After inspecting the applicants, he selected two candidates – the two men armed with Mannlicher-Carcano rifles. The weapons were Italian Army-issue. Bimbashi Hoolihan knew the rifles could be resupplied by capturing ammunition from the Italians, which was the only way Force N was likely to sustain itself now that they had no means to be resupplied by air drop from Khartoum.

There was no way Bimbashi Hoolihan was going to issue one of the prized Springfield rifles to men too cowardly to shoot back at lions ravaging their own village. He decided on the spot to issue M-1903 A-1s only to the dozen men who made the final cut after a selection process that was yet to be determined. These sorry-looking volunteers were going to have to supply their own weapons, ammunition and transportation until such time as they were "selected."

The two Patriots he accepted as potential Force N members were ordered to trade the mismatched ammunition in their bandoliers for bullets that chambered in their rifles. Kaldi supervised this process to make sure that those not chosen cooperated and that a fair exchange rate of one bullet for one bullet was established.

Bimbashi Hoolihan did not plan to allow any war profiteering on his watch.

In what could only be described as a stroke of military genius by the young Royal Marine, the other nine men were informed that they would be reconsidered for a position in the platoon if they showed up in possession of an Italian Army-issue rifle, complete with matching ammunition. With that simple directive, Bimbashi Hoolihan earned the honor of unleashing the first wave of Force N's guerrilla war on the unsuspecting officers and men of the Italian East African Forces.

Every native in the land was going to want to earn one Maria Theresa silver dollar per day. To qualify for a paying slot in Force N, they would do whatever was necessary to obtain a weapon that met the standard. Because Abyssinians were accomplished in the art of creeping upon and murdering unsuspecting people, Bimbashi Hoolihan's order did not bode well for the lone Blackshirt soldier armed with a rifle out for a stroll.

The nine men rejected departed immediately in search of the Holy Grail – in this case an Italian military-issue rifle. The best place to find one was the nearest Italian military installation. Abyssinian men routinely committed homicide for a trophy body part or the right to take a bride. They would stop at nothing for a chance to become Fat Lady millionaires. The word went out over the jungle telegraph – to serve in Force N, a man had to have a serviceable Italian Army-issue rifle and a mule to ride. Thousands of men country-wide would be looking for Italian Army rifles.

Force N's war kicked off.

When the order came to move out, the little band had grown by two volunteer Patriots plus their pages to carry their rifles, one to two women each to cook their food and a mule handler per man.

"Who are all these people?" Maj. John Randal demanded.

"My first two prospects, sir," Bimbashi Hoolihan explained.

"Yeah, Butch but what's with all the women and kids?"

"Each Patriot requires a page to carry his rifle and clean his gear. Sort of like the Knights of the Round Table, sir. Only these lads have beehive hairdos."

"Pages?"

"Abyssinian men feel it is beneath their dignity to cook their own food, sire. The women are their wives or female slaves," Kaldi added. "Some will cook; others manage the mules."

"I thought there was a shortage of mules."

"For one Fat Lady a day," Waldo interjected, "you're gonna' find out there's a whole bunch more mules hid out in this country than anybody knows about. The natives is hoarding mules, the nonsense about there being a shortage of 'em is all a money deal. We're goin' to be swamped with ridin' stock, you watch."

Using Abyssinian math – which does not always work the same way every time – recruiting two prospects for their fledgling guerrilla army resulted in Force N increasing in size by a total of nine people and eleven mules.

Before they moved out, Major Randal presented Lana Turner with Bimbashi Hoolihan's Royal Marine cap badge and Rita Hayworth with the regimental crest from his territorial regiment, "The Rangers." The girls happily pinned the badges on their multi-colored turbans – as delighted as if they had been expensive gifts of fine jewelry.

Now he had a way to tell them apart – Marine Lana and Ranger Rita.

According to Waldo, the Italians had informants in every village, in every tribe and even in each band of shiftas. "The boss man in each outfit knows they're there, but generally don't want to do nothin' about 'em, like shootin' 'em or turnin' 'em out because if he did then he'd have to deal with the consequences of the informant's family members gettin' riled up.

"The double-dealin', back-stabbin' politics out here in the Abyssinian bush is some kind of disease," Waldo explained. "And it's enough to give ya' a headache figurin' it out."

The informants were going to describe the parachute wings on the white men's Australian hats and the girl's badges when they reported to their fascist masters, which should give the Italian Army intelligence apparatus plenty to consider. From such tiny raindrops, a great flood grows.

Major Randal's guerrilla war was slowly but surely picking up speed.

As Force N moved out enroute to their next objective, Waldo was still lecturing non-stop, imparting his jungle lore as they rode along on their mules. "Now the most important thing to remember, Major, is I been a' teachin' you about lions. Simba is bad, but leopards... that's a whole 'nother story. Huntin' man-eatin' leopards is takin' it to an entirely different level of evil endeavor. For example, lions won't climb a tree to get at you, but a leopard will, and you won't hear the spotted devil comin' except maybe for the faint *tic tic tic* of its claws on the tree trunk.

"In the dark, a leopard sees twice as good as a lion, and a lion can see about 10 times better than you can.

"Leopards is real cunnin', and a lot of knowledgeable no-nonsense professional hunters think they have some kind of semi-supernatural powers. A couple I know – and I'm talking white men with big educations with letters tacked on the end of 'em, not superstitious natives who ain't never spent one day in a classroom – believe a leopard can actually turn itself invisible for short periods.

"Lions kill only when they're hungry – leopards kill for fun. I know of a case where one spotted cat carried off a woman, licked all the skin off her body with its sandpaper tongue while she was alive, then just left her there. Now that was a kitty with an ugly sense of humor.

"The most important thing to remember and don't you never forget it is – WE DON'T DO LEOPARDS!

"One time, back in the days when I was operatin' across the border over in German East Africa a' poachin' big ivory with P.J. Pretorius from the square heads before the last great debate broke out and we had to quit elephant huntin' so we could join up to be army scouts, there was a high-scorin', man-eatin' leopard operatin' in our huntin' area so old P.J., a' wantin' to make friends with the locals to get at their ivory, sent me to…."

22
TWO BAD PLANS

THE CARAVAN WOUND ITS WAY THROUGH THE HILLS TO THE NEXT village. The trip demonstrated loud and clear that Maj. John Randal's map of the area was not accurate. Captured from the Italians, the map showed towns where there were none; and some towns marked on the map consisted of only one or two stone and thatch, mushroom-shaped huts.

Waldo and Major Randal crafted a plan of action as they marched. When they arrived at their destination, Lana and Rita would set up their parachute tent headquarters while Waldo would go into the village to pow-wow with the head man. Major Randal would wait in the tent area until he came back with his report. Then the two of them would decide on the next course of action.

"You want to spend as little time in a native hooch as you can," advised the former ivory hunter, poacher, soldier of fortune, etc.

"They's got bugs – lice, mites, ticks, fleas, scorpions, rats, mice, the occasional snake and so forth. The natives bring in their sheep, goats, pigs, cattle and even their mules at night to keep the predators from gettin' 'em.

"Livin' under canvas… that's the way to go."

"Good idea, Mr. Treywick."

"With the radio busted and no way to bring in Fat Ladys and those Springfield rifles, recruitin' an army is gonna be tough. Abyssinians only follow a man they're afraid of or who they think can make 'em some money. Ya' need guns to get the money."

"If we only accept men with weapons that fire standard-issue Italian calibers," Major Randal said, "we can always capture weapons and ammunition from the Blackshirts."

"Yeah, I noticed how Butch done that. Weapons standardization with a ready source of resupply… now that's somethin' these dimwits ain't never thought of," Waldo agreed. "Ain't got the same visual effect as bringin' in new rifles floatin' down by parachute, but it'll work.

"Now, Major, the thing to do to establish your reputation as a big *tillik sau* is to make you out as sort of a mystery man at the same time as we build you up as a super hero."

"How do you plan to do that?"

"I'm goin' to take one of those proclamations the Emperor signed along with a copy of the official HIM photo they took of you two together. Butch showed me the folder, and it's a right nice shot of you a' wearin' your ivory-handled pistols a' squintin' into the camera like a real bad actor and the old Emperor all droopy-eyed.

"The chief ain't gonna' get to keep a copy 'cause this man is just a little fish, but I'm goin' to show it to him to establish you're bona fides."

"Think he'll buy it?"

"Can't say for sure; we got to always expect the head man, bein' a politician, will have one foot in the Italian camp. We can't count on many locals puttin' a lot a' stock in a coward that ran away and hid out like the Emperor done. Nothin' a coward hates worse than another coward, if you get my drift.

"On the other hand, the lawlessness that has flourished since the Wops done took over has probably got quite a few people a' hopin' the Emperor just might actually come back and restore some law and order. Keepin' in mind what Abyssinians call 'law and order' would generally be considered anarchy anywhere else. Your Italian Fascist has basically done a miserable job of winnin' the average Abyssinian heart and mind."

"Can we do better?"

"One baby step at a time," Waldo said. "It ain't gonna' be easy. We got to earn respect, and the way you do that out here is to kill somebody and let everybody know you done it."

"We shot those bandits holding you."

"There you go; that was a start. Your plan to kill man-eatin' lions ought to work even better unless the man-eaters gobble you up first, but with these ingrates it's always 'what have you done for me lately?'"

"Eliminating the man-eaters was your idea, Mr. Treywick."

"Like I done said," Waldo said, not wanting to take credit for a plan he was pretty sure was guaranteed to end bad, "we got to build you up big. Get you a rep' as a killer of hard men and bad lions with a little mystery thrown in.

"Bear in mind, the entire history of this country is a great big lie so it don't matter none if we always tell the whole truth or not. These whatnots has a long-established record of goin' with what sounds good, not what actually happened. So our story don't exactly have to be accurate; it just has to make you sound real impressive."

"Raiding Forces has a rule," Major Randal said. " 'It never hurts to cheat.' What do you suggest?"

"Well, I been a' studyin' on that ivory-handled mule swatter the Emperor gave you. It's got the official seal of the Lion of Judah engraved on the silver cap on the butt. I had the girls cut the tail off that big black monster that nearly ate you and replaced the original horsehair whisk with it.

"Everyone who sees it will know it's a lion's tail and that you killed that lion. In Abyssinia, the real big *tillik sau*... mostly Ras and up... tote whisks, sorta' as a badge of rank. You got one given to you by the Emperor his own self. Got his seal right there on it, and it's sportin' a demon lion's tail you done in by a' stabbin' right between the eyes with a dinky little hand-held knife in mortal combat."

"It doesn't count," Major Randal said, "when you're saving yourself. Besides, I don't have any recollection of knifing that lion."

"Well, these idiots don't have to know that," Waldo said dismissively.

"We'll say it's a magic weapon, sorta' like Excalibur — I'll work on the story... embellish it some.

"Now, what I'm sayin' is the man knowed what he was a' doin' when he gave you that mule-swatter; you ain't been playin' it up enough, Major. Wave it around; let people see you a' carryin' it."

"Can do."

"Now, remember... you're a killer of bad men and a' man-eatin' lions," Waldo ruminated as they rode in sight of the village. "What you got to do is constantly remind people of that little fact. This ain't no time for modesty.

"Killin' a man, or even a woman, is always good for your reputation, so don't pass up any opportunity to add to your personal body count. But anybody can do that the way these boys go about it, generally when the other party ain't lookin'. Killin' bad cats is what really counts and you done chilled three of 'em. It won't hurt the story none for you to be a real well-connected lion tamer. And that quirt you got says it all... your connections go straight to the top."

"I'll carry the thing."

"The silver pig-sticker," Waldo persisted. "The natives are really gonna' want to get a gander at that, they'll eat it up. Strap your magic lion saber on your chest holster so everybody can see it right off."

"Easy enough, Mr. Treywick."

"It's your calling card," the old soldier-of-fortune said. "Flash it around. Put on a big show."

While Waldo went into the village to meet with the head man, Bimbashi Butch Hoolihan and Kaldi wasted no time beginning the schooling of their two new barefooted prospects. The young Royal Marine started out by teaching the manual of arms while Kaldi interpreted his instructions. The result was a slapstick melodrama that thoroughly entertained Maj. John Randal as he sat on his canvas chair in the shade of a large tree cleaning his two M-1903 A-1 Springfield rifles with a shaving brush.

A number of the local men from the village drifted over to watch.

It was quite a show. Bimbashi Hoolihan was learning how to be a small-unit leader; Kaldi was learning the Royal Marine manual of arms, and the recruits were learning how to soldier. The ratio of chiefs to Indians was one to one.

Being skilled seamstresses, Rita and Lana fashioned the parachutes into two large pyramidal tents complete with mosquito netting stitched across the doors and around the sides. In short order, the two slave girls had organized a pleasant little campsite.

All the camp followers were put to work cutting thorn bushes and piling them into a high-walled boma where the mules could be driven at night. The thorn walls had to be high to keep the hyenas out and sufficiently thick to discourage lions long enough to shoot them. Protecting, feeding, watering, doctoring and maintaining the mules were never-ending tasks.

A cavalryman's work is never done.

After cleaning his rifles, Major Randal decided to conduct an inspection of the mule line. The mules they had captured from the shifta who attacked them on the drop zone and those of the two recruits, their pages and women camp followers were all extremely fine livestock.

Parachute, Major Randal's mule, was one of the best saddle-animals he had ever ridden, though a trifle high-spirited in the mornings.

Mules are tougher than horses, and also smarter, which is both good and bad in a military cavalry mount. Horses can be trained to be shot at and are good in cavalry charges, but mules – not being stupid – never grow accustomed to being shot at. On the other hand, mules can be trained to be shot off of and make rock-solid gun mounts.

Horses can be particular about their diet, but a mule will eat anything, including its saddle blanket.

By the time Major Randal had finished his inspection, Waldo was back in the tent area smelling of alcohol from his meeting with the village chieftain – rice wine having been lavishly dispensed.

"How did it go, Mr. Treywick?"

"You ain't gonna' believe this set-up, Major. You know I thought probably I'd heard just about everythin' but this is Africa, and I just listened to a tale that has to be tops in human egocentricity backfirin' and I do mean *KABOOOM*! I wish P.J. Pretorius was around to hear this story; he'd get a real kick out of it."

"How about running it by me?"

"Yes, sir, Major, sir," Waldo said, savoring the tale. "As advertised in their letter, this here village has a man-eatin' kitty problem all right – had it for 'bout three years. One day a pack of what the chief estimates to be five man-eaters shows up and commences to pick people off in ones and twos while they was out a' workin' the fields, herdin' the livestock or standin' watch over the animals at night.

"So the local elders hold a town meeting to come up with a strategy to deal with the killer-cat situation, a problem causing some civic anxiety. What the council decides is to organize a drive to run the lions out of their district, which on the surface is a reasonable plan. Then some bright forward-thinker raised the motion that instead of drivin' the man-eaters away, why not knock off two birds with one stone by drivin' the lions over to a neighborin' village."

"Really?"

"Yeah. The thinkin' was they could solve the local man-eatin' problem and at the same time get in a little payback for the blood feud that's been goin' on between 'em."

"That stud," Major Randal said, "might have possibilities as a tactician."

"Maybe not," Waldo laughed with a shake of his grizzled head. "The idea looked good on paper, but these dimwits didn't think it all the way through, which is the most important thing to remember when dealin' with man-eatin' cats.

"Turns out our local council here has two rival villages to choose from. The three villages is laid out sorta' in a rough triangle about a mile apart. All three of 'em hate each other's guts and have since the beginnin' of evolution.

"The head man arranged a large beat with everyone a' bangin' on pans and symbols and beatin' sticks together and all a' singin' and chantin' and they walked through the bush on line dressed right with military precision and drove those lions over to the neighborin' village they particularly detested the most.

"Well sir, the big cats went straight to the designated target and started right in a' eatin' the people over there."

"I thought you said it didn't work," Major Randal said.

"Well, it did and it didn't. The folks in the targeted village figured out what had happened, it bein' pretty hard to miss all that bangin', singin' and chantin'. Without wasting any time, they conducted a lion drive of their own to shoo them kitties right back this way, and the lions allowed themselves to get drove again. Only the cats was kind of testy from all the forced marchin' and had worked up a real big appetite. So, the lion chowed down on a whole bunch more people back here as soon as they arrived, which was definitely not part of the original idea."

"Poor prior planning produces poor results," Major Randal said, lighting a cigarette with his battered 26th Cavalry Zippo.

"Especially when huntin' man-eaters," Waldo agreed. "Back to the drawin' board. But not havin' all that much imagination, these boys come up with the same exact plan all over again. Only this time they organized a drive to send the lions over to the *other* hated village, who they despised almost as much as the first bunch – you followin' all this, Major?"

"I think so."

"Well, history done repeated itself all over again, which it has a bad habit of doin', and now all three villages is a' drivin' the pack of man-eatin' lions back and forth between 'em. The lions get drove and then right on cue they pitch in and start a' eatin' folks in whatever village they been pushed over to next."

"I see."

"Not yet you don't, Major. The way it all turned out is those other two villages eventually ganged up and decided they would form themselves a mutual man-eatin', lion-drivin' alliance. Now both of 'em beat the big cats back this way.

"These poor dumb folks in this here village is just a' gettin' eat up. The top knocker claims these killer kitties has done munched down over 200 people 'round here and that's not allowin' for bad record-keeping, faulty reportin' or the fact that they ain't good mathematicians."

"I hate it," Major Randal said, "when a plan goes south."

"Well, this one sure 'nuff backfired."

"What do you suggest, Mr. Treywick?"

"I don't rightly know, Major. These lions like eatin' people, not livestock, so it won't do no good to bait 'em. My guess is you don't want to try wadin' into all five of 'em in the dark with your flashlight. There could be more of 'em than that; these numb-nuts around here don't impress me as being real good at arithmetic."

"Come up with something."

"We could try trackin' 'em, only we ain't got any good trackers. Lion huntin' is an acquired skill, and a man has to survive his on-the-job training long enough to develop it, particularly trackers. Most aspirants flunk the test before they graduate, which means they get ate.

"Besides, we kinda' got to take it easy on you, Major. You still ain't healed up from that last lion fight you was in, and I heard you got yourself shot not too long ago in a gunfight."

"I'm OK."

"Maybe so, but trackin' lion is tough, dangerous business, and it ain't for the faint of heart – which you ain't, Major, but that tends to create its own set of problems."

"Cut to the chase, Mr. Treywick."

"The trouble with trackin' lion," the ex-ivory poacher elaborated, encouraged by the homemade rice wine, "is at the end of the trail you eventually end up face-to-face with the cat at close quarters with it havin' the advantage of the element of surprise. Generally ole' Simba ain't real contented at that point in time, not likin' to have his beauty rest disturbed. Unless, of course as in the case of his bein' a man-eater, he sees the person doin' the trackin' as a T-bone steak – then he's a real happy cat."

"Why don't we build a boma, like we do for the mules," Major Randal suggested. "Only you and I sit inside tonight and shoot the lions when they show up to check it out."

"You mean come eat us!"

"Got a better idea?"

"Major, you just might have the gem of a plan, though when you say it out loud the idea don't actually sound real good right at first. Go take a nap, get all good and rested while I dope out the details."

"I'll leave it in your hands."

"In the future, Major, why not come up with a suggestion now and then that don't have you – and more importantly me – as lion bait every single time."

"What did the chief have to say about recruiting?"

"We sort out this bad cat problem the big cheese promised to give you his personal bodyguard to go kill Italians. He don't seem real interested in restorin' the Emperor to his throne, though he was mighty impressed seein' you and ole Haile in a photograph together. Natives is funny about stuff like that sometimes.

"Plus, he's gonna' take an override on his men's Fat Ladys."

"Generous of the man."

"The chief wanted me to tell you he's lookin' forward to meetin' you in person bein' such a distinguished slayer of evil spirits, well-connected and all. I told him it's your policy to never palaver with the local potentate until after you've done draw'd first blood."

"The big lion landed the first punch last time."

"We're gonna' try to not let that happen again. Bear in mind," Waldo added, "the most important thing to remember about huntin' man-eatin' cat is never close with 'em."

"I'm with you on that one."

"It ain't like takin' an objective."

As dark fell, Maj. John Randal and Waldo took up their position in the small, 10-foot tall boma the villagers had constructed for them. They were seated back-to-back in two hunting chairs that had been built on poles that were approximately 12 feet tall. The hunters were able to see out over the wall. The team of native laborers, supplied by the village chief, closed off the thorn bush boma, sealing the two inside and then hurried back to the village cutting it pretty late, all things considered.

"Lions can't count," Waldo pointed out, not bothering to whisper, it not being necessary to be quiet, considering the plan.

"What?"

"It don't matter if the lions is out there watchin', and they probably are. Smoke 'em if you've got 'em, it ain't gonna' hurt none tonight. Lions can't count so they don't know how many people got left behind in here. The cat can smell us though, so the idea is for them to come in slow and easy, real quiet-like, to slink around the boma checkin' it out; hopin' for an easy meal.

"Then we turn on our lights safe and sound, real cozy behind our little stockade here and go to work with the rifles. We might get two or three of'em."

"Sounds like a plan," Major Randal said. "I'll follow your lead."

The night turned dark and surprisingly cool. Major Randal wished he had brought along his sand green parachute smock instead of leaving it in the tent. Mosquitoes came out in force, but tonight it was all right to swat at them for a change. Nothing happened for a long time. As previously noted, sitting in ambush is about as exciting as watching paint dry, though on this one it was permissible to smoke, which made the wait a little more tolerable.

Then a twig snapped, and neither man in the boma was bored anymore. Was there a hungry lion out there? The thorn bush wall was tall enough that a grown lion could not easily jump it, but that was not entirely out of the question. In practice, it is almost impossible to make anything completely lion-proof.

Tonight it did not need to be, the plan only called for the boma to slow down any curious lion long enough to spotlight and shoot it. Not to worry, the big cats would be coming after two highly-proficient riflemen. And the lion hunters were very alert.

"Cats is real cautious hunters," Waldo whispered over his shoulder, making the mother of all mis-estimates of the situation. "The kitties won't make a direct approach, they'll float in as silent as ghosts."

Like Waldo said, hunting lion is an art, not a science, and there are no hard and fast rules that apply to every single occasion. For example, when exactly were they supposed to turn on their flashlights? Timing is of the essence when out at night hunting something that is hunting you.

In the interests of ensuring the maximum chance of success they delayed activating the flashlights as long as possible.

Unexpectedly there was a giant thundering roar just outside of the boma. The first roar was responded to by another bone-chilling, terror-inducing howl on the other side. These sounds were followed by a blood-curdling chorus of hungry cats screaming all the way around the thorn bush fence. The piercing screams razored the night, leaving the two men quivering in their stand.

So much for lions being silent hunters; then again, the big cats were not actually hunting. They were simply announcing, loud and clear, their intent to kill and eat the two people in the boma. The man-eaters sounded like they were in an advanced state of rage. Why were lions always so angry?

At the first roar, both men quickly turned on the flashlights taped to their rifle barrels. The instant the lights came on, pairs of giant yellow eyes began to light up, completely ringing the perimeter. More than five man-eating lions were out there surrounding them... a whole lot more. Neither hunter took the time to count.

Suddenly, on silent signal, the angry animals launched a coordinated assault in a synchronized attack, as if executing a well-rehearsed battle plan.

The screaming cats ripped into the boma in a fury, fighting to be the first to tear the thorn bush wall apart with their razor-sharp claws. The flashlights illuminated furious lions standing up on their hind legs, tearing into the thorn bush fence. These monsters were not injured or in any pain, they were simply swept away by blood lust, howling like 500-pound tomcats in heat.

The horrifying sound reminded Major Randal of the dive sirens mounted on German JU-87 dive bombers, only worse – a Stuka was not going to eat you.

Enraged lions seemed to be competing with each other to see which one could fight their way in first. The cats were stark-raving mad. The tiny thorn bush corral had been constructed to keep cautious lions at bay long enough for the two lion hunters to spotlight and shoot them at their leisure – not to withstand a full-scale assault from all sides by a platoon of 300- to 500-pound monsters. The boma could not stand up to this kind of punishment, and was already beginning to give way in places.

Major Randal fired instantly, putting the ivory post just under the first set of glowing yellow balls of fire reflected in the beams of his flashlight. Behind him, Waldo opened with his Styer-Mannlicher 8mm short rifle. The two men fired steadily until their rifles ran dry; they immediately recharged their weapons using stripper clips, which makes for a fast reload.

The infuriated man-eaters were not the least intimidated or in any way dissuaded by the gunfire. Over the past three years they had been shot at and missed so often by the local villagers they did not associate the sound of gunfire with being life-threatening, which made them extraordinarily dangerous. In the fury of the assault, the giant cats did not realize the shots were killing their pride mates.

The animals never slowed their attack.

There was a crash on one side as the boma caved in, and howling lions poured in through the breach. One leaped at the two chairs. Major Randal nailed it square in the chest on the wing then he rammed in a second stripper clip of five .30-caliber rounds, and cycled the glass-smooth bolt on his Springfield M-1903 A-1 in time to shoot another big cat in the face when the roaring animal reared up on its hind legs and tried to swat him with a huge, claw-bared paw.

The vicious lion convulsed over backwards, screaming and snarling on the ground. There went the "no taking headshots" rule. Sorry, Mr. Treywick. A lot of diktats about lion hunting were being broken in this fight.

Behind him, the 8mm was booming steadily as Waldo hammered lion after lion. Another savage man-eater grabbed the side of Major Randal's hunting chair and started to shake it. He leaned over and shot it point-blank on the point of its left shoulder. The cat shrieked piercingly and bit at the wound in fury, then Major Randal shot the animal again, this time in the side of its tawny neck, and down it went.

The 8mm quit booming, and suddenly there were no more yellow orbs to be found in the flashlight beams. The night became deathly still. Not a sound was heard, not even the whine of a mosquito. The smell of cordite was heavy in the air. Things were very still.

"That was intense."

"Major, I ain't never listenin' to another one of your cat huntin' ideas ever again," Waldo croaked in a shaky voice. "You attract trouble like a dead zebra draws flies. Back when I was scoutin' for the army with P.J. Pretorius I thought he was a danger magnet, but I'm beginnin' to think you've got him beat all to hell."

"I should have brought Butch's submachine gun along," Major Randal said.

"Wish you had, with Butch a' totin' it instead of me sittin' here. This is my worst night in Africa, ever. I thought we were goin' under."

"Those lions were mad."

"I'll probably never get that horrible screaming sound out of my head if I live to be a hundred, which ain't likely if I keep hanging around you, Major."

When the procession of torch-bearing natives cautiously arrived, led by Bimbashi Butch Hoolihan and Kaldi, they a found an incredible scene of carnage. Dead lions ringed the boma, dead lions hung in the thorns on the top of the boma where they had been shot while attempting to climb over, dead lions were stuck in the thorn bush boma wall where they had tried to force their way through; and there were three dead lions inside the boma, lying directly under the hunting chairs. In all, there were a total of 14 dead big cats.

The torchlight revealed four blood trails leading out into the bush.

"Normally it's considered bad form to fire on an African lion unless you're absolutely sure of killing it dead," Waldo said, down on one knee studying the blood trails with his flashlight, "but as far as I'm concerned, that policy don't apply to man-eatin' cat, no sir."

"What?"

"There's different schools of thought on the subject. Under the rules of fair chase you ain't supposed to shoot at a lion you ain't sure you can kill clean with the first shot; but with man-eaters, go ahead blaze away, I say... take your chance shot... touch off a round, you might nick 'em. The wound could get infected, the cat could get sick and die. Besides, if you do only wing 'em, well, to my way a' thinkin' a man-eatin' Simba with a bullet in 'im ain't really all that much more dangerous than a hungry one that's fully physically fit."

"What are you rattling about?"

"Major, we got to track these four bad actors tomorrow," Waldo said. "And to think I used to live the peaceful existence of slave to a murderous, baby-rapin' bandit. Life has pretty much gone to squat since you showed up in this slice of the globe."

"The man said there were only five..."

"You ain't never goin' to dazzle anyone with fancy footwork," the ex-slave said, ignoring him, surveying the scene in the torch light, "but when the fight commences, you stay with it. I'll give you that."

"Next time we need to build the shooting chairs a little taller, Mr. Treywick."

"Ain't going to be no next time, not for me," the old army scout said. "You're on your own, Major, if you want to set up for killer kitty ever again. Makin' the world a safe place for democracy ain't worth a hill of beans if you end up bein' the Blue Plate Special in the process a' doin' it."

Waldo did not have the heart to say what was really weighing on his mind. He had never heard of any hunter or even a party of hunters who had ever successfully followed up and dispatched four wounded lions in a single day. Major Randal had his work cut out for him.

The cats that left these blood trails were certified man-eaters, confirmed.

Drums began to pound in the night, spreading the word over the jungle telegraph from village to village like wildfire in the long grass. The Emperor's *tillik sau* had killed 14 of the monster lion. Head men sitting in their mushroom-shaped huts all over south central Abyssinia began drafting messages for runners to carry in the cleft of forked sticks when the sun came up.

"Come at once to kill the devil cats plaguing our village."

On the way back to their encampment, Maj. John Randal pulled Bimbashi Butch Hoolihan aside, "Who in the hell is P.J. Pretorius?"

23
BAD NEWS

CDRE. RICHARD "DICKEY THE PIRATE" SEABORN AND CAPT. THE Lady Jane Seaborn met on the terrace of the Great Western Hotel in downtown Khartoum. The Commodore was the cousin of Captain Lady Seaborn's husband, and she and the Commodore's wife, Brandy, were as close as sisters. The Nile River flowed past the hotel, a constant reminder that Maj. John Randal was Missing In Action near its source in Abyssinia, somewhere south of Tanya Lake.

"Jane, I have a confession to make," Commodore Seaborn stated uncomfortably. "I have managed to land myself in hot water with General Wavell, and I am fairly certain I shall be in considerable trouble with you as well."

Captain Lady Seaborn stared at him levelly. This was not normal behavior for her husband's cousin, the least likely person she had ever known to get into any kind of trouble. He was a man who always went strictly by the book.

"Trouble?"

"General Wavell asked if there was a replacement officer I could suggest for the mission in Abyssinia. The man who was originally scheduled for the assignment had been turned down by the Emperor for political reasons. Since I knew John was in the Middle East Command area, I recommended him.

"Jane, my only motive was that I do not personally know of anyone better suited than John to raise a guerrilla army and ferment a native rebellion."

"Why would that create a problem for you with the General, Richard?"

"He has recently come to believe I did it to get John out of the way so you and Mallory would have time to resolve your marital difficulties. The General went so far as to imply I might have even wanted John dead."

"That's ridiculous," the Royal Marine officer responded sympathetically. "Why would you do something like that? John is your friend." When she saw the pained look on the Commodore's face, she pressed, "It *is* ridiculous, is it not?"

"Jane, that is where the confession part enters in. I am about to confide something to you, and you are going to have to promise to keep it a confidence between us for life."

"I am not quite sure I can make that kind of a promise."

"In that case, I shall simply have to tell you anyway," Commodore Seaborn said miserably, "and trust you will understand the dire predicament this revelation will put me in."

Captain Lady Jane was widely thought to be one of the most beautiful women in all England, though more than one observer had noted that her famous heart-attack smile had been strangely absent since her husband had been rescued. There was no trace of it today, and she was on full alert now. "What is it you have to tell me, Richard?"

"I want you to know that while it had absolutely no influence whatsoever on my recommendation to the GOC, Mallory did send me a cable inquiring if there was any way I could have John detained in the Middle East Command until he had time to put right his difficulties with you."

Women of Captain Lady Seaborn's class are raised from birth to show no emotion except pleasure. They simply do not make a public display, no matter how bad the breaking news. Lady Jane sat there as still as the eye of a hurricane. There was no doubt, however, that she was extraordinarily angry, and her fury made her appear even more striking.

"General Wavell found out about the cable?"

"No, he simply suspects my motive after he learned of your relationship with John. The General threatened if anything happened to him I would be cashiered and sent home. Jane, you simply have to believe me, I made the recommendation because I am tasked with the mission of clearing the Red Sea of Italian submarines, and the only way to accomplish that is to drive the Italians out of their ports in East Africa.

"John is vital to the success of my mission."

"He does not speak the language, and we both know John has never completely recovered from the wound he received in the Blue Duck," Captain Lady Seaborn responded in a clipped tone. Her vivid sea-green eyes were shooting sparks. "Does Brandy know about this?"

"I spoke with her before flying out to Khartoum."

"And...?"

"Brandy said if it were not for John Randal I would still be routing convoys in the basement of the Admiralty."

"She's right, you know. How do you think your son is going to feel when he finds out? Randy thinks John walks on water."

"I would rather not contemplate that at the moment."

"Let me see the note from Mallory."

"You know I cannot possibly do that."

"Poor Richard... buried in obscurity one day, a national hero the next, now a villain to your wife and family, possibly disgraced in the Navy. For what it is worth, I believe you."

"Jane..."

"Richard, you are the most honorable of men," Captain Lady Seaborn said, staring him straight in the eyes. "Doubtless, you did what you thought was best. You may be able to explain that to Randy some day, but you will never be able to convince Brandy. She and John love each other, you know. They may not even know it, but they do."

"You are quite right," Commodore Seaborn agreed miserably. "Brandy is never going to forgive me."

"And I shall never forgive Mallory for asking the favor," Captain Lady Seaborn said. "Richard, I believe it is time you reassess your relationship with your cousin."

"What do you mean?"

"Mallory has a way of sailing blithely unscathed through sheets of fire while those around him are mowed down. I had never noticed that side of him before. Not a very attractive quality, actually."

"That seems a bit harsh, Jane."

"Truly it's not," she said, not backing down. "Your career and reputation are in serious jeopardy of a stain from which it may never fully recover. John is in grave peril in an evil place, while Mallory achieved exactly what he wanted, as usual. Only this time it is not going to work out for him. I shall make quite sure of that."

"Believe me when I tell you," Commodore Seaborn said despondently, "the thought of my suggesting John for this Abyssinian assignment being interpreted this way never occurred to me."

A meeting was held in Maj. Gen. James "Baldie" Taylor's safe house. Present were Maj. Sir Terry "Zorro" Stone, Capt. Mickey Duggan, RM Pamala Plum-Martin and Sqn. Ldr. Paddy Wilcox, DSO, MC, DFC, OBE who had arrived from Canada where he had been recruiting civilian bush pilots for a Special Duties Squadron. Cdre. Richard "Dickey the Pirate" Seaborn and Capt. the Lady Jane Seaborn arrived a few minutes late from the Great Western Hotel.

Major General Taylor opened with, "We are here to begin the planning process for re-establishing contact with Major Randal's advance party and to continue working to make Force N operational. I am going to leave the tactical planning in Major Stone's capable hands. For the record, there is not one officer in the service I would rather have working on this project.

"From now on everything we do is classified 'Most Secret.' Do not discuss our plans with anyone who is not in this room. No one outside our command group has a 'Need to Know.'

"OK, Sir Terry – take it away."

The flamboyant Errol Flynn look-a like announced, "I have been giving this assignment some heavy thought and quickly came to the conclusion that the first thing I need to do is appoint a qualified intelligence officer.

"Pamala, I am hoping you will accept the assignment."

The snow-blond looked up from her chair, "Agreed, on one condition, Zorro."

"Name your terms, Plum-Martin. I rather need you to accept this assignment, actually. Promotion to Lieutenant goes with the job."

"I shall work for you here until we locate John, then I intend to be onboard the first aircraft flying to Force N to jump in with the replacement radio."

"Right, that's settled then," Major Stone agreed. "I essentially made the same arrangement with General Taylor. I took on this assignment as Operations Officer only until Force N comes back up on the air, and then I am off to command one of the native battalions."

"Squadron Leader Wilcox, you have been provided a thumbnail briefing on the situation," Major Stone said next. "John advised General Taylor to appoint you Force N Air Officer, then to stand back and 'let you do your stuff.' A suggestion I intend to follow down to the ground. What are your thoughts at this point?"

The middle-aged Squadron Leader was easily the most decorated man in Raiding Forces, the most decorated unit of its size in the British Army. He was literally dripping in medals from the last war in which he had been a triple ace. In this war, he had been forced to fly Search and Rescue missions because the cut-off age to fly fighters was 26.

Squadron Leader Wilcox had talked his way into Raiding Forces by dreaming up the idea of flying small raiding parties to land on isolated lakes behind the lines in German-occupied France.

The rotund birdman religiously sported a black eyepatch over one eye or the other even though he had perfect vision, claiming it "strengthened the eye muscles." The eye patch made him resemble a tubby pirate.

He had a penchant for nubile young women, in pairs.

"Well, gentlemen, and... ah... ladies, the air operations plan for Force N is a no-brainer," Squadron Leader Wilcox said without hesitation, as he stood up and walked over to the large map of Abyssinia pinned on the wall. "A blind man could see it. I would bet my favorite flying boots Major Randal did.

"Afraid to tell you General, but you have been going about this entirely all wrong."

The room became extremely still. Everyone present was aware of the Squadron Leader's exceptional flying skills. They had all flown with him. In her off-duty hours, Royal Marine Plum-Martin had taken flying lessons from him.

"Let's see, the Major dropped in roughly here, and we have not heard from him since," Squadron Leader Wilcox tapped the map with the stem of his pipe. "Now we need to figure out some way to establish contact with his party. After that we have to make preparations to fly in reinforcements and supplies. The idea, as I understand it, is to build up a guerrilla army deep in the middle of Abyssinia – a wild, unruly country notorious for having hardly any roads, only one rail line and bandit gangs roaming everywhere, not to mention a quarter of a million heavily-armed Wops – and support it by air."

"That's the idea," General Taylor confirmed.

"OK, here we are in the Sudan, which is an awfully long way from the scene of the action where the Major is. But, if we were over there on the other side of Abyssinia in Kenya Colony – where we ought to be right this very minute having this conversation – we would be a lot closer to our work.

"And, we would have this great, giant lake called Lake Turkana that we could use to establish a clandestine amphibious air base to launch out of to fly missions into central Abyssinia. You can see the northern tip of the lake actually stretches across the Kenyan border intruding into Abyssinian territory."

Everyone craned their necks to take a look at the lake he was pointing to. It was not clear to all present what the Squadron Leader was driving at. Lake Turkana appeared to be one of the most remote large lakes in the world. The salt lake was surrounded by hundreds of miles of tough, scrub-brush desert.

"Do the Italians operate naval patrol craft on any of the Abyssinian lakes, Commodore?"

"No, I believe they do not, Squadron Leader."

"You have to love those Eyeties… known for beautiful women, fast race cars and... ah... did I mention beautiful women? Awful sailors. Now, if we were to stage out of a secret base on Lake Turkana with flying boats, we would have our own private amphibious super highway consisting of a chain of nine lakes pointing straight as an arrow right through where Major Randal jumped in all the way direct to the enemy capital city, Addis Ababa. It's a hop, skip and a splash, which for the uninitiated is how you plan, stage and execute long-range, air-amphibious operations."

An already quiet room became a lot quieter.

"General," Squadron Leader Wilcox said, "my first recommendation as the Force N Air Officer is to relocate our tactical operations center to Nairobi, Kenya straight away, at the least the Air Division, sir."

Major General Taylor was instantly on his feet fighting hard not to interrupt so that Major Stone could continue to conduct the rest of the conference. He saw immediately what the Squadron Leader was talking about. The revelation was a game-changer.

The SOE Chief had stared hard at the map of Abyssinia for hundreds of hours and never recognized what he was now sure Major Randal had spotted at first glance. He missed the obvious because he had never been trained to think air-amphibiously. Few military men had. For a moment he felt positively giddy, which was not something that he would have cared for anyone present to know.

The map showed a belt of nine lakes that ran from the Kenyan border to the Abyssinian capital. An amphibious airplane could land on those lakes and establish clandestine supply dumps on remote islands, allowing Force N to stage lake by lake, ferrying men and stores forward, leap-frogging in measured bounds. Logistically, the plan was perfect.

No need to try to hack out any primitive airfields in-country with hand-held tools the way he had been planning. One advance company of Force 101 was already in Abyssinia right now, covertly struggling and failing miserably to build one.

Whenever anyone looked at a map of Abyssinia, the only lake they ever paid any attention to was Lake Tanya, the legendary source of the Blue Nile.

Not one minute of Major General Taylor's time had been devoted to studying the southern lakes. To the non-air-amphibious-thinking tactician like himself, the isolated lakes were meaningless. In fact, no one had ever paid much attention to them – they were virtually unexplored.

Now that he recognized the string of lakes for what they were, a dagger pointed straight at the heart of Abyssinia; for the architect of an insurrection, they instantly became the most strategic terrain features in the country, tailor-made for supplying a guerrilla force.

"What are you going to require in order to carry out your plan, Squadron Leader?" Major Stone asked.

"A squadron of Sutherland Short flying boats and five or six Walruses to ferry up the men and equipment should do the trick. We'll need to establish secret supply bases one lake at a time. At first look we may only have to use four of the lakes. Let's see… they would most likely be Lake Chew, Lake Chamo, Lake Awasa and Lake Ziway. We might eventually want to throw in a supply dump on Lake Koka, south of Addis Ababa, depending on how the operational picture develops down the road."

"Exactly how is this supposed to work, Squadron Leader?" Major Stone asked.

"Simple. The concept of the operation will be to fly in the military stores to the first lake, set up a dump there on a small, defendable island in the middle of the lake, then leapfrog forward. We'll need someone to command the supply base at each lake with adequate security troops to protect it. Pure, basic logistics… not much different from supplying a remote fly-fishing camp, only on a bigger scale."

"Commodore?" Major Stone asked with a raised eyebrow.

"My guess is there is not a spare squadron of flying boats available in the Middle Eastern Command. And if there were, we probably could not have them. The best I can promise you, Squadron Leader, is one amphibious aircraft… either a Sutherland or possibly a Catalina.

"Most likely I can scrape up all the Walruses your heart desires. No one but you seems to have much use for them. But the flying boats simply do not exist."

Squadron Leader Wilcox said, "Mark my word, sir, we will need more than one Sutherland or Catalina for an operation of this magnitude. We can't do this with single-engine Walruses alone, no matter how many you provide."

"I shall move heaven and earth to get you the aircraft you require, you have my word. Even if I can obtain the airplanes, quite likely you are going to have to find your own crew. The Royal Navy air arm is critically short-staffed. I doubt they will ever be induced to assign trained flying personnel for an irregular operation."

"Not a problem, sir. I recruited six of my old bush-pilot flying buddies for a Special Duties Squadron for Raiding Forces. You arrange for the airplanes and leave the rest up to me. But we definitely need more than one flying boat to airlift the volume of supplies necessary to support a revolution."

"I shall do everything in my power."

"Lady Seaborn?"

"I have several family properties in Kenya. My family was killed there years ago in a light plane crash. One is a remote fishing camp located on Lake Turkana. We can stage out of the camp.

"General?"

"I want to take this opportunity to say what has taken place here today is why working with Raiding Forces has always been a pleasure. You people pitch in and go straight to the heart of the problem. With a team as capable as this, I am confident we can overcome any obstacle, accomplish any mission."

Cdre. Richard "Dickey the Pirate" Seaborn made arrangements to return to Cairo to begin his quest for amphibious aircraft. Capt. the Lady Jane Seaborn and Lt. Pamala Plum-Martin flew out immediately on the C-in-C Middle East's converted Hudson bomber to inspect the Lake Turkana property. Capt. Mickey Duggan departed to send a radio signal change of mission to Lt. Harry Shelby and his "Shelby's Scouts," ordering him to alter course and divert to Lake Turkana.

Maj. Gen. James "Baldie" Taylor pulled Maj. Sir Terry "Zorro" Stone aside for a short, private conversation.

"Terry, there is this one thing that has bothered me since I briefed John for the mission."

"What is it, General?"

"The Major asked hardly any questions. Only one I can think of, and he never mentioned that string of lakes, but I am positive he saw them for what they were. What do you make of that?"

"I have no idea. Possibly he knew you did not have answers, sir."

"Or maybe John did not give a damn. You think he was counting on not coming back?"

"I should not wish to speculate on that, General."

"Was he hard hit by the rise from the dead of Lady Jane's husband?"

"I suspect he was."

After Major General Taylor decamped, Sqn. Ldr. Paddy Wilcox arranged a discreet word of his own with Major Stone before he too flew off to Kenya.

"I met with the Colonel at your club a while back, Sir Terry. He told me to give you his regards next time I saw you."

"The Colonel?"

"The old guy in the billiard room at White's, 'C.'"

"Oh," Major Stone replied vaguely.

"He informed me that I was working for him now, like you are. That's why I went to Canada to recruit my old flying pals. 'C' instructed me to set up a Special Duties Squadron using Raiding Forces as a cover. I'm still to fly for Raiding Forces as if nothing has changed, but I'm also required to have pilots on call to insert and ex-filtrate MI-6 agents into and out of France, the same way we do the Lovat Scout snipers."

"Well, Paddy, that comes as no great surprise," Major Stone said. "I suspect Raiding Forces has been working for MI-6, more or less, all along."

"The question is Terry, what's 'C' going to say when he finds I'm out here in Africa?"

"Nothing. We all work for the Colonel, every manjack in this godforsaken place. My guess is General Taylor has been MI-6 from the Gold Coast days, claiming to be SOE as a cover," Major Stone said. "Intelligence people do that sort of thing a lot, operate under a false flag."

"What should I do? Colonel Menzies is expecting me to be available to insert his agents."

"Here is the drill I recommend – send a small contingent of your pilots to Seaborn House, where they can be on call to fly missions for

MI-6. Keep the major portion of your fliers out here to support Force N. Then do your best to recruit additional bush pilots from Canada to fly the Force N mission, if at all possible."

"Consider it done," Squadron Leader Wilcox agreed without hesitation. "You're sure about MI-6 running things out here?"

"Absolutely, there are more officers from Eton on the ground in Khartoum ready to launch into Abyssinia with Force 101 than served in the Battle of the Somme. Eton equals Secret Intelligence Service. This operation has 'C's' fingerprints all over it, only no one knows, and you can never tell."

"You reckon 'C' masterminded the Major parachuting into Abyssinia?"

"Not likely. Colonel Menzies has to be as surprised by that little twist as we all are."

"You have to admit, Zorro, this is a strange situation we're in, and it gets stranger and stranger."

"In what way?"

"Raiding Forces works for MI-6, only Major Randal doesn't know it. We're secret agents. You're in charge of planning an insurrection to bring down an enemy-occupied country from within. The posh Lady Jane is out here in Africa instead of home with her miscreant returned-from-the-dead husband, searching for the Major who's gone MIA in a place where homicide is the national sport. Baldie, the down-and-out spy banished to the Gold Coast for blowing up a historic national shrine, has turned into a Major General, Abyssinia, the country we're planning to overthrow, has a history based on pure fiction. And the exiled Emperor, a runaway coward we intend to put back on his throne even though we don't want to, is served by a slave who carries the official State Umbrella even though slavery is illegal. Did you know the Abyssinian calendar contains 13 months?"

"Bring it to my immediate attention, Squadron Leader, the instant you run across the giant white rabbits," Major Stone said, "especially the ones wearing top hats."

"Wilco."

"And Paddy.... We never had this conversation."

The Emperor presided over the first official public ceremony he had held as the Abyssinian head of state in more than five years. The event was a grand affair. Refugees waving national flags paraded past his pavilion; lords going lunatic as they came by – capering and screaming in incredible piercing falsetto, bragging about enormous numbers of imaginary Italians they had slain, fictitious wounds they had suffered and great feats of make-believe derring-do they had performed in the service of His Imperial Majesty, the King of Kings, Lion of Judah, Elect of God.

The men strutted like cock roosters, jutting their heads from side to side, chests thrown out in pride as they pranced past the viewing stand.

"We are your vassals, your slaves," they chanted. "You are our UMBRELLA!"

A maypole-wrapping dance commenced, it being a custom in Abyssinia that had absolutely nothing to do with the month of May. Tradition stipulated that the pole, once wrapped, was then set on fire; when it fell over, in whatever direction it pointed when it landed, the Abyssinian Army would march out and attack that year (which paints a perfectly accurate portrait of the state of strategic target selection the Abyssinian general staff historically exercised when planning annual military campaigns).

Maj. Gen. James "Baldie" Taylor looked on as the pole (specially built by the Sudan Forestry Department whose chief engineer, acting on his orders, had gone to a great deal of effort to secretly construct it so that it would fall pointing in the direction of the Abyssinian capital, Addis Ababa) was prematurely kicked by an overzealous patriot, drunk on honey wine.

The pole fell down pointing straight as an arrow toward Lt. Gen. Sir Archibald Wavell's Headquarters in Cairo.

"The fate of the Free World," Major General Taylor reflected despondently, "rests on these idiots." From the way it was getting off the mark, OPERATION CANVASS had to be in the running to claim the title of absolutely most-fouled-up military campaign in the history of organized warfare.

Besides the errant pole, there was one other issue weighing heavily on his mind. Prior to the evening's festivities, he had been summoned to a private audience with the Emperor. The droopy-eyed little despot, looking as if he needed toothpicks to keep his eyelids propped up, had handed him the translated text of a message that a messenger had carried out of Abyssinia in the traditional cleft of a stick.

Lesson learned – the Emperor had his own sources of information.

Following the traditional, overdone salutations, the letter read:

> *The British officer who is not English arrived from the heavens. A RAS and five shifta struck down as by lighting. The Major killed many demons feasting on people. A bad lion bit the sheik.*

Reading it was a shock.

After being transported 600 miles across rugged terrain in all weather conditions and being held aloft in the fork of a stick, the document had seen better days. Like all Abyssinian messages, it was unsigned. There was only the seal of the sender. The way their postal system worked, if you could not read the seal you had no way to know who sent the message. This made forked stick-borne messages an "iffy" proposition.

Speaking flawless French, the Emperor informed Major General Taylor that the word "bit" in the original document was illegible and may have actually read "ate" and that the seal had degraded during passage to the point it was no help in pinpointing the origin of the message.

Lions have big sharp teeth, and even in the most optimistic, best-case-scenario, there is no such thing as a minor lion bite; but there is a big, big difference between "bit" and "ate."

The General's opinion of all things Abyssinian was not in any way improved by the quality of their message, writing skills or postal service. Feeling depressed, Major General Taylor decided not to share the report or the problems translating it with the Force N team at this time, though Maj. Sir Terry "Zorro" Stone would have to be advised about it eventually.

For certain, Major General Taylor was not going to allow Capt. the Lady Jane Seaborn to see the text of the message. No one in their right mind would voluntarily tell a woman as rich, powerful and politically connected as she that they had been responsible for getting her ex-boyfriend eaten up by a lion until it was absolutely confirmed.

Not that he was sure Maj. John Randal was her ex. Even though her husband had recently returned from the dead, Lady Jane did not demonstrate any great urgency to be back at home in England restoring him to health. Cdr. Mallory Seaborn was a lucky sailor, but he may have used up all he had with his wife.

Divorced three times himself, Major General Taylor wondered how the conversation had gone when Lady Jane retrieved the Rolex from her husband so she could give it back to the Major.

Early the next morning, Maj. Gen. James "Baldie" Taylor did show the text of the message to Capt. Lionel Chatterhorn, the professional white hunter and international explorer who had briefed Maj. John Randal and RM Butch Hoolihan on the state of wildlife they might expect to encounter in Abyssinia.

Captain Chatterhorn scanned the translation, "You say the team has no radio, which means that you shall not be able to send them Fat Ladys or rifles to use to raise an army?"

"Classified information, Captain. But between us, not to leave this room, that's the picture."

"In that case, those three men do not stand a chance, not in that lawless country, General. Abyssinians particularly like to murder outsiders. Without guns and money to use as tribute to bribe the natives, they shall be easy pickings."

"What do you make of the message?"

"I would hazard a guess that Major Randal was attempting to shoot problem lions, hoping to ingratiate his party with the locals and ran into trouble."

"Problem lions?"

"Man-eaters. According to reports filtering out, they're at plague-level across the wire. Abyssinia is overrun with the blighters, particularly lion. After five years of war, the way the Wops fight it out there, with dead people left where they fall, a lot of lions have become used to eating human flesh. Killing troublesome Simba would be a surefire way one could establish one's self as a *tillik sau.*"

"Which do you think it says – bit or ate?"

"Hard to tell… not that it matters all that much at the end of the day," the seasoned professional hunter said in a tone of final authority. "Any idea, General, what we old African hands call men who make a practice of going after lion on a regular basis? And I do not mean man-eaters, which are much more dangerous."

"No."

"Dead."

To be continued in Roman Candle – book IV in the Raiding Forces Series

HISTORICAL NOTES OF INTEREST

Chapter 1

The Huks were a problem for many years before their full scale uprising in 1947.

Chapter 4

OPERATION LIMELIGHT was a Political Warfare Executive black operation designed to confuse the Nazi Occupation Forces in France by dropping parachutes weighed down by blocks of ice. The ice melted leaving an empty parachute on the ground causing the Germans to believe an agent had infiltrated the area, which forced the Reich security apparatus to conduct a fruitless search for a non-existent parachutist, and creating a high level of anxiety when no agent was found.

Chapter 6

Pop is an elite social organization at Eton. Members maintain ties with each other for life. They can be found in key positions of government, military and business.

Chapter 16

OC's, short for Operational Centers, sometimes called Op. Centers, were to consist of one officer, six other ranks and thirty indigenous native troops. Their mission was to arm, train and pay guerrilla troops to act as force multipliers. OC's were the model for the US Office of Strategic Services Operational Groups (OG), which in turn were organizations the modern day Green Berets are patterned on.

Military attachés are basically spies. They collect items of military interest on their enemy and allies.

THE BATTLE OF THE PLAIN OF REEDS

THE RAIDING FORCES SERIES IS DEDICATED TO THE MEN OF A Company 2nd Battalion 39th Regiment 1st Brigade, 9th Infantry Division.

After an intensive six-week campaign of airmobile operations in the Mekong Delta, Alpha Company played a key role in the climactic Battle of the Plain of Reeds, which resulted in the 1st Recondo Brigade, commanded by the legendary Colonel Henry "Gunfighter" Emerson, being awarded the Presidential Unit Citation.

On 3 June 1968, the third morning of a four-day running battle in the Plain of Reeds, Alpha Company air-assaulted into a hot LZ; charged across one hundred meters of open rice paddy straight into the teeth of a dug-in main force Viet Cong regiment that was throwing everything at them but the kitchen sink; carried the enemy left flank, penetrating their first line of bunkers; and pinned the VC in their emplacements and fixed them in place until the rest of the 1st Brigade could arrive, encircle, and destroy them. This was accomplished despite A Company having landed outside the range of artillery support, with the company commander killed in the first minutes, and fighting in 110-plus-degree heat—with no shade, no water—armed with M-16 rifles that would not function in those conditions. They were outnumbered more than ten to one. The initial air strike had to be called in on their own position to prevent A Company from being overrun, which was complicated by the lack of even a single smoke grenade or any other signaling device to mark their location.

One senior officer described Alpha Company's charge and refusal to allow the VC to break contact as the "finest small unit action ever fought"—and maybe it was.

Six Huey helicopters flew out all the men in the company that were left standing.

ABOUT THE AUTHOR

Phil Ward is a decorated combat veteran commissioned at age nineteen. A former instructor at the Army Ranger School, he has had a lifelong interest in small unit tactics and special operations. He lives on a mountain overlooking Lake Austin with his beautiful wife, Lindy, whose father was the lieutenant governor to both Ann Richards and George W. Bush.